SAVAGE VANDAL

82ND STREET VANDALS

HEATHER LONG

For me, though mum doesn't know I typed that.
-Mini

FOREWORD

Dear Reader,

Thanks for picking up Savage Vandal. When I first started thinking about this book, I was as intrigued by an aerialist heroine as I was a group of male leads who are *not* heroes. Enemies-to-lovers come in all shapes and sizes, and I fell for these guys faster than I expected.

This is going to be a wild journey, and I can't wait for you to meet everyone. Trust me when I say that this book only skimmed the surface. I can't wait to see where we go next.

And now, as always, the housekeeping notes:

For those of you who have never read a reverse harem before, first let me thank you for picking this up and giving it a shot. Second, a reverse harem means the heroine will not make a choice in this book or any other between the guys in her life. It may take her a while to reach that conclusion, but it's the journey that drives it. There are many ways to frame this kind of relationship, currently reverse harem fits it very well.

Also, this is the first book in a series. While there may be no specific happy endings at the end of each of these books, there will be one to the whole series, that I promise you. Some of these books will have cliffhangers, largely due to the size of the story, but the happy ending has to be earned as part of the journey.

Thank you again for reading Emersyn's story and I truly hope you enjoy it!

xoxo

Heather

CHAPTER 1

"*E*mersyn." The waspish voice raked across my nerves. "You're late."

"I know," I informed Marta as I stripped off my soaking wet coat. "I know I am. There was an accident on the freeway. The car couldn't move for fifty minutes." I could have gotten out and walked, I supposed. It was only storming outside. Localized flooding, according to the radio report the driver had been playing. Why didn't I do that again?

Oh right, I didn't even know the name of the town we were in, much less how to get to the theatre. As if to remind us both, thunder exploded outside like bombs being dropped. I dragged the scarf off my hair, not that it had done me much good. The short walk from the hired car to the theatre had saturated the rest of me, despite the driver's best attempts to get me close. He'd wanted me to wait while he took us around front, but I needed to be backstage and I wouldn't melt. I swore he would have kept arguing, but I just wrenched the door open and thanked him before I darted inside. It might have been my imagination, but his swearing followed me to the door. The last time I glanced back, he was standing with the door open staring at me with such blazing intensity, it left me shivering as I ducked inside.

Marta glared. The woman had been with me in some form or another for over a decade. I used to be terrified of her. The other dancers used to tease me about my 'nanny,' but warden was more like it. Right now, this impatience only irritated me, and I found her need to scold me over every damn thing not remotely interesting.

"They wanted you out there for warmups."

"Well, I can continue to stand here while you verbally spank me, or I can go get ready and take my place. Which will it be?" The sugar in my voice might as well be saccharine. What vague sense of life that might have existed in Marta's eyes petrified as she turned that stony gaze on me.

"You are not entertaining, Emersyn."

"Ha!" I chuckled, amused for the first time really, even if I was wet *and* cold. "I'm hilarious." With that, I pivoted on a heel and headed down the long tunnel like hallway to the dressing rooms. This was an old theatre. We'd been in—fuck, I still didn't know the name of the town. We'd been here for a week. First, there had been electrical issues with the venue. Then some contractual mess. Finally, the equipment had been late. The decision to cut a stop and extend this one until we could perform had been a calculated one.

Despite what they thought I paid attention to, I understood a stop hadn't been cut so much as moved to the end of the tour. Now, instead of ending in eighteen weeks, it would end in twenty.

If I was lucky.

A sigh escaped me. I must be the most ungrateful wretch on the planet, but I'd been on tour every year for the last seven years.

I was tired.

Despite our 'break,' I'd spent every single day we could

2

rehearse in a dance studio, working. At least they'd found a school close enough to the hotel that I'd been able to walk back and forth to it. The last two days, though, I'd been here, running the routines over and over.

I could do the damn things in my sleep.

As I plunged deeper into the theatre, the scents, noises, and feel of the place began to seep into my bones. The scents of oil-based makeup, the all too familiar sawdust that inhabited every venue I'd ever performed in, and the ever-present must of sweat. Performers plus hot lights and hurried costume changes left a heavy perfume of sweat ingrained even into the stone walls.

It was familiar.

It was comforting.

I freed the cross strap of my bag as I nodded to some of the others already warming up. We wouldn't do our costumes for at least another two hours. Warmups and a quick run-through of specific acts were up next. The chorus had probably already been warming up.

One of the theatre techs had the door to my dressing room open, and he was doing something to the doorknob. Steps slowing, I studied him. He had his back to me, but there was no missing the tattoos on his hands as he twisted the screwdriver and tightened the knob.

"Is there something wrong with my door?" I did my best to ignore the pitted feeling in my stomach. The locks were all that offered me privacy when I was here. If they removed the lock...

The man glanced over his shoulder, and the startling slate gray eyes seemed to peer right into me. I forgot how to breathe for a moment as he straightened. I had to tilt my head to maintain eye contact. "No," he said slowly, the faintest hint of a drawl in his rough voice. It settled into my bones like a bruise that didn't hurt so much as ache.

I shook my head to free it from the awkward thoughts. "Then why are you messing with it?" It was probably his job, and the last thing I needed was to be harsh so I kept my tone even. At the same time, that dressing room was the one place I could legitimately call my own when I was with the company. My escape.

My freedom.

"Fixing the lock," he told me, and I shifted my workout bag. "I'll be done in a couple of minutes." He moved to the side to let me in. "But I wanted to make sure this was secure for you."

The volume of gratitude swelling through me was ridiculous. Smiling, I touched his arm as I moved past him. "Thank you."

The firm muscle of his biceps flexed under the brief touch, but I withdrew my hand and shut up my internal observations. Bodies, their build, their musculature, and how they moved always fascinated me. But most people didn't like it when I stared, so I learned to save it for when I was people watching or waiting in the wings while others went through their routines.

Safer that way.

"The other one was flimsy." His words came out as more of an accusation than anything else, but I only nodded as I hung up my dripping coat and dropped the bag on the little sofa. It was just another dressing room in a long line of them. A room not bigger than sixty-eight square feet, but it was mine. I took a savage kind of satisfaction in that.

"I know," I said absently. Two notes waited on my table. One had Marta's distinctive handwriting. The bitch had keys to my room. "Um..." I paused to glance over to where he still stood, staring at me. "Who else gets the keys to that?"

Keeping my gaze pinned to his unfathomable eyes rather than his beautiful muscles—where had that come from?—I unzipped the hoodie I'd worn under the jacket. Layers. Always layers. When I performed, I'd be damn near bare, but that was when I was on stage and moving with the music and the silk drapes. When I flew.

Otherwise, I needed my layers of clothing like armor. Except right now, when that armor was still wet enough to leave me chilled.

"Just you," he said as if he had to measure out the words, but I'd turned away to keep from staring and stripped the hoodie off. I wore just a tank top under it with a simple cotton bra. I'd be changing everything. The jeans had to go too. Speaking of which, I stepped out of my shoes.

The silence behind me grew intense, and I flicked a look up at the mirror. My guest glared at me, the heat in his eyes promising the kind of violence I was all too familiar with. Chills raced across my skin, and I swore. I shouldn't have started stripping with him right there, even if my clothes were damp.

Folding my arms, I pivoted to face him, but he'd already looked away. His movements were harsh and stilted as he finished his work. "I added a deadbolt," he said, motioning to the device. "It only locks from the inside." From this angle, the hint of a tattoo peeked out from below his collar, just the tip of a wing. I had to wonder what the rest of it looked like.

"Thank you," I said when I found my voice. Despite the dangerous expression he'd worn, I was grateful. Now, if he could just go…

"Emersyn!"

Only discipline kept me from flinching at Eric's voice. It was the only warning I received before he loomed in the doorway. Or would have, except for the fact that my gray-eyed visitor easily had two inches in height on him. He also shifted his position so that he all but blocked the open door.

Oh, I was going to pay for that later. "Sorry, Eric," I told

5

him in my most soothing tone. "The weather did crazy things to the roads, and it was a bear to get here. I'll be changed in ten."

At six foot, Eric towered over me. A fact he always used to his advantage, when he wanted something. Weirdly, the guy running interference was even taller and broader, but the icy-hot chill rippling over my scalp and down my spine had been utterly absent, even when he'd been glaring at me.

Maybe after all these years, something inside me had finally broken.

"Who the fuck is this?" Eric demanded as he motioned to the theatre tech. "What the fuck is he doing here?"

Yes, totally paying for it later.

"My job." The crunch of those two words echoed into the silence like he'd thrown them as punches. "Back up." Gone was any glimmer of the kindness he'd shown me. Kindness? His voice had been all kinds of rough and husky, and I was calling it kindness? The guy didn't take his gaze off Eric as he bodily invaded his space and forced Eric to either back up or have this guy touching him.

To my absolute shock, Eric retreated.

"Check the deadbolt," the guy told me over his shoulder without looking at me. "I want to know it works."

Instead of bristling at the order, I headed straight to the door as he forced Eric backwards and pulled the door closed behind him. I twisted the deadbolt, and the solid click of it driving in sent relief singing in my veins. Forehead against the wood, I let out a long breath, then tested the lock below.

"It works," I said against the door.

A second later, a piece of paper slipped underneath and a key sat in the center. "All yours."

"Thank you," I said, scooping up the key lest someone snag the paper and drag the key back. Someone being Eric. The metal bit into my palm as I closed my fist. A scant second later, a heavy hand hammered on the door, and I jerked away from it.

"Five minutes, Emersyn. Don't keep me waiting again."

Yeah, I was going to pay for the tech's attitude, but right now, I didn't care. With the show on tonight, Eric would have to be careful where he left bruises. We had performances all week. Turning away, I caught sight of myself in the mirror and sighed.

The mottled bruising under my ribs showed where the tank dipped low. My arms, neck, and face were clear. So were my legs. After I stripped off the rest of the damp clothes, I eyed myself critically. The black, blue, purple, and green bruises littered my chest and torso. The ones on my side were made from hands, but they were bruises layered over bruises.

The venue had wanted me in the minimalist outfit. The first set of numbers called for my stomach to be bare.

That couldn't happen. But I had the black one piece that was all mesh save for the circles to cover my nipples and a patch over my crotch. Even my ass would be visible through it, but the black would hide the bruises and titillate.

I rolled my eyes and then shook myself out of this negative headspace. I needed to focus. In a few hours, I would fly, riding the music, and the rest of the world would fall away.

At least for a little while.

If only the crash back to Earth didn't hurt so damn much.

I put on the solid leotard for the practice run and tied my hair up in a messy knot before tucking the keychain onto a necklace and hiding it under my collar. Fortunately, I could lock it by hand before I left. My tech—wait, he wasn't my anything. The tech was gone, as was Eric. The noise level had increased. More performers were coming down to grab food, drinks, and in some cases, smokes before they got ready.

That meant the stage would be available for my warmup.

Eric waited for me right in the center. His face was all hard angles and fierce in its beauty. The first time I met him, I'd half-fallen for his angelic looks. He could have stepped right out of a painting by Raphael or Michelangelo.

He was that perfect.

The cold eyes fixed on me as I strode toward him. Without me even having to say anything, the music started. Our bodies knew each other well, and when his fingers dug in brutally to my sides as he hoisted me up, my expression never changed.

What was one more set of bruises?

JASPER

Someone would die today.

Rephrase, I was going to kill someone today. The phone buzzing in my pocket warned me I'd lingered too long. But fuck that. If I hadn't, I wouldn't have seen what I just had. The plan for the day had just changed.

And that bastard's name was now on my list.

I shook one of the cigarettes out of the half-crushed pack. That was like pissing money, but I needed some measure of control.

"Take that shit outside," the foreman for the crew ordered, and I lifted my chin to acknowledge the words, even if I mentally flipped the fucker off. He knew better than to take that tone with me, and the flash of fear in his eyes told me he probably shit himself saying it. As long as he did, I'd let him play his role. I slammed the door open to the alleyway and stepped out into the damp cold.

It had been raining on and off for days. It was cold, damp, and stunk of trash back here, but it was also out of sight from the main stretch and gave me a chance to look over all the access points. I knew this theatre inside and out.

I'd been planning this for a while. But today had been all about getting in, getting a good look, and getting out. My phone buzzed again like a nag, and I pulled it out to stare at the message on the screen.

Fuck.

Rome: *F got pinched. He's not gonna be there.*

Me: *Get your ass down here then.*

Rome: *No can do. Sending the new guy.*

Was he fucking kidding me right now? Two days ago, Rome fucking lost his shit when I told him he couldn't come down here. Now he wanted to pull this crap?

Fucking Freddie.

Kellan and Vaughn were already in place. I couldn't pull Kellan, and I didn't want to pull Vaughn.

Might not have a choice.

I took a long drag on the smoke, letting it fill my lungs as I played out the scenarios in my head. This was what I did. I could see the possibilities. Tonight was a meeting, pure and simple. We would do business. We didn't even need to have a conversation. We were uptown because it was neutral.

Well, as neutral as anything got in Braxton Harbor. Still, the guy coming in didn't know our city. A handshake deal meant face-to-face. I could do it without backup. Freddie had a bit of a temper on him, but he was also the steadiest hand with a knife.

Guns weren't always an option in venues like this. Anyone coming in the front door would go through the metal detectors. Another reason I got the union to cover me being here for the day. An itch between my shoulder blades nagged at me.

Me: *Send the new guy. What are you doing?*

Rome: *Already sent. And how did you put it? None of your fucking business.*

I groaned and blew smoke straight up. Goddammit. Rome needed to get his head out of his ass.

Me: *Don't do anything stupid.*

Rome: *Fuck off.*

I thought about sending him another text, but fuck it. Rome was gonna be a jackass until he got over me telling him he couldn't come. He was too damn hotheaded, more inclined to impulsive actions.

And he'd have already painted that fucking stage in blood.

We needed cooler heads for this. I'd have some time backstage. I also had a key to the new lock I'd just installed.

The door behind me shoved open, and I pivoted easily. The faint sneer on my face froze as she pushed outside. Sweat dripped from her forehead and down her arms. She was dressed in nothing but a dark leotard that molded to her body so tightly, there was no missing the shape of her hips or her breasts.

Or the fucking bruises visible through the near sheer material. Something kept her nipples from peeking through.

"When you're done checking me out, could I hit you up for one of those?" She had slipped around to hide behind the door as it swung closed as though she didn't want anyone to see her. All that dark gorgeous hair was pulled up and away from her face, but I'd seen the lush waves earlier. The flush to her pale cheeks had added a definite warmth.

Fuck me. Those lips though.

Puffy. Full. And…

Fingers snapped in my face, and I raised both brows.

"What?" I grunted.

"Sorry to interrupt your ogling," Emersyn Sharpe said in a near lyrical voice, her sharp intonations far more amused than arrogant. "But do you mind if I bum one of those? I'll turn around and let you get a good eyeful of ass if that's your thing?"

I stared at her. I got hit by a baseball once. It slammed into the side of my skull. This was kind of like the same thing. The offer entertained me for all of about thirty seconds before I scowled. "You're not a slut, don't act like one."

Her perfectly manicured eyebrows rose. The honey-colored eyes lost every ounce of their warmth. "Never mind." She pivoted on those impossibly thin slipper-like shoes that had no business in this trashy alley, but I caught her arm before she could escape. Only to lose my own cigarette when I had to catch the swing of her free hand aiming for my face. "Let. Me. Go."

"Keep your panties on, princess." Not that she could be wearing panties in that get up. "You didn't get your smoke yet."

Tugging her back a step, I crushed the cigarette that had fallen under my boot. Then I let her go and shook out two fresh ones. The heat licking through her eyes promised she was not amused. Yeah, well, I wasn't here to entertain her. I put both in my lips and lit them, then I removed the second and held it out to her.

Yeah, I wanted her to have a little of me on her lips. Her nostrils flared, but she took it and pressed it to her mouth, and I tried not to think about her lips wrapping around my dick as she sucked in a deep breath. The cherry flared, and I withdrew a couple of paces to give her some air. When she exhaled with such emphatic force, I found myself studying her.

The bruises visible through the leotard were not the only ones. She had bruises on her thighs. Up close, there was no mistaking one was a handprint. Probably the big fucker on stage.

Well that was one hand that would be broken. I did a mental inventory, cataloguing every mark.

"Did I do something to piss you off since you installed the lock on my door?"

I shrugged. "No."

She frowned, but I wasn't going to elaborate. I wasn't even supposed to be having a conversation with her. I'd gone for the new lock after I got into her dressing room without even trying. Fuck that. Not in my town…

After a beat, she skipped her gaze away, and that irritated me. There was nothing out in this alley. Just a cold breeze and damp air. The sweat on her had begun to dry, leaving only some dark patches on the leotard.

When she finished the cigarette, she glanced around, and I lifted my chin. "Just drop it, I'll put it out."

At her side-glance, I shrugged and she nodded, then flicked it to the ground at my feet. Red ash flared against the damp ground. It was half-extinguished already. I put my foot on it to crush it the rest of the way.

The door jostled and she backed right up to the wall, and I narrowed my eyes as it shoved open and the brute from the stage stood there. I met his gaze as I sucked on the cigarette. He towered over her on that stage. Then again, so did I. But the fucker wasn't that big up close.

He glared at me, and I just gave him a bored look. If he took another step out of that door, he wouldn't be walking back inside. The fact Emersyn had plastered herself to the wall like that filled me with rage.

I didn't know what the fuck was going on, but it was going to stop.

"You alone out here?"

I made a point of taking a long drag and exhaling it straight into his face before I said, "Do you see anyone else?"

He scowled, then glared at me before he turned around and stomped inside. The door slammed behind him, and I slid my gaze to Emersyn. She blew out a breath so relieved, I flicked my cigarette down and stepped on it. The fucker couldn't have gone that far. I could start with breaking his smug fucking face and work my way through the other two hundred plus bones.

"Thank you," she said, then ran a hand over her hair like she had to straighten it. I didn't miss the way her gaze slid back to the door, and I could almost see her counting off the time since the asshole left.

"You want to tell me what the fuck that was about?"

"Not particularly," she murmured, then gave me the first real smile I'd seen on her face, and it slammed into me like a fucking truck. "Thank you though. For that, the lock, and the smoke…" She reached for the door, and I stood there like some moron as she vanished back inside.

Fuck me.

My phone buzzed, and I glanced down at the screen as I raked a hand through my hair, the crisp scent of burnt tobacco lingering in my nose along with a far sweeter scent tangled with the muskier scent of sweat. I didn't know what she used, but I was never going to forget it.

I had to focus. Work before pleasure.

But I'd be seeing her again, real soon.

That was a promise.

CHAPTER 2

EMERSYN

The knock at the door alerted me to my driver's arrival. My shoulders slumped, and I tilted my head back as I took a deep breath, held it for four seconds, and then released it. Shaking off the discomfort and unease, I schooled my features to reveal nothing. I double-checked my reflection, particularly after waking so sore this morning. It had taken everything I had to even roll out of the bed. A hot bath and Epsom salts had helped, but I stank of liniment.

I'd rubbed it on every inch of me. It hadn't helped as much as I hoped. Tonight was our very last show. We'd be leaving the next day. A second knock jerked me out of the reverie. Dammit. So much for composing myself. Blowing out a breath more exasperated with myself than the driver, who *insisted* on picking me up at my room and dropping me off here each evening no matter how late I ran at the theatre, I strode for the door and checked before I opened it.

It was Kestrel, my driver. Dark hair curled over his forehead, framing a pair of perfectly bright blue-green eyes. The square shape of his jaw could have given him too blocky a look, but he had a full and generous mouth and a perfectly tapered nose. The symmetry of his face was just...

What the hell was I doing? He had just lifted his hand to knock, a frown rippling across his brow, and the lift of his arm betrayed the gun he had on in an under the shoulder holster.

Fuck.

I jerked the door open, half-worried about letting him in, but that was ridiculous. He'd been here every night for the last four nights since he'd started driving me. And not once had he been inappropriate. Just because I noticed the gun didn't mean he didn't have it all along.

Hand still raised to knock, Kestrel gave me a careful once over and then shot his glance past me to the room. "You good in here, Sparrow?"

Leaning against the door, I searched for a plausible answer beyond I was exhausted and wished I didn't have to leave tomorrow among other things... Before the words could even begin to form, the scent of hot French fries and meat hit me like a sucker punch, and I swore I drooled.

A grin curved his lips as he lowered his hand and raised the bag of takeout. "Hungry?"

"I should absolutely tell you no," I informed him as I reached for the bag, almost unable to help myself. He must have had a burger and fries in the car the night I'd finished our opening performance. Bone aching weariness and sore from head to toe, I'd almost given in to the urge to cry for the food. All I could smell was the meat and the French fries and the salt... Those people who say salt doesn't have a real scent have never been on a low sodium diet and monitored every single calorie that passed their lips.

It had been years since I'd been allowed to cry. As it was,

only the fact I hadn't been alone staved off the desire then and now. I swallowed as he pressed the bag into my hand. "Your secret is safe with me." He glanced at his watch, then lifted his chin. "You have time to eat. I came early. I'll wait out here for you."

Just like that, he withdrew a step, and I gripped the bag a little tighter. "That's ridiculous, Kestrel, just come on in."

"You sure?" What might've come across as condescending from someone else seemed almost genuine from him. "I don't mind waiting. There's a guy down the hall that keeps shooting looks this way, and I wouldn't mind making life unpleasant for him."

Okay, maybe that shouldn't make me curious, but I leaned forward to peer around the doorframe at the man who stood in front of another door, keycard in hand but not going in. He was *glaring* at Kestrel like he wanted to report him.

Yeah. The hotel was fairly expensive and catered to a certain clientele. Part of the reason I'd booked here, even if most of the company was staying at a different hotel.

That, and Eric didn't have any access to my room here.

Win-win in my book.

"Yeah, you should definitely come in." I made the mistake of clasping his arm, and at his sharp look, I released him, even as I backed up. "Or not... I just don't want you to have to deal with hotel security that guy is likely to send up here."

When in doubt, fall back on manners, grace, and privilege. My mother drilled that into me from the day I could learn to talk. It didn't matter what I thought or wanted, they expected me to demonstrate a certain level of confidence and behavior, particularly in public. That included not making scenes or causing a disturbance of any kind. It also meant taking control of any situation.

And fuck it, I didn't want to think about either of my parents right now.

Kestrel eyed me from the doorframe, the warmth leaching from his eyes to be replaced by something far colder and infinitely more dangerous. With one glance to his left, he got rid of the man eyeing him. I didn't even need the sound of the door closing echoing down the hallway to know the man had fled that look.

I should probably want to flee that look. But I preferred it.

While Kestrel had been unfailingly polite to me, he hadn't hidden the darker side of him, and I preferred to see it on display. It reminded me that everyone was dangerous and I knew better than to trust them. But I'd invited him into my suite, and I intended to go with it.

If he was going to attack me, he'd have done it by now. Most of the predators I'd contended with didn't give me days to get used to them.

My stomach rolled at the thought, and I turned away, the paper bag filled with sinful delight clutched in my hands. The suite wasn't much more than a little sitting room with a sofa that turned out into a bed and a separate bedroom with an oversized queen bed in it. Both rooms had huge televisions, and there was a little kitchen type area that I barely used except to make tea when I got back here at night.

By the time I sat back on the sofa, Kestrel had actually come inside and he closed the door, then threw the security bar over the top and checked the bolt. I caught him prowling the room, checking the bathroom then the bedroom, like he expected someone to jump out at him.

"I'm by myself," I reminded him, not that it was any of his business if I hadn't been. But ugh, no thank you. The only one likely to have tried to be in here was Eric, and I'd worked hard to make sure he had no idea what hotel I was at.

Between the new lock on my dressing room door, the tech running interference for me at the theatre, and Kestrel making sure he didn't let anyone hitch a ride in my car, I'd had probably the best four days on this whole damn tour. Cross-legged, I bit into the burger and closed my eyes at the meat explosion in my mouth.

I was pretty sure I moaned.

Also pretty damn sure I wasn't remotely going to be embarrassed about it. He had no idea how long it had been since the last time someone smuggled me real food. The only concession I made was to chew it really slowly. I made sure to make every single bite count. I would fill up fast, but I could save at least half or more for after the show and just gorge on fries now.

They were less than tasty after they got cold.

On my third fry, I glanced over to find Kestrel leaning against the door to the suite, arms folded, staring at me with a frown.

"You could sit down," I offered around a mouthful of fries. Well, that was attractive.

"I'm good right here," he told me. The friendliness from earlier seemed to have disappeared behind a chilly façade. Yeah. Typical.

I stuffed my disappointment down with another French fry, then wrapped up the remains of the food. I hadn't eaten near enough, but I didn't want to throw up before I performed. I'd rather hold onto the burger for a little while longer.

Rising, I carried the food to the little kitchen and hid it away in the microwave. Housekeeping usually came after I went to the theatre, so hopefully, they wouldn't throw it away. My phone buzzed as I padded toward the bedroom.

A picture of my parents flashed on the screen.

Yeah. Pass.

I never wanted to talk to them when I had a show to put on.

I stripped out of the comfier pajama shorts and tank top I'd been wearing and pulled on the clothes I could wear like armor. Hair gathered into a messy bun and boots on, I snagged my dance bag and headed back out.

Kestrel was right where I left him.

"You should take the food with you."

"I should have left you to stand in the hall too," I reminded him. I didn't need him or anyone else ordering me around. I had my fill of keepers and taskmasters.

"You want your phone?"

I glanced back at it and then shrugged. "Not tonight. I won't have time to talk to anyone, anyway. It's our last performance, which means I'll have to stay after for an appearance at the afterparty."

He nodded, then said nothing as he walked me to the elevator. We were silent all the way to the parking garage. Kestrel towered over me, which was nice. It was nicer when he wasn't so ice cold and distant. I knew better than to take anyone at face value. Fuck, I'd gotten pathetic on this trip. Looking for friendship or interest in someone whose only job was to see me from point A to point B?

The screech of tires on pavement made me wince, and I turned just in time to catch the flash of headlights before a body plowed into mine and I hit the concrete. Every drop of air whooshed out of me, my layers of bruises let loose with a shriek of their own, and my stomach rebelled.

Dammit.

I nearly threw up the burger, but I managed to keep it down.

Barely.

"What...the...fuck?"

Kestrel was already hauling me up to my feet, and I glanced from him to the empty parking garage around us and then back to him. "That asshole was probably drunk," he snarled, and I swallowed back any response as he turned that icy gaze on me.

He ran his hands over me while I stood there, jaw clamped shut, staring at him.

"You okay?"

No. No I wasn't. "Yeah, I'm fine."

But I limped with my first step, and I scowled. Another limp.

"Fuck," Kestrel swore.

"I'll be fine," I told him. "Just a little bruise."

The next step, I didn't limp. Not for anything in the world.

I had danced on broken toes and flown in the silk with cracked ribs.

The show always went on.

My body could handle it.

Kestrel glared at me for a long moment as he held the door open, and I slid inside but leaned my head back and kept my expression calm. Finally, he slammed the door and moved around to the driver's seat.

The silence in the car weighed on me, but I concentrated on doing my own physical assessment of the aches and pains. Tonight would cost me on that stage, but I had never missed a performance in my life and I wouldn't start now.

It could have been worse. If Kestrel hadn't acted so swiftly, I might be riding in an ambulance now. When we reached the theatre, he glanced back at me. "Stay there."

Then he was out and stalking around to open the door for me. I met his gaze as I slid out. "Thank you. I should have said it in the garage…"

"Thank me by watching your back, Sparrow," he told me in a gruff voice. Then he lifted his chin toward the doors. "I'll wait here until you're inside. Don't leave with anyone else.

Don't even step outside until you see me. I'll be here after the show."

I hesitated. This was a terrible idea. But he had saved me, right? And I liked his smile earlier. "Do you want to come to the show?"

He stared at me, frowning. "What?"

"The show?" I repeated, a little stung at having to. Most people would jump at the idea of a free ticket. "Tell you what, don't tell me. Surprise me. But I'll leave your name at the office. You'll have a good table, near the front. The food isn't half bad, and I owe you for the burger."

Then I pivoted on my bad heel and nearly ruined the whole thing by stumbling. Only discipline kept me on my feet and marching up the stairs toward the doors. Marta clucked at me, but I fucking ignored her. Particularly because there was a tech with stormy gray eyes standing not two feet from the doors out front, smoking. Only he wasn't looking at me but glaring down at Kestrel.

I spared one look over my shoulder. Kestrel wore an unreadable expression, but he didn't move from his spot until I was inside the doors, just like he promised. I swore he glanced at me and gave me a little salute, but maybe it was wishful thinking.

"Stupid girl, what did you do to your face?" Marta demanded, and I rolled my eyes and stalked away from her. I'd need to ice my ankle, which meant I was going to have to diva my way out of the warmups with Eric.

From the walk on air to the dance of the statue, Eric and I executed our steps with flawless precision. The audience seemed mesmerized by the passion of our performance. Loathing and violence were very passionate emotions, I supposed. We rotated the numbers we performed with each tour stop. There were more than a dozen that Eric and I could do together. But that was only the first half of the show.

So whether I was the statue in the park come to life as a gift from the gods, as I'd been tonight, or the girl dancing aloft carried on the wings of her lover's admiration—excuse me while I gag—we delivered what the people who paid so much longed to see. I'd resisted throughout the first act and after each costume change from looking to see if Kestrel had accepted my invitation.

But at the midpoint, with the chorus on the stage delivering a rousing performance designed to titillate and give the audience time to finish their dinners and order their desserts before the second act started, I had time. The second act that was wholly mine. I'd fought for that when the tour began. I didn't want Eric in the silks with me.

If I had to perform with him on the stage, fine. I'd let him throw me around, dig his fingers in, crack my bones. I would trust him to catch me if I had to, flinging my body without a care, because whether I hit the floor or landed in his arms, the hurt would be the same.

But the air? That was mine.

Eric had been furious. But the show's backers had agreed to my request, because it also extended the show for me to do the full act by myself and I made them a lot of money. Power, as my mother often reminded me, should be wielded like a scalpel. Cut where it did the most good.

If I fell on the stage, I'd survive it.

If Eric knocked me from the air, I might not.

I'd take the power where I could.

The luck of tonight's dance card had me performing alone for the last five minutes, a solo en pointe as I leapt from 'flower' to 'flower,' a fairy whose wings had been clipped. I could let go when it was only me and the music. The world, its people, and my problems melted away, and there was only a state of being. Ecstasy maybe. Or some kind of trancelike state.

I didn't have a name for it, but this was where my soul lived. The one time my body, my mind, and my soul could exist in absolute harmony. When I folded down into the last flower and the petals closed over me, a stunned kind of silence filled the whole room, even as the music faded away.

I counted the seconds of silence.

At five, the audience erupted into spontaneous applause, whistles, and calls.

Five seconds of awe.

Five seconds where they were so utterly linked to me, the emotion overwhelmed them. The tears in my eyes burned a little as the stage swallowed the flowers and the petals opened so I could extricate myself.

The stagehand was right there, a hand out to me, though I'd only taken it a couple of times. I did tonight because my ankle throbbed in absolute fury, but for those few minutes on stage, I had even managed to forget the pain.

I already missed those seconds of perfection.

Hopefully, I would be back there once I was in the silks. For now, I stood in the rafters, alone. No one came with me. I would climb into the silks and descend in them without anyone hovering above. Another diva move, but I hated the idea of someone messing with my silks. If I were going to be vulnerable, I would do it on my terms.

So little else in my life conformed to such measures.

While the chorus girls danced, twirled, and performed their lifts, I searched the crowd. The theatre was not fully dark like it was when I was onstage, rather low lighting helped the servers who moved in and out, delivering desserts and coffees.

When I'd given Kestrel's name to the box office, they'd not even blinked. I never asked for tickets. Not once during this show. They probably couldn't know I didn't offer them to anyone else. Why was it important for me to see him out here? To see if he took me up on my offer?

I balanced my damaged ankle against the railing, keeping my legs warmed while I kept the ankle elevated. I'd gone to the medic for a cortisone shot. I didn't even have to make up a story about what happened. I just said I needed it and he did it. I shouldn't be performing on it, he told me in a tone so bored, I knew it was just a warning he had to say to cover his own ass.

There.

Dark hair illuminated under the lights as he waved off the waitress flirting with him, her hip jutting and her chest pushed out. Kestrel barely looked at her. Instead, he focused on his… Oh, he had his phone out. I glanced at what the chorus girls were doing. I didn't have enough time to shift my position, but he'd come to see the show, and warmth blossomed inside of me.

Absolutely ridiculous, like some schoolgirl crush I was far too old and jaded to indulge. Crushes would always result in hideous disappointment if allowed to get too close.

But he couldn't get close, could he?

In fourteen hours, this town would be in the rearview mirror and I'd forget about it. I didn't even remember the name now.

I could only hope I forgot Kestrel as easily.

A new town.

A new hotel.

New stagehands.

New drivers.

Same Eric.

Same pain.

For another few months.

Then I was free of it all. I could write my own ticket. No parents to appease. No agent to bow to. No producers to...

A single light flashed from the other side of the rafters. My cue. The silks hung suspended from their moorings, and I loosened the first length to wrap around me as I stepped up onto the railing. The music shifted below, and the audience applauded as the last of the chorus finished.

I'd chosen new pieces to open and close with tonight. Marta would have an apoplexy. So would a few others. I didn't care. I had to test them out somewhere, and here was where I would do it. Art, I tried to remind them, not that they cared, wasn't about commerce.

It was about emotion.

As I stepped off the railing and let the silks take my weight, I closed my eyes. My art let me break free from the shackles biting in my skin and the chains weighing down my soul. They let me fly, and a savage sort of satisfaction burst in me as the music began and I rolled downward, the silks unraveling until I hung, suspended.

A body.

A corpse.

A shell.

As I went slack, the silks twirled and I floated in midair. The lights didn't highlight me so much as leave me in shadow as the blues came up. Gasps of sound. But the audience faded as the first eerie chords of music began to play.

Haunting.

I stretched one arm upward as though awaking from that dark dream where I lived and arched my back. I lifted my eyes to the dark rafters above, but I didn't see scaffolding and catwalks, but rather a mystic wood and beyond them, the stars.

As I stretched my arm, I wrapped it around the silk and

then straightened my whole body. The silk moved around me, shifting with my weight as I increased or decreased the tension. Back arching, I hooked the silk around my calf and dangled so I mimicked a shadow of night falling from the sky. Then a twist, and I turned, gliding as if I'd caught wind, and everything faded except for the melody, the silk, and the cool air brushing my skin.

The black bodysuit I wore would leave me not much more than a shadow, though my feet and legs were bare. Dark glitter painted my face and sprinkled my hair, the ethereal effect turning to magic under the shifting blue lights striking not only the stage but lighting the air around me in gradients.

A spin and roll, and I hung only by my hips as I swirled, then I allowed my eyes to open, and for a moment, I locked gazes with Kestrel. I don't know how I timed it, but even amidst the shadows, I homed right in on him, and his lips parted as he stared at me.

Triumph seemed to unfurl, and I continued what would seem an effortless glide as I rolled through the motions, muscles tensing and then releasing as I navigated the steps. Like ballet, I had to float, even as it required every muscle in my body to control not only trajectory but my pose.

As the haunting melody drifted off, I relaxed back into corpse pose, but I stole a peek down at Kestrel, whose frown disappointed me before he vanished as the room plunged into darkness. Then the lights came up and the music changed along with the tempo, and I writhed to the rock song. This time, I would dance on the air as another set of silks descended, and when I let go of one to roll into another, the music drowned out the screams and applause.

Only discipline let me control my breaths whenever I had to rest my chest against the silks for suspension. The pressure on my bruised and battered ribs made gulping air a challenge, but then I'd curl my body up and I could forget.

Here, there wasn't pain or loss or loneliness.

There was the music and the feeling.

Sweat slicked my whole body by the time we neared the show's crescendo. I had them all now. They flew with me, we were a part of this performance together, and I'd never felt so powerful as the music shuddered and gave way to Rag'n'Bone's "Only Human."

Marta and the others hated this song. The raw rhythm and beat, they insisted, wasn't meant for this work, and I hung from the silks wrapped around my forearms as I moved like I was running against the air and heaven was dragging me back.

Or maybe it was hell and the audience was the surface I was desperate to reach. The cut of motion vibrated in my bones as I poured my anger and helplessness and frustration into the movement. The frenetic jerking snapped as I would tumble and then force myself up again. Twice, I snapped my limbs out like I was spread eagled and the screams hit me as I curved into a cross formation and then began to fall, the silks caught with the force I exerted, and I allowed myself a glimpse.

They were on their feet, and then I began my sensuous climb back up. But the tension in one of the silks gave abruptly, and my fall this time wasn't a part of the plan.

CHAPTER 3

JASPER

We closed the deal tonight. Three days of negotiation all taking place while the show went on and occupied all the expensive suits in the audience. They really came out for this show. The hottest ticket in town and she didn't even have to strip, but fuck me, watching her move with that bastard on the stage and wrapping around him and then letting go while he threw her around?

It left me with a bruised dick desperate to burst out of my pants and the violent desire for real bloodshed. I couldn't even be sure which made me hotter. But that fucker on stage was done touching her. Rodrigo leaned back against the wall next to me. The street rat had been filling in as backup all week.

The little prick adjusted himself twice, and on the second time, I pinned him with a look. "Go keep watch outside."

I hadn't missed the dick assigned to be her driver making

his way inside. Currently, he sat not far from the stage, his back rigid and his gaze pinned on the woman moving with so much grace, it was hard to breathe.

The punk nodded and slipped out. Like me, he was dressed in all black because as techs, we weren't supposed to stand out, which suited me fine. Technically, I didn't have a job out here, but no one bothered me. It was also the first night I'd really gotten to watch her perform that wasn't a rehearsal. If the show hadn't needed to go on, I'd have broken that fucker up there with her already.

His knuckles whitened every time he gripped her. Her expression, as flawless as her execution of her movements, never once faltered. It was like she couldn't feel what that asshole did to her. Maybe she couldn't anymore.

That just pissed me off.

At him.

At her.

At the fucking people who should be protecting her.

What the actual fuck was she still performing with that dick for? None of the pampered elite in this audience gave a flying fuck about that tool. They were here for her.

The room plunged into darkness, and when the single light hit the stage again, she was alone. I hadn't seen her practicing any solos this week, though I'd checked a few times and she'd totally skipped warmups today.

I couldn't look away. Everything in the room faded as she moved like a fallen fucking angel on that stage. The lighting and her body suit hid the bruises I knew were there. Bruises I'd memorized, but it was like I could feel the tautness beneath my skin with every step she took, and yet she moved with such effortlessness, it sucked the air out of me.

When she vanished into that flower and the stage went dark again, I stared dumbly forward. Only the sudden applause breaking through the room shook me out of the stupor. I scrubbed a hand over my face and then pulled out my phone as the lights around us began to come up and the chorus girls hit the stage.

Chattering and plates clinking filled in the empty spaces at the 'intermission.'

Rodrigo: *They're here.*

I pinned a look on her driver again. He hadn't moved, though he had his phone out. With a shake of my head, I slipped out the side entrance and headed down the catering corridor. A stream of bus personnel was moving at a clip, slipping in to empty the oversized trays of their dirtied dishes while servers navigated out with huge platters of desserts.

Ducking past them into another door, I headed to the backstage entrance. During the performance, this area was off limits. All the equipment for the first and second acts was secured here, but with the chorus on stage, it was a hive of activity packing away the first act and getting ready for the second.

I blended right in.

Fifteen minutes, and then she would be back on. I had zero intentions of missing the next half.

Emile Robert waited for me five feet from the loading dock, smoking a thin cigarillo and looking far too well dressed to be hanging out here. "Horan," he said as I descended the steps. We met with a quick clasp of hands, and I fell back a step. Like me, he was armed.

"Robert," I replied, favoring the French pronunciation of his last name, row-bear, which amused me. Because it sounded like something you'd call a stuffed animal. Emile Robert was not any kind of cuddly pet. His suit disguised his rough nature and brutal efficiency when it came to dealing with problems. "The terms are acceptable?"

We didn't need to dance anymore. The deal was done.

Tonight was literally a formality, one that Robert and his people wanted because they were old-school. They wanted permission to move product on our streets, and we wanted assurances they dealt in nothing dirty or tainted and that they also didn't deal to kids.

We took a cut off the top as part of their tithe, and they pocketed a tidy profit. Our streets. Our rules.

"They are. If this deal works out for us both, I want you to consider expanding it to other products. You have port access covered."

We did, but I just stared at him evenly. "It's a little late to be adding new items to the deal."

"Not a new item, not yet. Think of it as a promise of a future dividend." The man was too smooth. In a lot of ways, this was a good deal for us—we kept the Royals and the 19 Diamonds in their place and we got a new revenue stream, while keeping a firm grip on our corners and our neighborhood.

Didn't make me this guy's friend though.

"We'll see," was all I grunted. As for friendly reminders, he needed to also remember something. "First payment is due next week. Nothing moves until the deposit is in."

"You'll have it by tomorrow," Robert told me with a smirk, then he glanced back at the theatre. "I'm glad we met here. I'll get back to my table before the next performance. After seeing what she can do with her legs, I'd like a chance of bending her around me."

His fancy accent didn't make his words piss me off any less, but I couldn't respond. I gave him a shrug and lifted my chin, staring at him until he was the one to walk away. Rodrigo ghosted out from the shadows as Robert headed back around to re-enter the theatre.

Smart little street rat didn't say a word while I stared after the French gangster, the stinking trail of his cigarillo still lingering in the alley. My fingers itched to pull out a cigarette, but I would already be cutting it close. "Keep an eye on him. Make sure they leave after the show."

"Alone?" With that single word, the street rat earned a few points.

"Definitely alone."

The kid nodded, then pivoted on his heel and followed in Robert's wake. I wanted to follow too, but I only had a few minutes to get back into place before the second half of her show started. My phone buzzed.

V: *I have him in my sights.*

I nodded, then keyed in a response.

Me: *Don't lose him.*

V: *I won't.*

Rome was still maintaining his distance, remaining quiet and unavailable, while Kellan was being a little bitch. At least Vaughn and the kid were doing their jobs. Fuckers, every single one of them.

Inside, I threaded my way back to the caterer's hall and then drifted into the theatre proper just as the lights went dark. Settling in against the wall, I folded my arms. The first haunting bars of music filtered through the darkness, nearly silencing the faint conversations threading the room. The light shifted, blues pushing in around the ceiling. The catwalks and the scaffolding weren't at all visible from the dining tables, but I'd been up there a couple of times, just to walk the theatre.

I knew where everything was. The fastest routes between two spots. The place was a virtual warren of secret passageways, hallways, stairs, and ladders. All so that the performers and the servers could move out of sight of the patrons.

Definitely my kind of place.

My heart stopped when she appeared, suspended by just some silk, pale under the blue lights and absolutely still like a corpse. It began to pound again with her first stretch, but it beat against my ribs like a sledgehammer. If she was graceful on the stage, she was like a damn goddess in the air.

Her body weaved sensuously in the silks at one point, they shrouded her whole form and then she twisted and weaved. There was nothing between her and the hard stage except some twenty feet of air.

The rest of the room faded away as she moved. This... I'd seen it in videos online, but they were nothing like seeing it in person. Based on the hushed theatre around me, I wasn't the only one utterly trapped as she cast a bewitching spell. I didn't know shit about art or dance. I didn't care much about them either.

But this?

What she was doing up there?

Fuck, I was harder than I'd ever been if it were a titty dancer grinding on my lap. They had nothing on this utterly graceful creature. For one moment, she dropped, dangling like she was falling but not, and her eyes opened. Even at this distance, I could see her staring down at the asshole who was supposed to drive her.

Rage spilled into my veins.

She didn't need to look at him that way.

The moment seemed to last too damn long. Even after it ended, I wanted to push forward and be closer to the front, where she would see me the next time she opened her eyes.

How fucking stupid was that?

When the lights changed and the music shifted, I sucked in a ragged breath. This had been an epically bad idea. The last fucking place I should be was here. I dragged my gaze away from her by sheer force of effort. Where the fuck was Robert?

I found him, leaning back, his attention wholly focused

on the stage, and with brighter lights, it wasn't hard to read the raw lust on his face.

Yeah, fuck that.

The street rat stood like a silent shadow at the wall not far from him. His gaze was on the French fucker, not the woman on the stage. The pound in the music dragged me back in and the oxygen drained out of the room as she moved like she could actually walk on the air. The tension in every muscle was visible, but the cast of the lights hid the bruises marring her flesh.

Bruises that covered way too much of her and drained the lust out of me as I narrowed my focus on her ankle. She'd been limping on her way in earlier. There'd been a fresh bruise on her arm too. The reminder just incensed me all over again as she seemed to be shadow boxing in the air, fighting against the silks keeping her in the air, like they were keeping her trapped, not gravity.

The snap of her motion thrummed in perfect time to the beat, and then she pivoted and spun like she was going to climb again, but instead, she tumbled. A gasp ripped through the audience, and it took a solid three seconds for my brain to process what I was seeing, even as I pushed off the wall.

One of the silks floated down like a severed wing, and fuck me… The dark angel dangled by one leg, and that silk was sliding. It wasn't hooked around her like the others had been. More people leapt to their feet, and with my heart in my throat, I shoved past two guys on my way to the side door that would get me up there the fastest. I needed to be in place to pull her up.

I'd barely touched the door when the audience's gasps changed, and I whirled. She had hold of the silk with one hand, and then with deliberate precision like she'd practiced this for days—and who the fuck knew, maybe she had—she pulled herself up and climbed the silk like she was fucking

Spider-Woman. She wrapped it around herself as she pivoted and rolled. Pure strength carried her upward. Her strength. Her control.

It was a thing of absolute wonder.

I'd never seen a thing like it.

Ever.

The entire audience was on their feet, and then she stood, one foot in the strap she'd made out of the silk, her bad ankle out as her leg pointed like she posed, then she had one hand on her hip, the other gripping the silk above her.

The audience lost their mind, but I focused on her eyes.

Her lips were smiling, but her eyes were darker, especially with the way the light reflected off the glitter on her face. More...there was fear there.

That hadn't been part of the planned routine.

I found the dance partner fucker standing in the wings of the stage, *glaring* up at her.

Without looking at my phone, I pressed a single button and put it to my ear. I tracked Emersyn until she vanished above the stage as the lights went out.

"Don't let him out of your sight," I barked into the phone as I pushed into the hallway.

The show wasn't the only thing that was done.

I MADE IT TO THE DRESSING ROOM HALL IN RECORD TIME. There were dancers everywhere, and while I usually didn't mind so much skin on display, I had one goal. Her dressing room door was locked. I knocked once. Then pulled out the key and opened it when nothing moved behind it.

Not one single person questioned me. The black overalls relegated us all as stagehands and techs. The performers didn't notice us. Suited me fine. The interior of her dressing room was dark. There was a bloodied cloth sitting on her dressing table and a melted ice pack sloshing on the floor.

The duffle bag she normally carried in and out was still there. As were the street clothes she'd been wearing when she arrived earlier. There was blood on the pant leg. I hadn't noticed her bleeding, but she had been limping.

Someone was going to answer my damn questions.

My phone buzzed, and I answered it without looking at the screen. "What?"

"She's outside with the asshole. Side alley."

Fuck.

"Willingly?"

"I don't think so."

"Don't let him take her anywhere."

"Not planning on it."

I did a quick scan around the dressing room and grabbed the hotel room key, wallet, and make-up bag off the dressing table and dropped them all in her duffle along with the street clothes, and then I was out and on my way up the hall. The dour bitch who lorded it over the dancers and constantly seemed to be giving Emersyn hell glared at me as I strode past her.

"You're not supposed to be back here."

I ignored her.

"Where is Sharpe?" she demanded of another dancer, who skittered to the side to let me pass.

"I don't know," she answered. "Probably went off to fuck Eric somewhere. Not like she spends any time with us. Stuck up bitch."

I didn't have time to put the little cunt in her place, but my teeth ground as I ducked into another hall and then continued across the back passageway toward the north side of the theatre. There were two alleys framing the building—

the loading dock side on the west, and the alcove street alley where the trash went on the north.

It was also popular with the performers and the techs for stepping out to smoke or just escaping without having to wade through the richly dressed up front.

Not slowing, I raced up three stairs and then down another four before cutting a corner and sliding down the rails. I hit the door with a slam and pushed out into the alley. The darkness broken only by the milky light from the single unbroken overhead lamp created a dozen scattered shadows as dead fucker walking jerked around from where he had Emersyn crowded against a wall. The only thing keeping him off her was the fact Vaughn was right in his face.

While he might be shorter than I was or even the asshole ballerina who got off on hurting his partner, Vaughn was a brawler, old-school style, and built rock solid and thick.

"Fuck off," he ordered me like I gave a rat's ass about his opinion or his permission. Emersyn sent me a wild look. For the most part, Vaughn looked bored and cocked an eyebrow toward me like, *can you believe this asshole?*

Yeah.

I could believe him.

The overbearing prick walked around like he owned the world. "Get him away from her," was all I said.

Emersyn sagged as Vaughn smirked, and he shoved the asshole back. A flash of lights at the end of the alley warned of the car's arrival. The engine cut off as I caught Emersyn's arm. "Let's go," I told her. She shrank back at my touch, and I opened my fingers immediately.

Ignoring the sounds of the struggle behind me, all I said was, "Don't kill him."

"Fuck, really?" Vaughn swore.

Steps closed in on us, but I swept a look over her. She was

still dressed in that black bodysuit and nothing else. Her feet were fucking bare. Red decorated her toes.

"Emersyn," Kellan said. "Let me get you out of here."

Relief creased her face as she glanced past me, genuine relief, and even if she hadn't been looking at me with fear, she hadn't exactly been inspired. There was a new set of bruises on her arm and what looked like a burn.

The tearing silk came to mind and how she'd had to pull herself up and how she'd caught herself.

"You know," Vaughn grunted out as flesh impacted flesh, "a little help would be great."

I glanced over my shoulder as Kellan snorted, but Emersyn took that moment to dart past me. It was like everything slowed down, the world moved in stop motion.

The fucker wrestling with Vaughn slammed him with an uppercut, then plowed through. Kellan was moving to block him and so was I, but neither of us were fast enough. Emersyn hit the stone wall of the building with a soft grunt, and her head struck with a lot more force. I let go of her bag and slammed one fist then the other into the fucker's kidneys, even as Kellan caught him in the throat. Vaughn came at him, and there was a flash of the knife.

"No," I snarled before I slammed my elbow into the dick's skull. The pain shot through my arm, but the asshole went down. "He doesn't die quick."

Vaughn stared at me, then past me to where Emersyn lay. Kellan had already gathered her up carefully, his palm coming away with blood on it, and he glared at me. "Keeping him alive got her hurt."

"Keeping him alive is because he deserves a slow, fucking painful death. Look at her."

"I am looking at her." Kellan's expression was stone.

"Secure him," I ordered Vaughn. "Put him in the trunk."

"Jesus, Hawk," Kellan swore at me. "This isn't the plan."

"Yeah well," I told him, snagging her bag and looking at her, "I'm changing the plan. Someone tried to kill her tonight, and this bastard has tried every single day they've been here."

The fear on her face didn't come from one incident, but from a lifetime of them. That much had been clear to me the day I changed her lock. I should have just called it then, but they were right.

That *hadn't* been the plan.

"Fuck," Kellan swore, but he carried her toward the car as Vaughn dragged the bastard up and over his shoulder.

"Not going to help?"

I glared at him, then glanced around the alley. One camera, but it was pointed away.

Kellan already had the trunk open, and I helped them stash the asshole before I slid into the backseat with her. Vaughn dropped into the passenger seat, and Kellan glared at me in the rearview mirror.

"We should just take her to a hospital…"

"No, get us back to the club."

"This is a bad idea," Kellan said.

"You out then?" I dared him. We didn't walk away. None of us. We hadn't even when we'd had the chance. This wasn't even in the top ten of shitty things we'd ever had to do.

If anything, we were the white fucking knights in this situation.

"Fuck you, Hawk," he snapped, and I grinned before putting a gentle hand on her hair. I'd shifted her so she lay in my lap, and I took the towel Vaughn handed me to press to the back of her head. "I'm calling Doc."

I nodded. She needed to see him.

And I needed a detailed list of her injuries.

CHAPTER 4

KELLAN

*T*he drive across town took way fucking longer than I wanted. Still, I didn't dare speed. No drawing attention to the car. We had maybe an hour—if we were lucky, and so far, our luck had been absolute shit on this run—before someone noticed Emersyn was missing. I doubted anyone would miss the abusive jackass in the trunk.

Except, maybe the pair of tits he'd been fucking all week. Better that little slut than Emersyn. Not that he hadn't tried. I'd caught him more than once trying to get in the car with her and made sure he didn't. She didn't want him there, then he wasn't getting in. The bruises on her grew steadily worse all week. I wasn't blind.

Hawk ordered me to leave the fucker alone. A broken hand, a broken leg, a broken neck—they were all doable. But no, leave him the fuck alone. Fine. I just made sure he couldn't hitch a ride with her, and I kept it quiet about where she was staying.

That took me next to nothing to discern. She didn't tell anyone from the show the hotel of her choice, and no one from the show was at her hotel. I'd done some recon on their location, *miles* away. She'd also booked her room under a different name entirely.

The tags were spray painted everywhere. Only a moron couldn't read the warning in them, so why the fuck had Jasper let him get away with that shit? Course, he'd just answered that question tonight.

It was their last show, the final performance. They had one down day, and then they'd be moving on to the next stop on their tour. Our time with her would have been brief, but we would have protected her here.

Because whether Hawk okayed it or not, that abusive fuck in the trunk was not going to be continuing with the tour.

Accidents happened.

I'd make goddamn sure it happened.

The doc in the box had no lights on in the front. They closed at nine straight up. The neighborhood emergencies headed over to the Memorial if they made it that far. Pulling around back, I already had my phone to my ear before Vaughn slid out of the passenger seat.

Doc answered on the first ring. "We're here," I told him and then hung up. Out of the car, I tracked Vaughn as he eased Emersyn out of Jasper's arms. She was too fucking pale. Bruises seemed to underscore her eyes in the muddy light. How much of that was exhaustion? And how much real hits?

"Did he actually hit her before I got there?" I demanded, but Vaughn shot me a sharp look.

"Do you actually think I'd let him hit her?"

The door opening to reveal Mickey J or "Doc" as he went by now. In his late twenties, maybe early thirties, he had a grizzled look to him and a hard expression. He swept his gaze over us and then narrowed his focus on Emersyn.

"Get her in here."

Jasper cut ahead of them all and was inside. Fine, he could sweep the place.

I caught Doc before he could follow Vaughn and Emersyn.

"What?" the older man growled at me.

"I need a sedative. Something strong enough to keep a grown man down for eight to ten hours."

Doc nodded. Then gave a jerk of his head. "C'mon." He didn't ask me why or for who, just pulled up a syringe. "Intramuscular. You got that?"

"Yep."

"Thigh is best. Ass works too."

"Where does it hurt more?"

The slash of his mouth twisted into a cruel smile, and he tapped the side of his neck. "Don't hit the jugular. Leaves you with a bitch of a headache when you wake up, and the muscle spasms are vicious."

"Perfect."

"Who's the girl?"

"No one you need to know, Doc."

"Right," Doc said. "Hear nothing. See nothing. Say nothing."

I shot him a look. "Good plan."

With a snort, Doc strode away, and I headed out the back-door. With the key fob, I opened the trunk. Our asshole passenger was still out, and I jabbed the needle in right where Doc said to put it and pushed the plunger down. I suppose I could have cleaned the spot up, but did I really give a fuck if he got an infection?

No. No I didn't.

Done, I closed the trunk and then moved to do a sweep of

the area while I loosened my tie. I needed to ditch the suit here soon too. There was a little blood on my cuffs, so I left the jacket on. The mist of rain had begun to fall again, and there was a bitter chill in the air. Phone in hand, I hit Rome's number, but it went straight to voicemail.

He'd been doing that a lot lately.

"Hey, prima donna," I said by way of greeting when the beep sounded. "Get back to the club and clean out that room between ours. I have a feeling we're going to have company." Message left, I finished the circuit and headed back inside.

Vaughn and Jasper were toe to toe in the hallway, glaring at each other.

"This looks productive," I said as I bypassed them and headed toward the treatment rooms.

"He's doing X-rays," Vaughn said. "Stay out here."

"She awake yet?" Because if she wasn't...

"No," Jasper ground out between his teeth. "Another reason he's doing X-rays. He wants to make sure she hasn't done something significant to her skull."

I got kicked by a mule once at one of those stupid petting zoo things they bussed inner city kids to in order to experience nature. Cracked two of my ribs and left a bruise on me for weeks.

The idea she'd cracked her skull hit just as hard.

Swinging around, I glared at Jasper. "We should take her to a fucking hospital."

"Thank you," Vaughn snapped and then shoved Jasper back a step. "That's what I said."

"Doc can look after her," he argued.

"And then what?" I asked.

I knew.

I knew the moment he wanted us to put her in the car.

This was not how this week was supposed to go.

"Then we'll take care of her," Jasper said. "Keep watch here. Don't leave without telling me." He pivoted on his heel.

"Where are you going?"

"To check on our package—"

"He's out," I told him. Not giving him that excuse to duck this conversation. "Doc gave me a sedative for him."

Jasper making decisions on the fly was something I was long acquainted with, as was his gut. Sometimes, he just had to follow it, even when he couldn't explain it in logical or rational terms.

"Did your gut say take her?"

Scowling, Vaughn folded his arms. He'd spent the last week keeping a low profile behind the scenes, but he'd been there every single hour she was. He'd been the first to notice the abuse. Or at least the first to tell me. Who the fuck knew what Jasper had seen or when he had seen it.

The door opening behind me saved him from answering. Doc stuck his head out. "Tell me you punks picked up the asshole who did this to her?"

Jasper and I could hash this shit out later. He shoved past me to get to Doc, and I slowed Vaughn with a hand to his chest. "He's not gonna listen right now," I told him in a low voice. "You need to back off on picking this fight tonight."

"You always fucking say that," Vaughn snapped, though he didn't raise his voice. "He's always got some shit going on... but this is fucking different."

I caught his eye, and I nodded. "It is different. But back off. We need him to calm down so we can ease his grip out. Then we can get her where she needs to be."

As far the fuck away from us as possible.

Raking a tattooed hand through his hair, Vaughn nodded. "But if he doesn't chill this shit out, I'm gonna break his fucking jaw."

Yeah. I got that.

The last year, Jasper had gotten worse. More controlling. More tight-fisted. More invested in every single thing we did.

I got it.

I did.

But he wasn't making friends, and his attitude was grating on the friends we did have.

"Fine."

In the room where Emersyn lay on a flat surface that was more a table than a bed, I planted myself near the door. The unnatural stillness aggravated. Not two hours earlier, she was moving in those silks above the stage and freaking me the fuck out with those plunges and climbs.

Fuck. Seeing them in videos was one thing. She took my goddamn breath away in person, and I hadn't missed the moment she'd locked eyes on me. There'd been desire there. The same desire that flickered in her hotel room.

Better to nip that shit in the bud. Still, I couldn't get over how amazing she'd been up there, and now? Seeing her like this? Pale? Bruised? And lying helpless on that table? Doc better give us some goddamn answers.

"How many breaks?" Jasper demanded.

"Easily three or four," Doc explained. "Look..." He had the images up on a screen. "I'm not an expert, but I can read these well enough and I got a friend looking at them right now..."

I glared at him, but Doc just rolled his eyes.

"You can trust him."

"We don't trust anyone, Doc," Jasper told him in a cold voice. "You had to earn it too."

"Pretty sure that shit was the other way around, kid, but whatever helps you sleep at night. Now look..."

Then he walked us through a patchwork of injuries she'd sustained. It was like she'd broken or cracked nearly every bone in her body. Worse, there was soft tissue bruising. Have to do an MRI to get more explicit information, but he didn't have that equipment.

"Why the fuck is she naked?" Vaughn demanded, and I ripped my gaze from the screen to where she lay. There were blankets up to her chin, but I hadn't seen her dance leotard or pants lying off to the side before until Vaughn held the black mesh outfit fisted in his hand.

"Because I had to do a full exam."

"If you—" Jasper started, and it was Doc who glared this time.

"You finish that sentence, kid, you better do it with a bullet to my brain, because I've beaten men to death for less charges. She's a fucking child. Not to mention an abused one. She's barely got tits."

She had plenty of tits.

"What she does have are bruises over three quarters of her torso. How the hell she performed like that, I don't know. But she's got cracked ribs, that had to be impeding her breathing. She's broken every single one of her toes, some of them multiple times. She's had broken fingers. A broken wrist. Twice on the right. Old healed fractures to her arms and both legs."

My gut curdled with every single word.

"Someone is beating her."

The fucker in the trunk.

"And you better make sure he doesn't lay a finger on her again."

Oh, Doc didn't have to worry about that. I was going to cut every single one of his fingers off.

Jasper flexed his hands, his whole expression blank and his eyes icy. I knew that look. Nothing good came from that look. But I couldn't argue with it either. I glanced from him, back to Emersyn, then back again.

"You'll have to tell him," I warned him.

A single nod. "She goes back with us."

"What about her head?" Vaughn asked, the belligerence in his voice noticeably absent.

"Concussion most likely. Contusion from where she hit the stone, looks like she caught a corner. I'll do a couple of stitches, but I'm not seeing swelling yet. Need to get her to wake up and check her cognitive functions, but she's probably wiped, poor thing."

The sympathy in his rough voice was hard to miss.

"Gonna put her on an IV and get some fluid into her and do a couple of other tests. Then I'll get you some scripts. You taking her to the clubhouse?"

All three of us nodded at once. No way I could justify sending her back. That was a lot of damage for one asshole. Not to mention all those other assholes letting it happen.

"All right, get out then while I do this. Give me an hour." Doc turned his back on us, and I moved back into the hall after one more look at her. Vaughn didn't move, and Jasper jerked his chin at me.

Yeah, probably a better plan to leave one of us in there with her.

"We need to get rid of the car," I warned Jasper. "I can put him in the storage locker and deal with it. Then come back with a clean vehicle. Someone needs to pick up Freddie." Since he'd been left to stew all this time. His mood would be a real treat.

Not my problem.

Not this time.

"Secure him and take care of the car, but don't slip and let him die. We keep it quiet for now," Jasper ordered. "Family only."

"You were right," I told him as I headed for the door. "He doesn't die quick."

I didn't wait to see what he had to say to that. I checked my watch before scanning the area once more. The car needed to go, so I'd get Ripper to take it over to the chop shop. Fucking pity, I liked the damn town car.

I'd build another.

Inside, I started the engine and stared into the darkness. My phone buzzed, and there was a single word from Rome on it.

Done.

Behind me, a light flared as Jasper lit a cigarette. He was a sliver of a shadow against the side of the building that the headlights barely glanced off of as I pulled out. "Back in an hour," I called, and he lifted a hand.

Fuck me. Emersyn Sharpe was going to come home with us.

That just had "epically bad idea" written all over it.

Sending her back seemed worse somehow.

Go fucking figure.

ONLY AFTER I DEALT WITH THE FUCKER IN THE TRUNK, DID I hand the keys to the car over to one of the rats who wanted a spot. We didn't just take everyone, but Petrov wasn't a bad kid, just came from a shit home life, and who around here didn't? He was barely sixteen. The scrawny bastard was all arms and legs. He'd started hanging around a couple of years earlier. He made the mistake of trying to lie to Raptor about his age.

That didn't go over well.

We got it. Didn't mean we would let him get away with those kinds of lies. But he had a license. I knew, 'cause I taught him to drive and took him for his test. "No joy riding. Don't break any speed limits. Go straight to Bertie's, tell him it's the usual and to put it on my tab. Then have one of his guys give you a ride home."

Petrov smirked. "I can manage—"

I cuffed him in the back of the head and knocked the smug smile off his face. "When I want your opinion, I'll ask. Do as you're told, and do it now."

One sober nod, and the kid took off. I diverted through the converted warehouse we'd taken over, bought, and remodeled to suit us over the last few years. Some sections were still wide open and in need of work. Others shaped up nicely. The arcade and game rooms were probably the nicest because we spent the most time in them.

Striding past, I was stripping off the suit coat. I had time to change before I picked up the new car and went back for them, but slurping noises halted me mid-stride.

Someone had to be fucking kidding me right now.

Ducking my head into the lounge, I found one of the rats making himself at home with one arm stretched along the back of the sofa with a beer dangling from his fingertips and a busty little blonde going to town sucking him off. She was all but naked, save for a G-string.

Stripper, probably.

They weren't alone. JD was pounding himself into the ass of another stripper, one hand in her hair and her face tilted up in a grimace of pleasure or pain. Who the fuck knew.

We so didn't have time for this.

Not to mention… "If I were Hawk, you two would be dead."

JD's pounding hips stuttered to a halt, and he jerked around with wild eyes. The slut he'd been reaming let out a mouthy protest, and he raised his hand.

Yeah, not on my fucking watch. I caught his wrist before he even made the full backswing and hauled his naked ass off of her and ignored the sick little pop of him jerking free.

From her body. She let out a shrill sound, but I pointed my other hand at her. "Shut up."

Her mouth snapped closed, and I wrenched JD's hand behind his back. "That's a second warning for you, Rat," I informed JD, and he went stiff.

Well, his shoulders did.

His dick deflated.

Good, I didn't need the up close and personal. I flung him away. "Clean this shit up and get them the fuck out of here."

The slut in question shot me a hopeful look, and I snorted. No, I didn't take sloppy seconds. Thank you very much.

Shaun let out a grunt as he fisted his hand into his stripper's hair and emptied himself into her mouth before tugging himself free. "I figured I had a minute," he said with a huff. His face was flush, and his girl was dabbing at her mouth as she looked at me.

I did not have time for this shit. I wrenched JD's arm a little higher. His harsh exhale betrayed pain, but he didn't complain. At least not verbally. "Get the sluts dressed. Get them the fuck out of here. Get back to what you're supposed to be doing. I catch you in here again, and there won't be another chance."

Three warnings, and you were gone. They were lucky they were getting that much. One warning usually got you a job with a fifty-fifty chance of getting shot, and that took care of our problems.

Then right against JD's ear, so he wouldn't mistake the threat for anything else, I said, "You raise a hand to a woman or someone smaller than you again, and I'll break it the fuck off." Another hard wrench to punctuate the point, and then I shoved him off me.

Shaun already had himself buttoned up, and he threw his

girl's clothes at her. "You heard the man, party's over." He at least had the sense to shoot me an apologetic look.

We were going to have to burn that fucking sofa.

And the chair.

Hawk wasn't going to be happy about that, but I was pretty sure he wouldn't want to sit in JD's jizz. I waited long enough to see them taking the girls out. Shaun took charge of them. Good. Rome was here earlier, so he better have a good fucking explanation for why he ignored the rats fucking in the den.

They weren't blooded in, they didn't get privileges. As rats, they got protection, they got work, and they got a chance. It was up to them to make something of it. The cloying stench of sex clung to the air, and I waved a hand at my face as I headed for my room.

I paused only long enough to shoot Jasper a message.

Me: *Had to chase some rats out of the den. Heading back in 15. Status?*

Dropping the phone on the bed, I stripped off the shoulder holster and the holster for the gun I kept on my belt before discarding the rest of my clothes. Five minutes under icy spray chased away sleep and rinsed off the blood that had already turned flakey on my hands. I curled my fingers and resisted the urge to punch the wall. It wouldn't do my knuckles any good, and I had a feeling I was going to need everything I had over the next few weeks.

Five minutes later, I pulled on black jeans, a black T-shirt, and dragged a black jacket over the lot. The suit lay in a heap, and I inspected the blood on it. The dry cleaner's on 105th could probably get that out. I'd reserve burning it for later if they couldn't. I only had two good suits, and this one had taken me four months to save up for.

Keys in hand, I checked the phone.

J: *She's still out. Doc doesn't want her to leave until she wakes up.*

That didn't seem unreasonable.

Me: *You sure we can't make arrangements to get her into a hospital somewhere else?*

She was eighteen, right? Her birthday had been a month earlier, I was pretty sure. That meant she was free and clear of parental entanglements.

J: *No. She's coming back with us.*

I sighed and stared up at the ceiling.

A week.

I'd give him a week to get his shit together. That should give her time to bounce back and make her own call. We'd also deal with the abusive fuck too. Clean up. I slid my wallet into my pocket after checking I had the extra room key for her hotel. I'd slipped it off her. I needed to go and empty that room today. No one from the show knew where she was staying, but the hotel might report something. Better to just make it look like she checked out.

Jasper was risking more than himself with this move. Raptor would kill us all. And no way Jasper didn't know it.

Then again, I couldn't argue with his reasons either.

We were so fucked.

I paused to knock on Rome's door, but he didn't answer. I didn't open the door and walk in, even if it wasn't locked.

We didn't lock our doors, but we didn't barge in either. No one else belonged in this part of the clubhouse. The rats weren't even supposed to be in our lounge or den. A dull headache throbbed behind my eyes.

I checked the room between mine and his. I might need to install an external lock. Not my idea of fun, but a lot would depend on Emersyn. Inside, the room was clean, the bed made, fresh towels and pillows. It even smelled clean.

A desk and chair were also set up, and one of the walls

had a huge painting on it. When the fuck had Rome had time for that?

He didn't do canvas. Or at least I didn't think he did. But it was a sunrise. It was put right where a window would be. The room didn't have a window. None of our rooms did. That was a choice we made to avoid spies and snipers.

Paranoid?

Sure, but we were alive.

I was ready to walk out when I spotted the bear on the bed. It was a little ragged, but it had been cleaned up and a new bow affixed to his neck.

Yeah.

Fucked.

Totally fucked.

I didn't know the half of it though until I made it back to Doc's. The drive in my baby—a 2017 Dodge Challenger SRT Demon, sleek, black, and growling with power—had settled some of my misgivings. It did not in any way prepare me to walk into the standoff taking place in Doc's clinic.

A tousled and wary-eyed Emersyn, pale as death with dark shadows ringing her eyes held up—what the fuck was that? It wasn't a knife. No, it was some kind of steel tray. She wielded it like a weapon. Vaughn had a hand over his mouth like he was trying not to laugh, and Jasper shot her an exasperated look.

But Doc was actually talking to her in a soothing voice. "You have a concussion. No one here is going to hurt you…"

Only Emersyn's whiskey brown eyes weren't on Doc anymore. They pinned to me.

One minute, she had the tray in the air, the next, she stumbled straight to me and threw herself in my arms. I caught her, especially after the way she staggered and pain creased her face. She only had on a T-shirt—Vaughn's—and her dance clothes were still in a heap.

Fuck, I should have brought her some clothes back.

"Kestrel," she gasped, and I closed my arms reflexively. "You didn't abandon me."

Fuck.

Fuck.

Fuck.

Jasper glared at me, and I just stared back at him as I held her.

I told him this was a bad idea.

"You're safe," I tried to assure her, but she stiffened in my arms and jerked away a little. I tried again. "You're safe."

This time, she blew out a breath, then shot a nervous look toward Jasper, then Vaughn, and finally Doc. Some color flushed back into her cheeks, and her mouth tightened.

"Where the hell am I?"

CHAPTER 5

EMERSYN

"*W*here the hell am I?"

That had been my first question when I woke up to the chilly room, naked beneath a blanket. The second had been the icy realization that not only had I awoken in this foreign room, it was some kind of hospital or clinic.

The last place I wanted to be stuck again was a hospital. No, just no. Worse still, no sooner had I slid off the bed in search of my clothes than my ankle screamed in protest and so did my head. Hot hands had gripped me, and it had just gone downhill from there.

He'd dragged a shirt onto me, and then more people had walked in, and frankly, I didn't know any of them. Well, I knew the one tech guy—both tech guys—sort of. I had no idea what their names were or why they were here. The redhead had helped me I thought, or he'd tried to when Eric cornered me.

Fuck, my head hurt so bad, I swore my heartbeat pulsed inside my skull. My wrist hurt, and so did my leg. Every muscle on my body had a protest, and they were screaming. I could barely focus. When they'd tried to make me get on the bed, I'd grabbed the silver tray and hit the redhead across the shoulder and swung it at the older guy when he suggested sedating me.

Hell no.

I had to get out of here.

If they called my parents...

The tech with the arm sleeve tattoo and the colorful hands—they were nice hands, broad palms and thick fingers —had just asked me if I would sit down when Kestrel strode through the open door. I'd never been so relieved to see someone in my life.

I hurled myself between the other two in a rush to get to him. My driver had had my back all week. He caught me as I all but fell into him, and I had to swallow back the pain clawing up my throat.

"Kestrel." I had to shove the words past the pain. I wouldn't cry. I wouldn't betray how much it hurt or the fact my stomach lurched with every swaying breath I took. How hard had Eric hit me this time? "You didn't abandon me."

No sooner had those words slipped out of me than I wanted to take them back.

Had they seen it?

Of course, they'd seen it. Why else would I be *here* with a bunch of strangers?

"You're safe," Kestrel soothed, and he closed his arms around me. The cage of his arms was strong enough, it pressed me tight into him without squeezing me. Even the labored huff of my breathing warned me my ribs were hurting. "You're safe."

No, I wasn't. The words had me stiffening. I shouldn't

have bared a weakness, especially when I still didn't know *where* I was. I pulled away from Kestrel and ignored the white-hot pain shooting up my leg. I'd performed on worse, and frankly, nothing compared to the hammering inside my skull.

Which brought me back to the question no one had answered. "Where the hell am I?" I repeated, swinging my gaze from the redhead with brown eyes so pale, they bordered on topaz, to the tech who'd installed my lock and gave me a cigarette. He had longer hair and a beard, but they didn't detract from his appearance in the slightest. The appeal of the sexy bad boy wasn't lost on me, but I had long since learned my lesson.

Everyone lied.

Everyone betrayed.

Everyone wanted something.

I dragged my gaze off his chilly gray eyes and looked back at the redhead. Shirtless, most of his tattoos were on display. That wasn't a good idea either, so I swung around to face Kestrel again, suddenly aware of his hand on my arm, and that was one step too far.

My stomach revolted, and my leg buckled in the same breath.

"Fuck," Kestrel swore, but he didn't let me go. If anything, he caught my weight and turned me away. Redhead with the beautiful eyes slid a pan in front of me, and to my utter humiliation, I threw up into it. Every gag brought up nothing but bile—thank fuck I never ate before a performance. Usually. Luckily the burger was hours before. The worst part though was the spikes retching drove through my skull.

The world swayed, and as soon as the gagging stopped, strong arms lifted me, and it took me a minute to identify who held me. Even then, the panic clawing through me wanted him to put me down. "No," I ordered him and had to fight crying out when I tried to pull away and bashed my arm. Pain shrieked along it to compete with the cacophony in my brain.

"Stop," a harsh, gravelly voice ordered, and then there were cool fingers on my chin. The man lifting my gaze up was the oldest one in the room, I thought. He had a dusting of stubble over his face, and his eyes were dark and intent. While his fingers were gentle, they didn't let me pull away. "That's enough," he said. "You have a concussion and a lot of other damage. I'm going to look after you, and you're going to let me. I'll throw these three fuckers out if that's what you need to rest, but right now, you stop flailing about. You're going to hurt yourself, and we can't have that."

The combination of command and humor helped, but the panic was a real thing shuddering inside my skin. I really needed Kestrel to put me down. He was sexy and sweet and he'd even come to the show and then he was here, but... "Put me down," I said in a voice shaking way more than I liked. "Please."

The man holding my chin gave me a studying look and then said, "Let me help you back onto the bed, all right? Would that be all right? We just need to make sure you don't hurt anything else."

The shaking seemed to be coming from deep inside.

"Put her down, Kestrel," the man ordered. "What's your name, sweetheart? None of these idiots bothered to tell me."

I should totally lie. But my head hurt too much. "Emersyn."

"Nice name," he commented as Kestrel set me on my feet. My ankle protested violently, but I forced my footing to stay steady.

"I'm Mickey," the man said as he held out a hand to me. "Most of them just call me Doc, but here, brace yourself on my arm and we'll get you squared away."

I didn't know if it was the pain or the soothing patience in his voice, but I put a hand on his arm just like he said and started forward. The sensation of hot and cold washed over me in waves and my stomach rolled, but I had always been good at ignoring the protests my body made. If only my head would stop.

"Easy there, Emersyn, that's a sweetheart, almost there. Lean more on me and keep your weight off that foot."

A shuffle of movement had me stiffening, and I jerked to find gray eyes right behind me. Where had Kestrel gone?

"Back the fuck off, Hawk," Doc ordered in a tone made of corded steel. "Ignore him," Doc said to me in a far gentler tone. "Kestrel was right—you're safe here, and they're backing off now."

"I'm not fucking leaving, Doc. Stop telling her bullshit."

We were finally at the bed—though it was more of a table. The cool air on my bare legs reminded me I just had on a T-shirt. I had to assume it was the guy with the pretty tattoos all over his chest and arms. But I didn't much care right now.

Hawk.

Kestrel.

Why were they all named after birds?

Wait, Doc wasn't named after a bird.

"If she needs you to step the fuck out, Hawk," Doc growled out, "then you'll damn well do it, and if you fight me on this, you'll lose. She comes first. She's the patient. You're just an asshole."

That was almost funny, only the room kind of blurred around the edges. I put my hand on the table, and all at once, I couldn't figure out how I was going to climb up there. My tongue felt thick, and my lips numbed.

"I don't feel so good."

The first time I'd dropped from the silks, I'd done it

under orders. You couldn't learn to fly if you didn't know how to fall.

This was a lot like that. Everything went weightless, and I crumpled.

Only instead of bouncing into the net, I found myself staring up into a pair of fierce gray eyes so filled with fury, I was kind of glad I was about to pass out.

Whatever I'd done to piss off this man, I had a feeling they wouldn't find my body.

Maybe that wouldn't be such a bad thing.

The next time I opened my eyes, the room was dim with almost no light, save for a sliver of it on the far side of the room. The bed was soft under me, softer than most of the mattresses I'd ever had. I needed something firm to support my back. Soft encouraged laziness. The cool air was still there, but the antiseptic smell was gone. I couldn't sort my thoughts into a straight line, but when I tried to sit up, my stomach lurched again.

"Easy," a warm, almost honeyed male voice said, and there was a steadying hand on me. "Got the pail right here if you gotta upchuck again, though I'd really appreciate it if you didn't."

I frowned. "You're not Doc." My voice came out super scratchy and rough. Had I swallowed glass?

There was something icy and cold at my lips, and I opened my mouth to take the ice, half aware of the warm fingers chasing the ice in so it didn't fall out. Fuck, I was all kinds of sloppy. Why couldn't I focus?

"I'd offer you water, but we have you on an IV," the honeyed voice told me. "Doc's orders. He'll be here in a couple of hours to check on you."

He had to go?

"Want me to settle another pillow behind you, let you sit up some?"

"Please," I said and tried to focus, but I couldn't see anything. He lifted me with care, and then there was another soft pillow behind me. When he settled me back against them, he did with such smoothness, my stomach didn't protest.

Before I could ask anything else, he pressed more ice chips to my lips, and I sucked on them gratefully. A few more of those, and my next words weren't so harsh. "Why is it dark?"

"You have a concussion," he told me in that melodious voice. The rich, deep timbre of it was something I could listen to for hours. "Doc explained the light in the clinic probably contributed to your symptoms worsening when you woke up earlier. So we'll keep them off for now. I can see what you need."

That shouldn't be comforting. "Where am I?"

"Somewhere safe."

I licked my lips. "That's not an answer."

"It's the only one you're getting right now, Dove."

"That's not my name."

"But it suits you." There was an element of laughter in his voice. Was he laughing at me or with me?

The thud of my skull made trying to puzzle that out hard. I was so tired. "Who are you?"

"My name's Vaughn," he told me.

"So you're not named after a bird?" Oh what was it with them and birds?

He chuckled for real this time. "Sometimes they call me Falcon. But my name is Vaughn."

Huh.

I thought I might have fallen asleep, but when I jerked awake, he was right there again, all soothing, deep voice in the dark. "You're safe, Dove."

"Stop calling me that."

"Nah," he said, almost teasing. "I like it. Besides, you're more like a wounded bird right now."

Wounded. "Has someone called my parents?" Dread curled through me. "Or the company?"

"Nope," he told me. "No one knows where you are."

The sinking sensation gave way to relief and then to sinking all over again. If the company didn't know where I was, then Eric couldn't bribe someone and show up. If my parents didn't know, then they hadn't dispatched some handler to deal with me. But I didn't know these people...

"You're the one who gave me your shirt."

"Yep," he said. "Looked good on you too. Though it kind of fit you more like a dress."

I wheezed a little laugh. "I should say thank you."

"Nah, you were having a shit night. Pretty sure you still are, Dove. You should try to sleep. Doc came and checked on you a little while ago. He's wrapped your ankle and your wrist. Checked the stitches in your head. And I'll go back to putting ice on your chest and sides here soon. We're in the twenty minutes off portion."

"I'm so tired," I admitted. "But I need to..." I needed to do something. But fuck if I knew what. I thought that I could handle Eric, that he would do what he did but he wouldn't go any further. I never expected him to drag me out into the alley or whatever he was going to...

"You don't need to do anything but rest, Dove. We'll take care of everything else."

That sounded too good to be true.

"Why?"

Instead of playing dumb, he just said, "Why not?"

"That's not an answer."

"You're a petulant little thing, aren't you?" That rich tone of amusement drifted back into his voice. "Go to sleep, Dove.

Plenty of time to argue tomorrow. Soon as you can handle it, I'll get you another steel tray to whack me with."

I laughed, and it hurt. I couldn't quite keep the gasp of breath to myself. Almost immediately, he stroked a warmed calloused hand over my cheek and up to my hair. "Shh, easy," he murmured. "No more jokes. Sleep is the best thing for you."

"I need…"

"What do you need?"

"Nothing." Nothing I could ask for. I didn't even know why they were doing this. Or who they were…but he was stroking my hair, and my eyes got heavier and heavier.

"It's all right, Dove, you sleep. Nothing is going to touch you here." At least that's what I thought he said before I plunged back into darkness.

CHAPTER 6

EMERSYN

The headache awaiting me the next time I opened my eyes promised me the night before hadn't been a series of stop-motion filled nightmares. I was still in a soft bed, in a mostly dark room, though the light in the corner was a little brighter and the sliver had become a soft pool. Everything hurt, not as bad as it had, but the body aches stretched and threatened me as I rolled over.

Instead of an IV in my hand, there was a Band-Aid across the back of the right one. My left was coated in a splint while also being wrapped in an Ace bandage. I shifted again and my ankle immediately protested, but I could feel the wrap on it and how it extended over my foot.

Stiff didn't begin to describe me. Every other time I'd woken, Vaughn had been here, a soothing presence in the dark, a melodious voice to chase away my nightmares and my protests. He told me very little, even while he spoke a lot.

I half expected him to appear and begin stroking my hair again. I'd made it halfway to sitting by curling my abs, even as my chest and sides protested when I realized no, I wasn't alone in the room.

There was an oversized chair in the corner turned slightly sideways so the guy sleeping in it could stretch his legs out onto the foot of my bed. The puddle of yellow light highlighted the stranger sprawled there. He had a notebook pressed against his bare chest. Paint splattered his arms, and there were some in his blond hair. His arms were thick with muscle, and what I could see of his chest promised the same, but his legs were leaner. More like a runner.

I made it all the way to sitting and took a moment to catch my breath. He let out the faintest of snores, and relief spilled through me. I didn't know who he was or why he'd taken Vaughn's place. I'd asked about Kestrel at one point, but I couldn't remember his answer.

Pushing the blanket away slowly, I tried to keep my movements controlled. I didn't know this latest keeper, but if I could manage to move and get on my feet, then I could get to that door.

Escape was the first item on my list.

The dull throb of my headache pulsed with every movement, as if a warning. While my stomach didn't lurch and the room didn't waver, I paused frequently to let the pain ease back before I got my legs out and I stared down at my ankle. It had been taped well, and the bandage circled the arch of my foot to give it steadying support.

Unless I'd actually broken it, when I didn't think I had, I should be able to walk on it. Besides, my chest burned with every breath I took that threatened to try and expand my abused ribcage.

How much worse could the ankle be?

I was wearing a T-shirt and nothing else.

That was a momentary flicker, but then I'd only been in a T-shirt in that clinic room I'd awoken in too. I didn't feel any wetness on my thighs, and I had to pause right there at the edge of the bed and grip it with my right hand as I fought back the panic clawing up through my wheezing lungs.

There was no wetness. Not once had I woken to Vaughn *in* the bed with me. He'd always been next to it, and I'd been under the covers.

Head bowed, I forced deeper breaths. I couldn't afford to freak out. Racing pulse and hot-cold sensation notwithstanding, I could do this. *Up, Emersyn. On your feet. Focus on that step, then the next, and the one after that. Keep going until you can't. Then get up and move some more.*

The mental litany did the trick. My heart still beat too fast and I still wanted to gulp air like I was drowning, but dance was as much about controlling my breath as my body. I needed to get out of here.

Shooting a look over my shoulder, I checked that my blond guard hadn't moved. The angle gave me a better look at him. There were definitely different colors of paint speckled over him, and one of his fingers was nearly blue like he'd been finger-painting. Or whatever.

His ripped jeans were also stained liberally with paint. The rest of him was bare, from his blond head to his tapered waist. He had tattoos too, but I couldn't make them out as more than shadows on his skin.

I was pretty sure one was Celtic knotwork of some kind. I loved knotwork. I'd wanted one, but my body was always on display and why would I make a mess of it?

Yeah, not sure how they justified the bruises when that was the bullshit excuse about tattoos.

I was eighteen.

Fuck it. I'd go get one as soon as I got out of wherever the fuck here was. I didn't have to follow the rules anymore.

Rising, I put most of my weight on the good ankle rather than the bad. No point in landing on my ass less than thirty seconds after I got out of the bed. The whole room swayed, and I wanted to curse. Curling the fingers of my right hand into my palm, I swallowed with a grimace. Or tried to.

There was no spit in my mouth, and my throat, like my head, ached. The room teetered a little, and even with what little light there was in the room behind me, my eyes still watered.

If I couldn't stand up for long, I'd never make it out of here. I didn't know why Kestrel and his friends took me, but kidnapping wasn't out of the question. The last thing I wanted was to be ransomed back to my family. Yeah, I was sure that would go over well.

Maybe I could offer them money to let me go without talking to my family. They'd said they hadn't called anyone, and I vaguely recalled Vaughn assuring me no one knew where I was. That had been important in the dark, head screaming and not able to focus.

Right now, though? It worried me.

The room had finally stabilized, so I headed for the door. Whether I had just a shirt on or not, I didn't want to chance waking up my guard by looking for clothes. Every step was like sending a knife through my skull. My ankle wasn't much better, but it held if I balanced more of my weight on my uninjured leg.

I gripped the knob, but it didn't turn. Frowning, I tried it again. Was I locked in here? I smoothed my fingers over the knob, looking for a lock of some kind to release, but nothing. Then I just pulled it if the knob wouldn't turn, but the door didn't budge.

Frustration swelled through me as I yanked it harder. Not that it changed the result. The scrabble of panic clawed its way up my spine again, and I swallowed back a sound as I yanked it again.

"That's not a real door."

Fuck.

The scream I'd been holding in burst out of me, and I twisted to slam my back against the door. My blond guard stood a couple of feet away, one hand raking through his disheveled hair.

He jerked at my scream, and for a moment, a slash of a smile penetrated the shadows hiding his face from me. He half-twisted so the light hit him. "It's not a real door," he repeated. "The bathroom is over here." He motioned to the other wall where a door stood ajar.

Still fighting the breathlessness, I stared at him.

"You okay?" He cocked his head to the side. "You don't look steady."

"You scared the shit out of me."

When he raked his hand through his hair this time, I glanced away from the motion, only that was a mistake. I focused on the ripple of muscle along his chest and arm. The light playing over the muscle seemed to emphasize not only his physique, but also gave the paint flecks a bit of a glittery appearance.

Frankly, his body was fine, and it wasn't like I hadn't seen good bodies before.

"Didn't mean to scare you," he said, giving me something of a sheepish look. "But you were going to hurt yourself and you looked scared."

I scowled. Pushing off of the door, I straightened and ignored the thundering in my head and the pulse of pain in my ankle. "I'm not." I didn't care what I said earlier.

"Okay." Just like that. "You want the bathroom?" He cocked his head and nodded toward the open door. "Need a hand?"

"I can manage." The words came out on a rasp. What I wouldn't give for a little spit. That said, to get to the bathroom, I had to pass by him, and he squinted at me like I was some kind of puzzle.

"Okay," he said, repeating the earlier word, yet neither of us moved. With a sigh, he rubbed that hand over his face. "Are you going to go?"

"Are you going to move?" I bit the words off one at a time. His hand dropped from his face, and he pressed it against his chest. A hint of mockery touched his smile as he took a step to the side and then extended his arm as though *please, go ahead*.

That would put him at my back.

But if I kept making a big deal about this, it was going to let him know I really was afraid. I couldn't afford fear. I'd have licked my lips, but the dry mouth made that almost an impossibility. We both stood there for another long minute, and I had a feeling he wasn't going to budge until I did.

Fine.

Fuck it. It wasn't like I could get away at the moment. I just had to conserve my energy if I had to fight or to at least get a little stronger. Trying to act like it didn't matter, I forced myself to walk without a limp. I swore he moved a little closer as I passed him because I had tried to leave distance between us, but there was no missing the heat radiating off of him.

Not slowing, I half stumbled at the bathroom door and wanted to swear. I didn't fall though. No, the hand on my arm and the other on my lower back steadied me.

"Okay?" That word again, only this time, he asked it and there was a hint of laughter in the way his lips twitched and his eyes creased. They were deep blue-green, like the ocean. Or maybe that was just the lamp and I needed to stop worrying about what these guys looked like.

Sure, describing my kidnappers sounded like a fine idea.

"Yeah," I said and tugged my arm. To my immense relief, he let me go, and then I was through the door and had it closed. Sinking back against the door, I didn't give a damn that the bathroom was pitch dark. All I cared about was that there was a door between me and him.

I could have my freak-out here in the dark, where no one, not even me, could see me fall apart. A roaring in my ears blotted out all sound, and I kept my eyes closed whether the light was on or not. My heart beat so frantically at my ribs, I wouldn't have been surprised if it left fresh bruises and cracks for me.

How long I just stood there, I didn't know. Then he knocked on the door, and I leapt away from it.

"You okay in there, little one?"

The trembling in my limbs threatened to drop me on my ass, so I felt around until I located the toilet seat and perched on it. The cold on my bare ass helped get my mind unstuck. "I'm fine," I called. "Just—I need a minute."

"Take your time," he told me. "But I'll be right here."

Right there? Right outside the door?

I tilted my head back, I had to think. I was having a hell of a time with the headache though. Since I actually had to pee, I stood and then moved to the wall to flick on the light switch.

The brightness cut into my vision like a knife, and I squinted my eyes closed as those new spikes began to burrow their way into my brain. Teary, I sniffed and squinted until I could locate the toilet again. The bathroom was pretty plain, all white tiles, and it looked clean. There was a rod, but no shower curtain on the tub. A toilet. A vanity. The only items in the bathroom besides the fixtures was some toilet paper.

There wasn't even soap or a towel.

It took me no time to finish my business. And it wasn't

until I started to pee that I realized how badly I needed to go. I rinsed my hands because there was no soap and then shook them off.

I still had to squint in the light but at least the screws being drilled into my brain had slowed down. I stared at the closed door.

On the other side was one of my kidnappers. Or whatever they were. They weren't attempting to hide their faces and they had taken me to a doctor, so maybe they were well-meaning kidnappers?

I would have slapped myself if I didn't already hurt. There was no such thing as a "well-meaning kidnapper." They wanted something. Something to do with me or my too wealthy parents.

But the fact they let me see their faces? And I even knew their names? They weren't letting me go. I could identify them.

Pressing my forehead against the wood of the door, I fought back another wave of tears before I straightened and opened the door.

As promised, the blond stood just a couple of feet from the door. The light from the bathroom gave me a better look at him. The tattoos were Celtic knot work and a series of little birds along his chest like they were scattering. They were all tiny though, so I had no idea which birds they were.

"Better?"

Well that was an improvement over okay.

Maybe.

Up close, I couldn't ignore the way he smelled either. Cedar and sandalwood, like the theatres with their big wooden stages, with hints of a citrus scent like polish. Weird, but I kind of liked it. There was something a little harsher under it. Paint, maybe? It wasn't bad, but it made it hard to focus.

My brain was so messed up.

"Is there more ice?"

"Yeah, I can get you some," he offered. "But there's water too."

I frowned, and when the room swayed, it took me a minute to realize it wasn't the room, it was me.

"Back in bed."

"I don't want to," I argued. "I just—I need to go."

"Yes, you need to lie down before you fall down. Get in the bed, okay? I'm trying to give you space since you're a fretful little magpie, but you're killing me with this."

I was killing him?

I glared at him and glanced around for the other door, since the one I'd been at wasn't a real door. Who left a door in a wall like that? The other door wasn't far from where he'd been sitting. The whole room seemed oddly laid out, but I started for it, and tall, blond, and irritating got in my way.

"The bed's over there," he told me.

"I know where it is. I'm leaving."

He sighed, and when I tried to side-step him, he blocked me again. Aggravated, I slammed my hands against his chest to shove him out of the way and regretted it instantly.

Pain ripped up my arm, and I stumbled. Once again, he kept me from hitting the floor as he picked me up. The pressure of his arm against my back actually fucking hurt, and I couldn't suck in a deep breath.

"You're a fucking brat," he told me as he set me in the bed gently, despite the growl in his words. I half expected him to just drop me.

"Fuck you," I snapped back up at him. "I don't even know who you are, so why the hell would I listen to you?"

What little emotion had been on his face vanished behind a blank mask.

"Because I'm one of the guys helping you," he told me in a

flat tone as he loomed over me. "You're hurt. Doc's been in and out of here a few times. One of us has been with you since you got here. Stop being a spoiled princess."

Spoiled princess.

Asshole.

Curling up to a sitting position, I ignored the pull of my muscles and slapped him before he could jerk back. At least this time, I remembered to use my uninjured arm.

When he lifted a hand, I scooted backward and did my best to ignore my screaming wrist as I tried to scramble out of reach. Everything about him went still, and he touched his fingers to his face. My pulse jump-started, hammering away, and I swore I could feel it pounding a path into my brain.

He stared at me for a long moment, then dropped his hand. "I'm Rome," he said.

"What?"

"My name," he said in that inflectionless voice. "My name is Rome."

I licked at my lips, desperate for even a little moisture. His eyes hardened, and he turned away. I sagged, blowing out a breath. I knew better than to hit, it always invited retaliation, but I wasn't a fucking princess.

I'd never been a damn princess.

Instead of leaving the room though, he went over to the chair, and there was a rattle of plastic before he lifted a bottle of water. He had the cap twisted off before he handed it to me, and he didn't come any closer than arm's reach.

A part of me wanted to refuse the water, but I needed it and I needed every resource I could on my side until I could get out of here. His fingers didn't touch mine as he passed the bottle over. I drained it in four swift gulps.

All Rome did was raise his brows, and then he went and got another bottle of water.

I choked a little on this one, coughing as it went into my

windpipe, but I didn't let it slow me down. The water felt great in my mouth and on my throat. The whole time, Rome stared at me, his expression still blank and his eyes hard points of color.

"Are you hungry?" he asked finally, and I started to shake my head, then thought better of it.

It already hurt enough. "No."

"Okay."

Still, he stood there another long moment before he moved back to the chair and picked up his notebook or whatever it was. It looked like a pad of paper. He stretched his legs out and placed his feet on the end of the bed.

Pencil in hand, he focused on the pad in his lap and started writing something.

"Did it help?" he asked after a long silence. I was still sitting up against the headboard, exhaustion weighing down my muscles.

"The water? Yes." Then, because they'd been ingrained in me since before I could talk, I added, "Thank you."

He snorted softly, and I glanced over to find him shaking his head, almost a flicker of a smile on his face as he continued scratching his pencil against the paper. "I meant telling you my name."

Oh.

I eased down a little. Maybe if I pretended to go to sleep, he would, and then I could go for the real door—over there. Near him.

The light from the bathroom kept the room brighter, but that didn't seem to kill my eyes as much.

"Well?" Rome asked again as I finally laid my head back on the pillows and managed to drag the blankets back up over me. "Did it help?"

"I don't know," I told him honestly, and then I closed my eyes and tried to turn away from him. It hurt to twist about, but I didn't want to look at him and I didn't want him looking at me. Still, no matter how long I lay there, the pencil scratches didn't stop and I finally closed my eyes for real.

One little nap.

One little nap, and I'd get out of here.

CHAPTER 7

EMERSYN

*T*he next time I opened my eyes, Kestrel sat in the chair Rome had occupied. Relief threaded through me, at least until it hit me that even if I'd trusted him, they'd still kidnapped me. He'd still kidnapped me. I had shifted in my sleep, and I faced toward him instead of away. He was also staring at me, so there was no disguising the fact I had awoken.

"Hi," I croaked out and then grimaced. How did my voice sound even worse than it had in the middle of the night?

Pushing out of the chair, he was at my side in an instant and had the water cup with the bendy straw at my lips. I really shouldn't trust any of them. But they'd all helped me in some way, and my throat ached and my mouth was so dry. I sucked in a few drops, and the minute the cool water hit my tongue, I sucked in some more.

Before I knew it, I'd finished the whole cup, and I let out a sigh as he tugged it away. A frown tightened his brows, and his blue-green eyes seemed darker somehow. More green than blue. But he turned away as I tried to sit up.

Oh man, if I'd thought I hurt when I woke up the night before, I really hurt now.

"Let me help you," he said, but he didn't just reach out and grab me. That was something. Still, I shook my head. I'd managed on my own for a long time. All this sleeping and lying around had caused me to stiffen way too much. Bruises would stiffen worse if I didn't get some movement in.

One upside—shaking my head only made the room sway a little. I didn't want to puke either.

Score a point for me.

I crunched my way up to sitting, even if my abs protested the movement and my ribs let me know in no uncertain terms they were on strike. Yeah well, we'd dealt with worse. We could do this. I blew out a breath as Kestrel glared at me. Undeterred, I stared right back up at him. Without a word, he whipped around and stalked into the bathroom.

Ignoring the way his jeans shaped his ass was probably a good thing. In all the days he'd driven me, he'd always been nicely dressed in a dark suit. Always put together. Now... now he looked rougher somehow. The only light in the room came from that lamp by the chair. At the sound of the water turning on, I did a quick inventory.

My wrist was still splinted and wrapped. So was my ankle. I was still wearing that same T-shirt. Still no panties. Joyful. I grimaced. Even after the water, my mouth tasted like ass, and my hair was all kinds of ratty feeling and I stunk.

Stunk like I'd been sweating in rehearsal for hours then gone to sleep like that.

Or maybe like I'd been performing?

The water cut off, and I pulled the covers back over my legs before Kestrel emerged from the bathroom. He offered me the cup, but when I tried to take it, he just held it steady while I took another drink.

The whole time, the weight of his stare rested on me, and I finally let go of the cup and licked my lips. Yeah, the water was great. What the hell died in my mouth?

Instead of moving away, Kestrel set the cup down on the nightstand. Crouching, he put a hand on the bed next to my leg, but he didn't touch me. "How are you?"

I frowned, then had to stop because it just added to the dull ache in my head. "How the hell do you think I am?"

"I don't know," he said slowly, then exhaled a heavy breath. "If I knew I wouldn't have asked. You've been in and out of consciousness for the last three days."

Three days?

My stomach bottomed out. "The show…"

"You don't have to worry about that right now."

"Right now? That's my life." What the hell did he mean right now? The dull thud of the headache seemed to be gaining some force.

"It was a job with shitty people who you let treat you shitty." The judgment in his voice dried up my next words before I said them aloud. "Fuck." He pushed upward and stalked away from the bed. I wasn't sure who that last comment was for—me or him.

He raked a hand through his hair and then turned around to glare at me. *Again.*

"What?" I demanded. "What did I do?"

"You're here."

"That wasn't my choice. In fact," I continued and shoved the blankets back, "I'll just leave if it's bothering you so damn much." I swung my legs out, and if he ended up seeing my bare ass, too damn bad. The world swayed once I stood, and I still kept my weight off the bad ankle.

"Sit down."

"Fuck off."

He glared, and I glared right back. "Emersyn—"

"No."

"Excuse me?"

"You can call me Miss Sharpe or ma'am or a fucking cab, but you don't get to use my name." I'd asked him to do that when he'd been so damn kind that first night. But it was just another act. I should have learned my lesson by now. I had the absolute worst taste in…

"Sit down before you fall down. I don't want you to get hurt any further."

"Then why not take me to a hospital or a…" Wait. They had taken me to a doctor. No. They should still have taken me to the hospital. Called the cops. "Where am I?"

"Somewhere safe," he said. "Sit down, Ms. Sharpe."

"Why are you so pissed at me? What did I do to you?"

Head back, he stared at the ceiling for a minute. "You got hurt."

"Well, I didn't do it on purpose."

"You sure about that?" He bit off the last word with a growl, and I just stared at him.

"Seriously, what did I do to *you*? And when can I leave?"

"Sit down."

We were going in circles.

"Tell me when I can leave."

"I can't."

"Then I can't sit." And we were at an impasse. As badly as everything ached…

The door opened, and I turned to find another room on the other side of the door. I could see the bed from here. The man standing in the doorway, however, was strangely familiar. "Well, it's about time you woke up, sweetheart. You were starting to worry us."

"Doc?"

"Excellent." A genuine smile stretched his lips as he continued into the room. The door behind him remained open, but all I could make out was a bed with a dark cover and a bit of a bookshelf. I shuffled forward a step. "Uh-uh," the doctor said as he circled my bed. Well, not my bed, the bed I'd been using. "That ankle is still swollen, and you're not putting weight on it yet. So let's sit down and go over some things."

Maybe it was the fact he smiled or he was a doctor. Or maybe because he wasn't the guy I'd trusted in the first place, but I sank down on the bed, suddenly aware of my lack of dress, not to mention my shitty hygiene.

"Whatever you do, can you get these things off me so I can shower?"

"Maybe," he said. "If not, I can wrap them in plastic and we'll get you cleaned up."

We? I shot a look at Kestrel, who fixed such a narrow-eyed, almost hostile look on the doc.

"Ignore him, sweetheart," Doc told me as he sat on the bed next to me. "Seriously, ignore him. Look at me."

I shifted a little, but that would require pulling my leg up onto the bed. Not missing a beat, the doc snagged part of the blanket and dragged it over my lap.

"Would it kill you boys to get her some different clothes?" he asked without looking over his shoulder. He had a small penlight in his hand.

"We have her clothes," Kestrel answered, then folded his arms.

They had my clothes? Really?

The light in my eyes hurt, and I winced.

"Yeah, you're still a little photosensitive. But that's to be expected. You had a hell of a concussion."

I swallowed.

"He said I'd been out for three days."

83

"In and out," Doc agreed, all confident business. I focused on his face. It was a kind one, if a little stern. The stubble on his face was thick enough to offer the promise of a beard, and it was reddish-brown like his hair. His eyes were a light brown, and they focused on me. I swore he seemed to catalog every reaction, so I tried to keep my expression calm. "I'm going to touch your arm…"

And he went from there. Every action, he announced, and bit by bit, I found myself relaxing. Well, not relaxing so much as focused on what he did. Follow the motion of his finger. Raise my arms. Not flex my wrist. Though he did test the sensation in my fingers. Next came reflexes. Then my ankle.

He unwrapped it and checked it side by side with the other. Nothing he did, however, came as a surprise.

"All right," he said as he rewrapped it with careful sure fingers. "That wrist may yet need a real cast. It's in rough shape, and you've still got swelling in this ankle, even after three days of essentially being off it. The concussion is looking better. You've got good tracking with your eyes, but they're still light sensitive and…" He placed two very gentle fingers against my jaw and tilted my head a little. The hands were calloused but careful. Everything he did was perfunctory and professional, and at the same time…almost friendly. "Still dilated. I want you to keep taking it easy. I'm concerned about you being dehydrated. I didn't want to keep you on an IV without a catheter…"

I made a face, and he chuckled.

"Not my favorite thing either. Trust me, I've been there."

Oddly, that didn't seem as difficult, even if I couldn't trust him. I couldn't trust any of them. "I believe you." Damn, my voice still sounded rough. "I'd rather skip that."

"Agreed. So Rome told me you got up and used the bathroom. Vaughn helped you in there last night."

"Rome was kind of an ass."

Kestrel scowled, but Doc only chuckled. "He can be."

I didn't remember... "Vaughn was the one who gave me the shirt." I plucked at the one I was wearing.

"He did."

He'd been really nice to me. I had some vague memories of him talking. "He has a pretty voice."

For some reason, Kestrel looked even more pissed. Someone with a stick that far up their ass shouldn't be as handsome as he was, nor as attractive. Fuck, I'd flirted with him, and now...

"Well, I wouldn't know about that." Doc's gentle retort pulled my attention back to him. "But I'll take your word for it. How are *you* feeling?"

"Like I'm trapped."

"Understandable, but I meant physically." So. No help there.

Good to know.

"It doesn't matter," I told him, and his eyebrows rose. More, his gaze hardened as he fixed me with a look.

"If it didn't matter, sweetheart, I wouldn't ask. This is how this works, I'm Doc, you're the patient. I ask questions, and you answer them. That way, I can compare your assessment with my observations, and we can make sure we're not missing something."

"I mean it doesn't matter because I'm still a prisoner."

An impatient sigh escaped Kestrel. "You're not a prisoner, Emersyn."

"And you're not allowed to call me that, bird boy." Aggravation swarmed through me, but I didn't give him the satisfaction of looking at him. Instead, I focused on Doc. "As for you, Doc, you're clearly on their side. So I'd rather keep my information to myself."

Rubbing a hand over his face, Doc shook his head. "Kestrel, get out."

"No."

On his feet, Doc pivoted to face the other man. I stole a look at Kestrel's expression. If anything, it had grown darker, and a storm brewed in his blue-green eyes. Even from here in the crappy lighting, I could make that out.

"Not asking. Telling," Doc said, and his voice became as inflexible as Kestrel seemed. "She's the patient. You're being an ass. You're also getting in the way of me treating her. So get out."

The standoff stretched for several long seconds. Finally, Kestrel looked at me. "Do you want me to go?"

I didn't know Doc, but I did know Kestrel. A part of me really wanted him to stay, to be a familiar face here. To be the one I'd be safe with, but that was just another lie. Another illusion. I knew better.

I should know better.

"Yes." Even if every other part of me wanted him to stay, I needed him to leave.

"Fine. I'll be right on the other side of that door. No funny business."

What the hell did he think we were going to do?

But Kestrel didn't wait for us to say or do anything. He stalked out, and the door closed with a solid, if almost hushed, thump.

"Better," Doc said as he pivoted to face me. "Now, I get it. You're not happy with this situation. Neither am I. Those boys… Well, the less said about that at the moment, the better. You're safe here, for the most part, and they're more interested in keeping you that way than anything else."

"If they wanted me safe, why didn't they take me to a hospital or…"

"Or?" He folded his arms.

"Or back to my hotel or something." I had been about to say back to the show or back inside, but considering Eric had dragged me out there in the first place... "Oh shit... What happened to Eric?"

"I have no idea, and I don't care. He's not my patient." I'd say that felt suspiciously like a lie, only he didn't even flinch as he said it. "As for the rest of that? Why do you think they didn't take you somewhere else? The injuries you have? The cracked ribs? The bruising?"

I flicked my gaze away and firmed my lips together.

"Yeah, I've seen abuse before, kid."

"I'm not a kid."

"Right," he said, doubt heavy in that single syllable. "I've also seen torture."

I pinned a look on him. He was tugging his shirt out of his pants. "What the hell are you doing?"

"Making a point."

With that, he tugged the shirt up and off. Half of his chest, all of his left arm and shoulder were completely covered in tattoos. He took one step closer to me as he said, "I know what scars are—the ones that are visible and the ones that aren't. And like I said...I know what torture looks like." Then he turned away, and I had to swallow bile that crawled up my throat.

His back, like his front was also tattooed, but only on one half. But this close, there was no mistaking the ridge lines hidden in the tattoos. They looked like grill marks.

Back still to me, he said, "I went over your X-rays. I know how many breaks you've had, and I've seen your current injuries, including the cracked ribs and the bruising. Some of those, you could have gotten from dancing. The older injuries. Some from performing, absolutely. Your current injuries?"

He turned then and faced me.

"No." With that, he pulled on his shirt once more. "So cut the shit and be straight with me."

"I hurt."

"That's a start," Doc said on an exhale. "Where does it hurt?"

Everywhere. "My chest. My wrist. My ankle." I met his gaze. "My head. But most of all…my skin is crawling because I smell and I'm wearing some guy's shirt and nothing else and I'm locked somewhere I don't know…in a place that has no windows." Because I'd finally had a chance to look around at all the walls.

It was a cell.

A cell with a comfortable bed and a parade of rugged, attractive men, some with sinful voices and all of them… Who the fuck knew what they wanted?

"Okay," he said slowly. "Anything else?"

I almost laughed. "Isn't that enough?"

"Maybe," Doc agreed, cocking his head to the side. "But is there anything else?"

So many things. None of which I had any intention of saying. "No."

"We're going to have to work on that."

I frowned. Work on there not being anything else wrong?

"Let's start with what we can fix. I'm going to put plastic on that ankle and that wrist, then I'm going to run you a bath. I don't want you trying to stand in a shower, and unless one of us is in there with you, I'd be concerned. And I don't think you want anyone in there."

Fuck no.

"As for the bath, if you'll trust me, I can get you in and out and we'll keep it professional."

My breath backed up, but there was nothing heated in his gaze. Nothing invested at all, just…patience.

"What about them?"

"Don't worry about them," he said. "I can handle it. I'll get you in the bath, you can wash, then we'll address the pain. I have a feeling that's going to wear you out. I do want you to try and eat, and then you're probably going to sleep."

Great.

"So what do you say, sweetheart? Let me help you? Maybe earn some trust?"

I glanced at the door again. Then at Doc.

"If it helps, all you'd have to do is scream, and I'm pretty sure Kestrel would do his damnedest to bust my head in."

"Not sure how that helps."

Doc shrugged. "It was worth a try."

Fuck. He wouldn't be the first man to see me naked. "Please," I said. "I would very much like to not stink and to change my clothes."

And to put some fucking underwear on.

He smiled. "Then let's do that. Hang tight, and I'll run that bath. You like it hot or just warm?"

"Scalding." At that admission, we locked eyes, and for a moment, the first real emotion crept into his face, but I looked away from the rough sympathy. I needed to concentrate on getting better.

Because I was going to get out of here.

I didn't escape one trap only to fall into another.

Not this time.

Not again.

I glanced back at Doc when he didn't move, and when I held his gaze this time, he nodded.

Maybe he was an ally

Maybe he wasn't.

One step at a time, Emersyn. You might have to fall before you fly.

CHAPTER 8

EMERSYN

"*E*ase forward," Doc said, and I leaned in with care, my good arm wrapped around my thighs. Doc had helped me into the bath so I didn't get my ankle bandage in the water. When I eyed where my leg was propped, he'd loosened the wrapping and then removed it so I could at least put it in the water. As scalding as it was, he hadn't wanted it in the water long, but I couldn't begin to describe how good it was to boil myself.

You knew it was bad when you began to offend yourself and the smell of old sweat and pained sweat had turned sour. How any of them could stand to be around me, I had no idea. Once I was in the water, I used my good hand to wash. The soap and washcloth weren't fancy, but I didn't fucking care. They were clean.

Even the bathroom was old, the tile cracked and the wallpaper peeled, but the tub itself was white porcelain and very clean. Even the knobs on the wall were shiny. The smoothness beneath my ass was a relief, but to be honest, I wanted to be clean too much to be fussy and I'd stayed in my share of bad hotels over the years. Just because the company made money now, didn't mean they always had.

"Ready?" Doc asked. He cupped water in his hands as I nodded and began to soak my hair down. I'd tried to just lie back, but that was impossible in the size of the tub. I wasn't exactly tall, but the tub was like four and a half feet and it also doubled as a shower. If my wrist wasn't in a splint, I could have just done this myself, but I had to keep that arm out of the water and Doc wanted my foot out soon.

So he was going to wash my hair, and I wanted it clean too bad to argue. Frankly, he'd been perfunctory since we got in here. He'd helped me out of the borrowed shirt and given me a cursory, if professional once over. My nipples puckered in the cold, but he hadn't even stared at them. When he tested my ribs, he kept it light and gentle. Then with a great deal of care, he'd lifted me up fully and set me in the tub rather than let me climb in.

The minute he added shampoo to my hair, I almost cried. The gentle scrape of his blunted nails against my scalp sent a wave of release through the tension bunching my muscles. He moved around the tender spot on my head like he knew exactly where it was. He was the doctor, so he probably did.

I hurt. A lot. The bruises seemed to throb, and that was probably the water. If I could have stood an ice bath, I'd have done that first. I might have to do it yet. Somehow, I didn't think Doc would be on board.

He didn't say anything for the length of time he scrubbed my hair, until, "Close your eyes and relax, I'll dip you back and then up."

It was surprisingly easy to do as he asked, I went slack like I would for a lift, focusing my center of gravity on where he held me, and he dipped my back until my hair was under the water but my knees and the rest of me weren't. He rinsed it, and the water turned soapy around me, then sat me up again. He squeezed the hair.

"I can do conditioner, but it might not rinse out in the water." I blinked past the droplets of water escaping down my face to stare at the water. It was nowhere near as clean as when we started. There wasn't a shower curtain, but I cut a look up at the shower head.

"Maybe just put a little on the ends," I said, and the weariness swimming through me made it not worth pushing this. "Not that anyone is going to care, but it will be easier to comb." My hair was ridiculously thick.

"Okay." He put a smear of it in big palms and then worked it through my hair, not just the ends but all of it. "I'll help you comb it after we get you out."

"Thank you." The words came out a little quieter and with a lot more helplessness than I ever wanted to admit, but Doc had helped and I felt so much better, even if I could sleep for a week.

The bathroom door slammed open, and the impact of it crashing into the wall made me jump, the jerk sending a fresh throb of pain through my chest. The gray-eyed man glared down at us. Well, me really.

"What the fuck do you think you're doing?"

"Taking the dog for a walk, asshole," I snapped. "What does it look like?"

Shit, I'd almost gotten rid of my headache, but it was back full force with that jerk and jump. The dump of adrenaline chased away the fatigue like I'd just done espresso shooters.

"Cute. I wasn't talking to you." He cut a look at Doc. "What the fuck do you think you're doing?"

Doc rose to his full height and rather than glare, just looked at the other man. "Dial it down, Jasper. She was miserable and needed a bath. And I wasn't leaving her in here to do it by herself."

"You had no fucking business doing this."

"She is my business."

"No," Jasper snarled. "She's not. She's not your business or your concern. You do her meds, you check her injuries, you get out. You do not get her naked and molest her—"

"What the hell is wrong with you?" I demanded, and to hell with the audience, I grabbed the towel rack bar and dragged myself up.

"Dammit, little bit," Doc said as he reached out to steady me. Probably not my finest hour, but I wasn't just going to sit there while some asshole threw his weight around and was a total dick to Doc for helping me.

Who the fuck did he think he was?

"Don't fucking touch her." Jasper grabbed Doc's arm and hauled him back. I nearly fell on my ass, but I locked my good hand around that towel bar and held myself up. Hopefully, it wouldn't rip out of the wall.

Doc slammed his elbow into Jasper, and then they both crashed into the wall. "Are you trying to hurt her?"

"She's all skin and bones and bruises," Jasper snarled in that shitty tone of his. "I don't want to do anything to her."

Yeah well, the feeling was mutual. They grappled for a second, and in a move I didn't quite catch, Doc twisted Jasper around and yanked his arm up behind him in what had to be a punishing hold. I flinched. My arm had been in a hold like that once.

That was the second time I broke it.

They vanished into the bedroom with a series of grunts and then came more punishing blows. Dammit. I clung to the wall and then took a deep breath and stepped out on the bad ankle with my good hand flat to the wall. It would hurt. But I could handle it.

I made it out without passing the fuck out and over to the doorway in time to see Doc slam Jasper into the ground and then Jasper had a gun tucked right up under Doc's jaw and everything in me froze.

"You want to think about that, Jasper," Doc told him in the steadiest, calmest voice ever. The door to the other room was open, and a guy I'd never seen before wandered inside. Leaner than anyone else I'd met, he had brown hair cut short with the sides of his head shaved and a pair of curious blue eyes.

"Did I miss the party invite?" he asked, an easy grin on his face, and then he looked at me. "Well hello, gorgeous. I definitely missed the party invite, or I'd have been right up to see you." The twang of his Southern accent was far too smooth to be manufactured. "You're looking a little rough. The guys do like to throw their girls around, get all dominant and shit. Now me? I'm a slow and easy ride, I'll take you real gentle like."

"Freddie, fuck right the hell off," Jasper snarled. "She is not here for your entertainment."

"Well, no shit, Boss, I can see that. Though I think you should be a little easier on the ladies. Just 'cause we pay 'em don't mean we need to slap them around."

I wasn't sure who was more appalled by the statement—Doc or Jasper. But at least Jasper pulled the gun away from Doc's face, and Doc rose to let the other man go. Surging to his feet, Jasper glared at Freddie, who made no pretense of looking me over. Maybe I should've cared that I was standing there naked, dripping, and chilled, but that would require more energy than I could muster.

"Out of curiosity, do you laser or wax?" Freddie asked. "I mean, that's the smoothest pussy I've seen in a long time."

I stared at Freddie. Had he seriously just… Had he really just asked me about my grooming? That spurt of adrenaline had gotten me out of the bathtub, but it was already fleeing.

"Put some fucking clothes on," Jasper snapped at me, and I sighed. It would take some effort to wrap a towel around me, so I just said fuck it and limped out of the bathroom.

"Yeah, you do whatever you want, Boo-Boo," Freddie told me with a wide grin. "I don't think I'd want to put on clothes over any of that, either. If you want, I can just shuck my clothes, then we can be naked together. Solidarity."

I probably shouldn't have laughed, but that was kind of funny. My bags were in the corner, which meant I had to go between Jasper and the doc to get to them. I concentrated on putting one foot in front of the other as I made my way over. My ankle protested every single step, but I refused to do more than the faint hobble.

All of the bags were on the floor, which meant I'd have to bend or squat. Great, I guessed everyone was getting a show. Bending hurt, but squatting would put pressure on my ankle. I leaned to grab the hand of one with my good hand, and a grunt escaped me.

"For fuck's sake." Jasper brushed my hand aside and grabbed the bag. The gun he'd had before wasn't visible anymore. He tossed the bag on the bed and then shoved Freddie backward. "Get out." He looked at me. No, not me. Doc. "You too."

"I think I'll wait. I still need to rewrap her ankle and she needs help…"

"I could help," Freddie offered from the other room, but neither of them looked over to the door. Instead, they just glared at each other. The tension in the room crackled. Yeah, I'd been in the middle of these situations before. Better to just keep my head down and get dressed. Then I could probably quietly pass out.

At least with the bag on the bed, I could unzip it. Everything was packed inside of it as neatly as I supposed they could manage. There were silk shirts that were rolled, and I tried not to grimace. I didn't really think I needed to worry about silk blouses or cocktail dresses right now.

Hopefully this bag had… I felt around the edges and then snagged some lace and pulled it upward. Panties. Those would do. They weren't practical, but anything would be better than the nothing I had right now. I stared at the panties for a minute and then sighed. Doc took a step toward me, and Jasper growled, honest-to-God growled, and he had a hand behind his back.

If I were to place a bet, I'd say he had a gun back there. I shook my head at Doc. I didn't want him getting hurt for me. Clearly, he worked for my kidnappers, even if he wasn't one of them. He might have already put his neck out too far. I leaned against the bed with my back to Jasper and then bent, good foot first while hoping the bad could take it for just that long. That done, I got the bad foot through and with care, pulled it up.

Probably not the most graceful put on of panties ever, but the moment they covered my ass, I swore I felt a thousand percent better. Sure, I was still topless, but fucking hell, my bare ass wasn't hanging out for everyone to see.

"What's going on?" The beautiful, melodious voice rolled right over me and eased some of the distress brought on by the fight. *Vaughn*, my brain very helpfully supplied. He'd been the one soothing me in the dark, chasing away my nightmares. "Freddie's bitching you're not sharing, Hawk."

I glanced over my shoulder at a crunch, and there was Vaughn and I finally placed the melodious voice with a face. It was the tech who'd helped me out that night before Eric had shown up. He'd actually tried to get me clear.

He was one of them.

Disappointment inched through me. So far, every single

person who'd been nice to me in this shitty little town was linked to this kidnapping. Good to know I attracted a type. He took a bite of the apple in his hand, and the crunch of it echoed through the silent room. My stomach growled at the sound, and my gaze fixed for a moment on the way his lips came together and the hint of juice on them.

It sounded like it would taste fantastic.

With one arm, he pulled the dark blue T-shirt he'd been wearing up and over his head without losing his apple, and then all I could see was the ripple of densely packed muscle under a colorfully inked skin. Someone had used him as their canvas, and my panties went damp, and not just from the water still dripping from my hair.

"Here," he said in that soft voice, like this was the most natural thing in the world as he bypassed both Jasper and Doc. "Let's get this on you. You look cold and a little miserable."

I laughed. It was a weird little sound and it kind of hurt to let it out, but laughing was better than crying. Biting the apple and holding it in his teeth, he wiped his hand against his jeans and then tugged the shirt over me, maneuvering my arms with ease, and then I was surrounded in his scent again.

"You hungry, Dove? I can fix you something." He offered his apple though, not the side he'd bitten into. Fuck it, I was hungry and so I took a bite, and damn if it wasn't juicy, crispy, and sweet. The taste flooded my mouth, and I closed my eyes, almost swaying.

"Fuck." Jasper's sharp curse had my eyes jerking open in time to catch him storming out of the room. Sure enough, there was a gun tucked into the waistband of his jeans. A cold shudder went through me.

"Look after her," Doc ordered. "I'll be back."

Then he followed after Jasper, and there was a sound of another door closing. When I looked back at Vaughn, he gave me a small smile. The copper of his hair seemed to gleam in the light, and his grin was easy, like they did this every day. "They'll figure it out. C'mon, get back in the bed and you can have the rest of my apple."

As nice as he was being and as pretty as he was...he wasn't my friend or my ally.

"Need a hand, or you got it?"

Exhaustion hit me all over again, and I sagged against the bed. Not even the warmth of his shirt or the richness of his scent around me was a comfort now. I was still trapped here —wherever here was—with armed, tatted up men, who probably wanted to hurt me. Or at least wanted *something* from me.

I pulled myself on the bed, and Vaughn let me do it, even when I grimaced. Once I settled against the headboard, I was ready to just close my eyes and pass out all over again. God, I was tired.

"Here," Vaughn said, holding out the apple. As much as I'd have liked to refuse his food, I needed my strength, so I took it. He nodded once I took another bite, and then he moved the suitcase back off the bed after zipping it up. I suppose I could have asked him to get me something of my own out to wear, but I had on my panties.

That would do.

He vanished into the bathroom, and the water began to drain from the tub. He came back a minute later with a towel. With it in both hands, he nodded to me. "Sit forward a little, I'll get the rest of that water out of your hair."

"I don't care if I'm wet."

"Well sure, it's fine now, Dove," he said, agreeing with me easily, and I hated how his voice just seemed to beckon me to relax and my fucking body did it. "But you're going to crash soon, and then your pillows are wet and it's uncomfortable and a whole thing."

"Is it?"

"Yeah," he told me. "And I'd really rather not have to go steal pillows from one of the other guys, 'cause then they whine and bitch. Not to mention, it'll smell like them."

I swallowed. "You could give me yours."

"Those are mine, Dove."

"Oh."

He grinned, and it softened his whole face. No one who was that big or that muscled should look that sweet when they smiled.

"Sorry."

"Don't apologize, not your fault. Rome pinched them and put them in here 'cause I have the nice pillows. I'd rather you used them anyway. But it's better if we keep them dry."

He had a point.

Fine. I eased forward, and he leaned forward until all I had was an eyeful of his gorgeous chest as he worked the towel over my hair with the kind of care Doc had taken when he washed it.

"You got a lot of hair, Dove."

I shrugged and then winced. Fuck, that hurt. "It's just hair."

"Yeah, I guess." Then he didn't say anything while I took another bite of apple and tried not to focus on the way the muscles of his pectoral flexed and danced as he worked the towel. But when I dipped my gaze lower, I couldn't stop staring at the tattoo on his navel—the crossed blades, the blood drops, and the way the snakes wrapped them together in an infinite loop.

"Vandals."

"Hmm?"

I probably shouldn't have said anything. "Nothing."

He leaned away from me and then glanced down at himself, then back at me. "You asking about the tattoo?"

"Just reading it."

He gave me a moment, then nodded before he flung the towel in the direction of the bathroom. The rest of me was mostly dry, even if the sheets were a little chilled from the fact I'd been wet when I got on the bed.

"Finish up the apple, and I'll go find you real food."

I was eating the apple, but I'd finished nearly all of it while Vaughn stared at me. It should've been uncomfortable, but the silence worked for me. When I was down to the core, he took it and I licked my fingers clean.

When he headed for the door, I had to admit, I was honestly surprised. They hadn't been leaving me alone.

"I'll be right back," he said. "Don't go anywhere."

I didn't comment. I didn't owe them anything.

He sighed. "Dove…you're safe here. We won't let anything happen to you, but I need you to trust me."

I stared at him.

"Just stay here."

I held up my cast wrist and motioned to my throbbing ankle. "Where am I going to go?"

He sighed, one arm on the door, and it was hard to miss the roses along his biceps and the pistol on his forearm and the Captain America shield on the inside of his biceps tucked right toward his underarm like it was a secret.

Every tattoo had a story.

Vaughn had a lot of stories.

"I'll be right back," he said and pulled the door closed after him. I debated getting off the bed and trying to wrestle on pants and then seeing if I could get out of here. The click of the lock told me that would be wasted effort, and I sagged back against the headboard and the pillows again.

Dammit.

Fine. Rest. Bide my time. Eat.

Then get the fuck out of here.

CHAPTER 9

EMERSYN

*A*s much as I could, I kept track of the passage of time. The lack of any actual clocks or windows eliminated the sense of whether it was night or day. I relied on meals to give me some ideas. The guys were not cooks, that much was obvious. Some meals were just beans on toast, and I'd eat it because I needed the fuel. It wasn't terrible, just bland. Grilled cheese was popular, so was microwavable pizza. The sheer volume of carbs was useful, but I needed more proteins.

I didn't ask.

They didn't offer.

Water, I had plenty of, though my cup was now plastic because I'd thrown a glass at Jasper's head. Damn near hit him. Fuck his reflexes.

I slept a lot the first couple of days after Doc's visit. That was another thing—Doc hadn't been back since the incident with Jasper and the gun. After he came back up with food—a burger and French fries—Vaughn had rewrapped my ankle for me and helped me comb my hair before I pretty much passed out.

I woke up to Kestrel being back in the room, and they continued their rotation. Oddly though, Jasper was there more than any of the others. While Vaughn would keep an easy patter of conversation going when I was awake, expecting nothing from me at all, none of the rest did. The minute I realized I was disappointed that Rome had arrived instead of Vaughn, I wanted to slap myself.

These people weren't my friends.

They refused to let me out of this room, and it was making me crazy.

Three meals a day helped me map out the hours over subsequent days. My ankle was better, but my legs were sore because I wasn't working them. I was used to hours of daily training, whether we were performing or not. Being idle wasn't good for me. If anything, I think it impeded my recovery, not helped.

When Jasper appeared on what I figured had to be the eighth day since they'd taken me—over a week since anyone had seen or heard from me, were they worried at all?—I glared at him. "Where's Doc?"

Eyebrows raised, Jasper closed the door slowly and stared at me. I hated when he looked at me like that. Like he could see right through me. I'd grown to hate the gray color of his eyes. They were cool, even when he was hot. A muscle could tick away in his jaw and a vein pop on his forehead, but those eyes? They stayed ice cold.

It was unnerving as hell. Even if I forced myself to not look away. Showing fear did nothing for me. Not being defiant hadn't gotten me far either. One thing he hadn't done was act any differently if I was belligerent, so belligerent it was.

"What's wrong?" He flicked a glance over me. I had changed out of Vaughn's shirt after the first couple of days and unearthed a ratty old T-shirt of my own and pajama bottoms. At least my legs were covered. The more clothing I had, the more armor. I'd also managed to find some more practical panties than the see-through fuck me lace. Bad enough I'd given them all a peep show, I didn't need to send the wrong message.

"I just asked where is Doc? He hasn't been back to check on me, and I would like to take a bath." I hadn't had one other than a cursory wipe down with a washcloth while leaning against the counter in the bathroom. I'd been testing my ankle in there without their observation. It was stronger every day, but without a proper workout, I was rapidly losing muscle.

Even a handful of days down could take me a month to work back from. At the rate we were going... No I couldn't handle being dependent for the length of time it would take me to rehab. If I got out of here—when I got out of here, I needed to be at full strength.

"He has a job," Jasper said. "And you don't need Doc. Just take a shower."

"Wow. If only I had thought of that." The sarcasm should be burning through the carpeted floor. At least the floor was carpeted, even if it was loose at the edges. I wasn't complaining.

"Glad we resolved that." He smirked, then moved to sit in the chair. That was their favorite station to take up, like they were on sentry duty in my boring as fuck room where the only entertainment was me.

Joy.

"With what tools, genius? There's no shower curtain, and I'm not supposed to stand. I also need plastic or something to wrap my wrist so it doesn't get wet along with my ankle."

Half hovering over the seat, he straightened with a snap. Frowning, he stalked over to the bathroom and glared inside it like it had the temerity to do something wrong. It would be comical if not for the fact that for the last few days, I'd had to make do and there wasn't much else to use. I thought Doc would be back and at least I could trust him to help me get another bath.

"Stay here," Jasper said before slamming out of the room. I loved how they all said that. *Stay here*. Like, where did they think I would go, if they weren't in this room watching me?

I'd tried the other door a few times when they'd left me alone. If it opened at all, I had no idea how. As soon as Jasper was out of the room, I slid off the bed and hurried over to the door. It hadn't locked. Or at least I hadn't heard the lock when he left. Turning the handle with as much care as I could, I braced myself for any sound that might possibly betray what I was doing.

Not hearing anything, I managed to turn the handle until it gave the faintest click and then swung inward slowly. I glanced out at another bedroom. Laid out similarly to the room I was in, it was done in darker colors. Black comforter. Black sheets. Black light in the corner. That was weird. Even the walls were plain like my room, with a couple of posters of cars on them.

Oddly, like my room, it also had no windows. There were two lights close to the ceiling that illuminated the room in low light like they had in mine when my head had been hurting. What was their problem with windows? Had they ever heard of fire codes?

I rolled my eyes at myself. Right, because guys who kidnapped people were going to worry about city code violations.

It wasn't much more than I'd already glimpsed the few

times the door had been open. The room itself had *three* other doors. Fuck my life. Really?

I leaned a little farther out but heard no one, and there wasn't anyone readily apparent. Did I risk it?

Check one door. At least eliminate a possibility. I had a one in three chance of finding the right door the first time.

I glanced around the room and chose the door to my left. It was on the opposite wall of where my bathroom was situated in my room, and I tested the handle. When no resistance met my effort, I pulled the door open a fraction. A hallway was visible through the sliver, dark with splashes of yellowish looking light. A faint smell of sawdust, sweat, and old gyms hit me. I'd trained in enough, that scent was too damn familiar.

"Freddie, where the fuck do you think you're going?" Kestrel's voice drifted up the hall. "You heard Jasper. You don't go in there."

"C'mon, Hawk's lost his damn mind. Boo-Boo has to be going insane."

"Stop calling her that and get your ass to work. You miss another day, and you're going to get shit-canned." Kestrel sounded so aggrieved.

"Probably for the best. I'm really bored there anyway, and the manager is on my ass every night."

"Maybe you shouldn't have fucked her then." I could practically hear the eye roll, and despite the fact I was supposed to be checking for a way out, that actually made me want to laugh.

"Dude, the tits on this chick. I mean, I've seen yoga balls that didn't have that girth. I had to come in between them. Then she was all about me eating that pussy. But been there and done that, and now I'm in the mood for something a little more delicate and maybe, you know, slender."

"Freddie, if you go near her room, I'll cut your balls off

and feed them to you." The ice in that threat came straight from Jasper, and my heart jerked at the unrestrained violence.

"Damn, Hawk. You have got to get *laid*. You are so tense."

I closed the door as easily as I could and then fled back into my room and shut that door. I'd just sat back on the bed and fixed my gaze on the ceiling when the door handle jiggled. Jasper cursed and flung the door open abruptly, and I jumped, not quite able to strangle the stupid scream as the door slammed against the inner wall and an angry Jasper filled the opening.

He glared at me like it was my fault.

"What the hell?" At least it explained my sudden rapid pulse and uneven breathing. The adrenaline rush of nearly being caught had nothing on the furious man radiating barely suppressed violence.

"You're still here." The incongruous statement surprised me.

"Where was I supposed to go?" Yeah, I knew which door in that other room led to a hall. I didn't know where that hall went or what building we were in or even *where* we were. So yeah, where would I go?

That was a tomorrow Emersyn problem. I still needed to get more mobile and work on building up my strength.

I was getting out of here.

One way or another.

He blew out a breath and finally dragged that icy gaze off of me, and I could breathe again. That was when I noticed the chair he had in one hand and the plastic sheeting in the other. Well, not just plastic, but cloth with rings on it.

A shower curtain.

Stepping in, he closed the door with his boot and carried the stuff into the bathroom. I leaned forward as the chair legs scraped porcelain. Then there was a snapping sound and rustling. A minute later, he came back out and pointed at me. "Stay there."

I raised my hands. No, I'd already tested my luck for today. Staying right here would be fine.

He gave me a firm nod, then slipped out. This time, he wasn't gone near as long as he had been before. No more than three minutes. So I doubted he'd left the hall. When he returned, he had an oversized duffle bag.

With a little flourish, he set it on the bed. "We got this for you. I just didn't realize it hadn't been brought in here."

I didn't recognize the bag, but that didn't mean anything. Despite the terse tone, he folded his arms and rubbed his thumb against his lower lip as he watched me. Normally, he'd been in button-down shirts, but today, he had on a dark green henley with the sleeves pushed up and beat-up jeans that had seen better days.

Easing forward when he gave me a look like *get a move on*, I pulled the bag open and pulled out huge fluffy towels. Three of them. They were soft, much softer than the threadbare one I'd used the other night. They were also gray, kind of like the sheets on the bed, but a softer, dove gray and pretty. Included with the towels were a pair of washcloths and some hand towels. Beneath all of that was shampoo, a salon brand I recognized but rarely used, and it was scented like citrus. More, there was vanilla soap, exfoliator, and lotion. Also body cream.

It was all very sweet. Most of these brands had been in the bathroom at my hotel, but not all of them. The body cream I'd had in my dressing room at the theatre. I glanced up to find Jasper studying me steadily with no expression on his face.

"Thank you," I said slowly. "This is very…nice of you."

Was there etiquette for expressing gratitude to your kidnapper? Yes, I'd behave because you brought me some nice shampoo and conditioner. That was totally worth the price of my freedom.

Right.

"You're welcome." A ghost of a smile seemed to hover over his lips, then vanished as he grabbed the stuff from the bed. "I'll put all this in here, and I've got plastic to wrap up your splint. I can remove the wrap."

He disappeared into the bathroom, then reappeared a moment later.

"Well c'mon, I want to make sure you can reach everything before I leave you in there to do it."

Oh.

With care, I slid off the bed and limped into the bathroom. I took my time and played it up a bit more than necessary. They didn't need to know I was getting better.

In fact, the less they knew, the better.

He had the towels hung up and arranged all the bath products along the shelf in the tub. The chair was in the middle, facing the shower head. I'd have to lean forward to rinse my hair.

Beggars didn't get to be choosers.

"Can you get in the tub?"

It took some maneuvering, but I managed to get in, though it was a near miss 'cause I had to hop a little to get my good leg over faster.

Jasper scowled.

"Sit."

I was tempted to ignore the barked command. I wasn't a damn dog, but I had to admit, I was also curious. So I sat. He vanished. This time, he was gone long enough, I started to wonder if he intended for me to just shower while he was gone. I could reach the controls and the bath products.

Opening the vanilla body soap, I took a deep breath of it. It was sweet and clean and probably the nicest thing I'd smelled since they'd brought me hot spaghetti and garlic bread the other night.

My stomach growled at the memory. It had been a while since lunch, I thought. Maybe longer than normal, but my jailer was currently occupied with another task.

I managed to strip off my pajama bottoms when it seemed like he really wasn't coming back. Bracing my foot on the edge of the tub, I began to unwrap it. I'd figure out the splint in a minute.

Jasper appeared in the doorway with a drill and some metal rods and a few other items. Kestrel was right behind him. "Move her," Jasper told Kestrel, and the other man shot me what I thought might be an apologetic look and held out an arm.

I gripped it and stood, ignoring the fact that once again, I was in a T-shirt and panties. At least they were pink and solid this time. He braced me as I climbed out and then maneuvered me back out to the bedroom.

"Want me to grab your bag so you can get out clean clothes?" Kestrel asked as soon as I was perched on the bed.

Though I opened my mouth to respond, the sudden whine and scream of the drill in the bathroom filled the room. Holy crap, that was loud. Kestrel actually rolled his eyes and shook his head with the first real hint of a smile I'd seen since this damn odyssey began.

With great exaggeration, he motioned to my bags and then to his clothes before he made a strangling motion at the bathroom and flipped it off.

That shouldn't have been funny.

Nothing about this situation was humorous.

Yet, I laughed. 'Cause that was the Kestrel who'd been driving me around for a few days and whose intensity appealed to me alongside his wry sense of humor. His expression sobered at my laugh, and I tried to wipe the smile from my face, not that I had a terrific amount of luck with that one.

The whine of the drill climbed again, then cut off as Kestrel set the bags on the bed. I concentrated on collecting a change of clothes, clean panties, and still skipped the bras 'cause I wasn't asking anyone to help with it, and as much better as my ankle was, my chest wasn't. The cracked and bruised ribs protested nearly every movement.

Hammering from the bathroom made me jump, but Kestrel just folded his arms and waited. A couple more whines of the drill followed by a couple of minutes of hammering, then Jasper reappeared in the doorway, covered in fine white dust. It coated his henley and his beard.

"Gotta clean this up, then you can test it."

Kestrel rolled up the sleeves on his shirt and went into the bathroom. The water ran, then turned off. Jasper reappeared with the drill and the bag of tools I hadn't seen before. He'd cleaned off his face. The bag went outside the door and then he went back.

It was weird as fuck sitting on the bed while those two did whatever in there. The water came on a couple more times and then Jasper called, "Come give it a try."

In the bathroom, I found the new bars he'd installed. One on the wall right next to the shower, another fixed into the wall inside the shower, and a third one mounted to the edge of the tub. I could literally use it to climb over and hold my weight on my good arm without risking slipping.

After putting my clothes down on the closed toilet, I used the first railing and climbed right in.

"Perfect," Jasper said. "Can you reach everything?"

I nodded. "I tested that when you were gone."

"Okay, now you can shower. No more complaints." Then he shoved Kestrel out and closed the door behind them.

No more complaints.

I flipped the closed door off, and at the same time, I looked around the shower. There was a small box in the corner with plastic sleeves in it. I dragged it out and pulled it up and over my splint. It had a little tape seal to tighten it closed. Not perfect, but it would do.

I got out of the shirt and panties pretty easily, then dragged the curtain closed and turned on the water. This close, I was gonna get hit by that initial cold spray, but that would be good for my chest and my bruises.

Wait…

A slow grin pulled my lips wider. It would be great for them. Especially since they were letting me shower alone. I'd bet they had no idea how long my showers should or could be. They probably expected me to be a spoiled princess like Rome had called me that night.

My lip curled. Still…I cranked the water on cold and hissed when the icy spray hit my chest. It was so cold, it almost made it hard to breathe.

That was okay.

Cold would help with the bruising. I could warm it up when I needed to wash.

Thirty minutes of punishing cold was about all I could stand and I was fucking shivering, but I couldn't feel the bruises anymore. I switched up the warm water and even tepid was warmer than what I'd been using. It took me time and some maneuvering, but I got my hair washed, rinsed, and conditioned. By the time I soaped everything and rinsed off, I was beat again.

What a waste, but then again, I had more data than when I'd started.

And more access.

One step at a time, I reminded myself.

I was going to get out of here one way or the other.

CHAPTER 10

EMERSYN

The next two days after Jasper fixed everything for my shower, I took to showering twice a day. They didn't need to know it was for the cold and the fact that it did wonders for the bruising along my back and ribs. I did my damnedest to avoid being naked around any of my caretakers. Morning—or what I assumed was morning because I really had no idea—of the third day, I woke alone.

Totally alone.

When I first opened my eyes, I was curled on my side facing the chair where my current keeper would usually be seated. A single dim light remained on in the corner. It was the light Rome used when he sketched. Rubbing a hand against my face, I sat up slowly. The combination of cold showers in addition to the enforced rest had at least minimized the bruising effects I'd suffered. For that, I was going to be grateful.

I tested my ankle as I stood. It was wrapped, but the

sharpness when I put my weight on it was missing. Two steps, and it barely twinged. I pushed up on my toes and lifted my good leg, forcing all of my weight onto the bad.

The strain was there. My muscles objected to the activity after being so disused. The ankle held though. Setting my foot down, I stretched my arms over my head. The pull on my chest and back ached, but I'd had worse. I stretched my arms behind me and clasped my hands as best I could before I bent. The crack of my spine popping and the scream of muscles protesting invigorated me.

Step by step, I stretched until I was warmer and looser. The wrist was still problematic. I hated the damn splint. They hadn't put me in a cast, so that had to mean something. At the same time, I hadn't seen Doc since he helped me bathe. Apparently Jasper or "Hawk" as the others called him —what the hell kind of name was that?—had blocked him for some bizarre, possessive jerk reason.

I wasn't an idiot. I got that guys got crazy stupid about that stuff and he was warning off Freddie with very violent threats. The image of the gun Hawk had placed under Doc's chin shivered through me, and I frowned. Had Jasper done something to make sure Doc didn't come back?

Fuck.

And if he did, why?

He wasn't doing anything more than stare at me when he was in here. Well, except for the shower thing—and the dresser thing. My clothes weren't in suitcases anymore. They'd hauled a dresser in here and put my stuff up.

There was the book thing too. He'd brought me a stack. No television or phone or Internet, but I had books.

Most of them were fantasy, a couple of spy thrillers, and at least one romance novel. They were well-thumbed too. Not new.

Fine, Jasper had done more than stare. Still, they hadn't

told me anything about why I was here. Or what was going on, and when I tried to broach it with Vaughn, he changed the subject. The one time I brought it up with Kestrel, he'd just gone ice and shut me out.

Yeah, so, there was that.

I stared at the closed door.

It was weird that no one was in here.

I hadn't woken up alone more than once since I'd woken up in this room. That one time, Rome had been in the bathroom. The flushing of the toilet was what told me someone was still here.

Speaking of, I got fresh clothes out of the drawer and clean panties. I was down to my last two pairs. The laundry was stacked in the corner, so I supposed I could rinse some of the panties out and wash them in the sink. I gave a little shudder. I could do it, but I'd rather actually wash my clothes.

THE DAY HAD GONE FROM MEH TO WORSE. NOT ONLY HAD I woken up alone with no captor in sight, I woke up to my period. I should have done the math, I wasn't expecting it though that would explain some of the soreness and discomfort. There was nothing in the way of supplies. So I rolled up toilet paper and made do after my shower.

I would've killed for coffee. And some Midol. Maybe a heating pad.

I could've gone for getting the fuck out of this room too. I'd been cooped up here for so long, I knew exactly how many cracks there were in the wall and that the painting I'd been staring at was not only painted directly on the wall and not on a framed canvas at all, but that it had the kind of depth and majesty that belonged in a museum.

Sheer. Raw. Talent.

I also wanted to go to the grotto depicted. It was beautiful. The only thing I couldn't figure out was whether it was sunrise or sunset. And I'd genuinely thought it was a framed canvas. Ugh.

Not even staring at it would relax me. I paced around the room. I'd picked up the books, thumbed through them, and put them back down a dozen times. I probably shouldn't move so much, I was intimately aware of the toilet paper serving as my only barrier to staining another pair of panties. I had one pair soaking in the sink in the bathroom.

A part of me couldn't wait for one of the guys to see them. Hopefully, it grossed them out. Or something.

Time dilated, or maybe it really was an hour later, but I'd had it. I wanted out of this room. No food. No people. No coffee. Just. Out. Of. This. Room.

I stalked over to the door and raised my hand like I was going to knock, then hesitated. I hadn't actually tried the handle, so I twisted it and it opened with a soft click.

Shit.

Now, I felt stupid for not having tried it earlier. The door opened, and I checked the room on the other side. It was dark. No lights on. The other door was six steps to my left.

A shaft of light from my room cut across it and there was a shift of movement in the bed. I froze and then backed up slowly and turned off the light in here. Then I waited. The rustle of sheets ceased and regular, deep breathing filled the silence. There was just a touch of a snore.

Breath slowing, I concentrated. I didn't want to make too much noise, so I stepped deeper into the room and pulled the door closed silently behind me. The faint click seemed like a crack of gunfire in the darkness, and I winced.

The figure on the bed didn't stir.

Six steps to the door. The carpet beneath my bare feet

was soft and muffled my steps. Braced for all hell to break loose, I turned the handle, but it wouldn't budge.

Fuck.

Running my thumb over the knob, I found the lock and turned it. My door didn't have a lock on the inside, just the outside. My door was also only accessible through another room. Nice and sneaky. Assholes.

Unlocked, the door opened easily, and light filtered in from the hall. It wasn't a lot brighter, but enough to make me squint. I stole a look back at the bed. Sure, it was a horror movie cliché, but I wanted to know who was sleeping there.

A tousled blond head was all I could see beyond a long, muscled arm. So Rome.

His breathing didn't change, and he didn't move. Good. Turning my back on him, I looked back out in the hall. Nothing moved, and there were no sounds reaching me. I hadn't gotten past here the last time I slipped out.

No time to waste. Sooner or later, one of them would come to find me. If I was going to escape, I needed to do it now.

The floor of the hallway was wooden and cold beneath my feet. In fact, the temperature beyond the room was a lot chillier. Right or left? The voices the other day had come from the left. So were there stairs or a door there?

It was a hallway with no windows.

Seriously, what was their problem with windows?

Tucking my wounded arm against my middle, I chose left and hurried. My ankle protested some, but I ignored it. I passed more closed doors, but I didn't want to open every single one to check. Surely there would be stairs or some-thing that—fuck, there were stairs. I almost slid to a halt on the wood. It was rougher here and bit at my feet.

Thankfully, I had callouses. At the top of the stairs, I peered down. Six steps, then some kind of landing. The light from the single bulb hanging above cast bizarre shadows. The walls were rougher looking than in the room too. Old. Dilapidated.

It also kind of smelled out here. Moldy. Disused. Wet.

I glanced down at the floor again. There were stains on the wood. But it wasn't damp. That was something.

A shiver worked up my spine, and I looked back the way I'd come, then the other way.

Yeah, I really had no choice but to keep going. I wanted out, and I probably wouldn't get this chance again. Not if they caught me.

That sent a far worse shiver up my spine. And my gut clenched.

Down the steps I went, slowing at the bottom and glancing around the wall to look down the next set of steps. Still nothing.

If this were a movie, the creepy music would've started playing right now. I descended the next steps and stared at another hallway, but this one wasn't as long and there were open archways that revealed a pool table and carpeted area with sofas, chairs, and a television.

Well, look at that. There were posters up on the wall too. These were more of half-naked and never mind, all naked women with generous breasts and curvy hips. There were bottles of beer on the table. But no people.

Where the fuck were the guys? And how big *was* this place?

You know what, Emersyn, you don't care. You want to get out of here, not sightsee.

Good talk.

I ignored the room and the other open archway and started looking for an exit. There was more light coming from the other end of the hallway, so I headed for it. A window. A door. I just needed one way out. The end had a door—with a window—that opened up into a *warehouse*?

Pulling the door open, I stared out into the drafty looking warehouse. It was all plays of shadow and light, with the light coming in from skylights along the ceiling that was easy two or three stories above me.

Son.

Of.

A.

Bitch.

The place was huge and ugly as sin. There were also cars parked inside. What were the chances those cars had keys in them?

That shit only happened in the movies.

I also had no idea how to drive.

I mean, it didn't look hard, but I'd been driven every-where, and the only free time I'd ever had had gone into my dancing and performances. Driving to school would have been a waste of energy.

Oh, the last thing I needed was her voice in my head, so I slammed the door on that and stopped hovering. If cars were in here, then there was an exit point. I did a slow one-eighty and there, with light shining down on it like it was a sign from the heavens, was a pair of huge doors. I didn't waste any more time. I hurried across the open expanse and past the cars and the pair of motorcycles. The concrete was like ice beneath my feet, and I narrowly avoided a scattering of broken glass.

The door at the end started opening, and the grind of the automatic chain above pulling had me stumbling to a halt.

I jerked my head toward the only other door nearby and raced over to it. *Please be unlocked. Please be unlocked.* I shoved it open and ducked inside. It was like a huge utility closet. I'd barely closed the door when the smell of exhaust tickled my nose as the rumble of engines—more than one—rolled past.

Masculine voices rose up. Some loud, some softer. Most of them angry.

Or at least they sounded bent.

I couldn't quite make out what they were saying.

Come on, go away. The sooner they parked and went inside, the sooner I could get out. But even as car doors slammed, the voices didn't dissipate.

Dammit.

I glanced around the room I was in and then up. It had a low ceiling, probably faux since it was all warehouse. I could go up through it and onto it, maybe. Then watch for when it was quiet. Another door nestled at the back. It had a giant bar lock on it. The kind you used to keep someone from opening it from the other side.

Like on emergency exits. You could pop them from the inside, but they had nothing on the other. What I thought was a closet, was more of an office. Well, a dusty one that didn't seem in use.

There was a desk. An old ratty chair. Some buckets with stained cloths in them.

Probably better to not know what that was.

I leaned against the closed door and listened. Two men were arguing. I really wished I could *hear* what they were saying. But they didn't sound in a hurry to end it.

Fine.

Fingers crossed, this door opened to the outside. I didn't think it was close enough to the outer wall, but I'd take a hallway and some windows right now. The lock was hard to pop, and I had to twist it to release the bar. Shoving the door open, I narrowly swallowed a scream as the lights came on overhead and in the room that I'd opened. A cold, stone room, with one person sitting on the floor, slumped really.

Half of his face was swollen and bruised, nearly unrecognizable. His wheezing breaths told me he was alive. There was blood on his feet. And his arm hung oddly, or he was clutching it to himself in a weird way.

Bile crawled up my throat because the room stank of piss and shit and blood.

I really was in a horror movie.

Then he opened his eyes, and I slammed a hand over my mouth to keep the sound inside.

"Emersyn," he wheezed.

Eric.

Oh God.

It was Eric.

"You…"

What had they…

"…cunt."

The door behind me slammed open, and I jerked, retreating into the cell with a monster to get away from the monsters coming for me.

It slammed shut behind me, leaving me trapped in darkness.

A scrape of sound against the floor like he was getting up. Then the door shoved open, and Jasper filled the entrance, his gray eyes fixed on me and then jerked toward Eric, who was up.

Shit.

He lumbered right at me, and dammit, better the monster I didn't know in this instance. I went to Jasper, even as he caught Eric by the throat and slammed the man back against the wall.

"Don't look at her," he ordered, and I stared as he rammed his forearm into Eric's trachea, choking him.

Eric was a big guy. He'd always towered over me and used that strength and size to his advantage. Until this moment, I hadn't realized that Jasper and Eric were almost the same height. Jasper might actually be taller.

Then Eric whimpered, and the sound cracked right through the center of the fear floating in my veins.

"Cunt...caused...this." The choked words and spittle flew out of his mouth like Jasper squeezed them out with the force of his hold.

Instead of answering him, Jasper drove his fist into Eric's side. Once. Twice. On the third, there was a faint snap, and I flinched.

The crack of a rib was a familiar noise.

I retreated, the bile burning in my throat and souring my stomach, threatening to make me sick, when warmth pressed right up against my back. I flinched again and yanked away, only to be caged by a pair of colorful arms, trapping me against him.

"Easy, Dove." The familiar croon of Vaughn's voice washed over me, and I nearly sagged. The adrenaline rush from the escape crashed, even as the fear and disgust at finding a beaten Eric trapped here as well swam through me. "Easy, we got you. Big stupid dancer boy is not going to hurt you again. Promise."

Wait...what?

"Get her the fuck out of here," Jasper said over his shoulder, but when I looked up, he was staring right at me, not at Vaughn. Despite his harsh tone, his expression was neither twisted nor furious. "Go."

Was that a request? Not an order?

That didn't make any sense.

I was still trying to sort that out when Vaughn walked backward, taking me with him. He didn't drag so much as just lifted me and moved. Then we were back out in the main warehouse, and there were a dozen guys staring at me.

Including Kestrel, who looked angrier than he had when

he'd snapped at me for being here in the first place, and Doc, who shoved past him and headed straight for me.

I would have made for him, but Vaughn spun me away. "Ah-ah, Doc. Let's not start more violence. Dove's already feeling a bit under the weather after the stench in there. Told Hawk we should have taken the garbage out."

Kestrel swore, and Doc grunted. But the door behind us slammed shut, and Jasper was in front of me. Only this time when Vaughn tried to swing me away, Jasper said, "Give her to me."

"Hawk…"

"When I want your opinion, Kestrel, I'll ask. Give her to me, Falcon. The rest of you, get your asses to work."

"It'll be fine, Dove," Vaughn said against my ear before he handed me over. Jasper gripped me by the biceps of my good arm, but it wasn't a harsh grasp, and even as he started walking, he didn't hurry. If anything, he shortened his steps to mine.

"Move," Jasper said, and suddenly, all those people had somewhere else to be. I glanced at Doc as we passed him.

But he didn't intercede on my behalf, and Kestrel looked away.

Good to know that alliances were fleeting.

If they existed at all.

Jasper walked me back inside and right past the little living room and the pool table and the television, but instead of going upstairs, we went into a kitchen.

Um.

He pointed to a table as he let me go and dragged out a chair. "Sit."

Prickling at the order, I glared at him.

Jasper let out a growling groan and met me stare for stare. "Sit. Down." I honed in on the speck of blood on his cheek. It wasn't huge, but…he'd had Eric by the throat.

He'd cracked his ribs.

I sat.

I was trembling like hell, and it was taking everything I had to keep my teeth from chattering.

What was it that I'd said about the monster I didn't know?

CHAPTER 11

EMERSYN

*J*asper stared at me for a minute, the frozen tundra of his gray eyes locking me in place. He raised a hand to his mouth, then paused. The minute he looked at his hand, air whooshed out of me.

"Fuck," he swore.

Jerking my gaze to follow his, I swallowed back bile at the red coating his fingers. I knew what I'd find the minute I looked, and still, I glanced at my upper arm. Where his fingers had gripped me were bloody marks. Still swearing, he scrubbed his hands in the sink, then went over to the ugly ass fridge with its boring beige exterior and yanked it open. Bottles rattled and he pulled out two, then walked over to the table.

He did that thing where guys rest the bottle cap lip against the edge of the table and hit with his fist. The lid popped off and he slid the first bottle to me, then popped the second and took a long pull from it.

Despite the fact that I hadn't eaten, it had been a fucking day. I took the bottle and downed about half of it. It was awful, and I coughed at the harsh bitterness of the dark beer.

"Might try sipping it," he suggested, and I just glared at him. The guy had blood on his hands, and he had Eric in a storeroom out there while he was holding me hostage in here. Not looking away, I downed the rest of the bottle.

I didn't cough this time. I'd choke on it before I gave in.

One eyebrow up, he took my empty bottle and replaced it with his. Then stared at me as if daring me to repeat it. I took a drink and ignored the fact he'd just had his lips on the same place. Disgusting as it was, it hit my system like a shot of valium, quieting the quakes and soothing the rougher edges.

"Hey, Hawk," a guy said as he stomped into the room. He had tattoos over both arms, long sleeves of them, jungle foliage with animals peeking out at me. His arrival earned a colder stare from Jasper than he'd been giving me. "What do you want us to do with the stash?"

"Put it away for now. We'll deal with it later. Clean up. Then you and JD head out and grab food." Jasper cut a look at me. "Fried chicken."

I didn't say a word. The fact they lived on a steady diet of fast food was killing me. Particularly with me not working or training.

"Actually, get a little of everything."

"Sure thing," the tattooed guy said before he glanced at me. "Do we get to ask who the chick is?"

"No, you don't, Rat." Kestrel stood in the doorway to the kitchen. "Get lost."

The guy actually ran a hand over his bald head. He caught me staring at him and winked. I rolled my eyes and looked away.

"I said go." Kestrel half-growled the words, and Jasper smirked. The guy was out, and voices came from down the hall. Shouts and laughter. Then the television cranked up, and somewhere else, music began to thump.

I'd spent days in a room wrapped by silence with only one of my stone-faced and snappish captors for company.

"Hey, Dove," Vaughn said as he sailed into the room. "You hungry? I'm starving."

Well, except for Vaughn. He'd been attempting to engage me.

"Sent the rats for food," Jasper said as he returned to the fridge. "Where the fuck is Rome, and why wasn't he watching her?"

"Good question," Kestrel said. "You want to fill us in on his whereabouts, Ms. Sharpe?"

The use of my last name was a little verbal jab, even if he was following my wishes. Jasper let out a soft snort as he pulled out another bottle. He repeated the process of opening it.

"She doesn't talk," he said. "So go check her room. Maybe she clocked him with something." There was almost some amusement in his voice.

"I'll do it," Vaughn said before Kestrel could reply. "And if the rats get back with food, save me some. I've got work in a couple of hours, and I've got appointments all afternoon."

The silence he left in his wake had me turning the beer bottle in my hand, drawing little circles of condensation against the tabletop. So close.

I'd been so close to getting out.

So close.

"Sparrow," Kestrel said almost on a sigh, and my shoulders stiffened at that endearment. It had been sweet when he'd been my driver. My ally. My almost friend.

Okay, admit it, when I wanted to climb him like a tree and take just a little bit of pleasure for myself. I liked that he had a pet name for me. Kind of like Vaughn's 'Dove.' But unlike Vaughn, Kestrel turned out to be a lie. Everything about him had been a lie, and that made that name just another lie.

Tears burned behind my eyes, but I took a long drink of beer rather than give into them.

"You can pretend we're not here all you like, doesn't change facts."

"Really?" I glanced at him slowly. He stood close enough I could touch him, but it also forced me to crane my neck to look up at him. Arms folded, he cut an imposing figure. It didn't help that he wore filthy jeans and a shirt with grease stains on it. Gone was the expensive, tailored suit that he'd sported when he'd been driving me.

I guessed he didn't need it here.

"Really," he confirmed, one corner of his full mouth turning upward. Normally clean-shaven, he had a fair amount of scruff on his face and another dirt stain on his cheek. Like he'd wiped the back of his hand against his face. His hands were also pretty filthy with grime seemingly embedded on his nails. The hands had always been big and calloused, I just assumed from some other labor in addition to his driving.

Maybe working on the cars too?

"Let's talk facts," I said as I forced myself to meet his blue-green gaze. "Fact—you posed as my driver to get close to me. Fact—your friend here got a job working backstage for the same reason. So did Vaughn. Fact—you kidnapped me. Fact —you're holding me hostage. I assume for ransom, though if you'd demanded it, it would have been paid by now. Fact— you're holding Eric in a room out there and torturing him. Fact—I want to leave, and if you want to tell me how much the ransom is, I'll pay it. I have access to money."

Not as much as my parents had nor as much as in my trust, but I'd been secreting funds for four years. Four years to plan my escape. I didn't realize I'd need it so literally, but surely I had enough to persuade them.

"Fact," Jasper said when I paused. "You don't give a shit about that asshole, as long as he never touches you again."

I shrugged.

"Not particularly, no."

The fact I could say that without a lot of feeling was a testament to just how much I loathed him. Maybe it was cold. Maybe it made me a monster.

I'd been raised by them after all.

Jasper stared at me, surprise flickering across his face for the first time since I met him, and he dug his cigarettes out of a pocket and lit one up, even as Kestrel flipped a button on the wall that started an extractor.

Then it was my turn to be surprised as he held the cigarette out to me. I had to leave the beer on the table to take it, and for a second, my fingers trembled as they brushed his as I took it. The first drag, like that first full beer, also helped settle me some.

Moving back to his chair, Jasper sat, lit another cigarette and then leaned back as he stared at me. A groan from behind Kestrel pulled Jasper's attention, but I didn't look, instead I just sucked on the cigarette and tried not to look at the blood on my arm. The cramps from my twisting and tortured uterus were a lot harder to ignore.

The beer settled my nerves but not that.

Dressed in gray sweatpants and nothing else, Rome walked into the kitchen yawning and scowling.

"Sleeping beauty didn't even notice she'd left her room, and he hadn't locked the door," Vaughn explained, and I swore he shot me a near apologetic look when he mentioned locking the door.

Rome shrugged, his whole back a ripple of golden muscle. The long lines of the tattoo decorating his spine pulled my attention before he slanted a look at me and grunted. He went to the fridge for a beer, and Jasper scowled. I twisted a little as the light of the fridge hit Rome on the chest.

The flock of birds tattoo was missing. Not just…

"Where the hell is Rome?" Jasper demanded. "Why did he leave you watching her?"

The man who was *not* Rome smirked as he pulled out a beer. "You're welcome that I came over to do a favor. I didn't have to show up you know."

Jasper's expression had turned thunderous, and Kestrel let out an aggrieved sigh. "Where is he, Liam?"

"I didn't ask," Liam said as he grinned at me. Though it was more a grimace with a lot of teeth showing. "You don't look so fragile and scared to me."

Maybe it made me a cliché, but I just blew smoke at him and the guy with Rome's face laughed. Twins. Identical. But they had different tattoos. There were also a few scars along Liam's abdomen and on his back. Rolling his head from side to side, he cracked the vertebrae and took a long slug of beer before he said, "I don't know where he had to go. Just said he had something he was working on. Man, you know how he gets when he has a project. He said the squirrel didn't do much and I just needed to be on hand until you got back. I was fucking tired, so I slept."

As much as I tried not to look at him, it was hard to miss the bruises on his knuckles as he closed in on the table. Kestrel was right behind me. He'd shifted his weight, and the heat from him seemed to press against my neck. The only other place I could look was cracked linoleum, otherwise I was staring at Jasper, Vaughn, or Liam.

The room seemed to shrink with all of them in it.

Jasper snubbed his cigarette out, then nudged the ashtray toward me.

"Vaughn…"

"No," the colorfully painted man with all his tattoos and thick brawn said with a shake of his head. "I am not going to look for him. If Liam doesn't know where he is, I'm not wasting hours hunting all over town. I have appointments booked all afternoon. I'm eating, then I'm out of here."

"Don't look at me," Kestrel said. "I've got Sparrow duty."

"Sparrow?" Liam snorted. "She's not a sparrow." He studied me. "You're quiet, but you're tough. Or you wouldn't be sitting there bleeding without an ounce of complaint."

I frowned at him as Jasper jerked to his feet. "What the fuck do you mean she's bleeding?"

Kestrel yanked my chair around, and Vaughn shoved Liam to the side. Why the hell had he told them that?

"I'm fine," I snapped when Kestrel put his hand on my leg. Sure enough. I'd bled through the tissue and it was soaking my leg. Shit.

"You're bleeding, that's not fine." Jasper glared at me. "Why didn't you say something?"

"Because I don't generally discuss my period with others much less my kidnappers. I'm not injured. I just don't have any products, and I had to make do with toilet paper."

I jerked my leg out of Kestrel's grasp. Mostly because the warmth of his hand on my thigh seemed to have left an electric imprint and burned all the way through my clothing to my skin.

Vaughn had frozen and so did Liam. Jasper stared at me as if I'd sprouted a second head, while Kestrel raised his hands in mock surrender. Yeah, typical guys.

"I just need a bathroom for a few minutes or a trip to a drugstore."

Somehow, I doubted I'd be going to a drugstore. And if I went to the bathroom in my room, I wouldn't be getting out again. This had been my one escape attempt. So...maybe what I needed to do was make friends?

Ugh. I could do this.

I had to pitch myself all the time at fundraisers.

Maybe that could work...

"Doc was here," I said slowly. "We could just ask him."

Vaughn shoved off the counter and was already through the door before Jasper said, "Don't..."

"Too late," Kestrel murmured. "And she's right—Doc probably has supplies. He's always got stuff for the girls over at the center."

The center?

Jasper ran a hand over his bearded face and then focused on me. "Are you sure it's just that? It's not...something else wrong? Something that asshole did?"

I stared at him, then shrugged as I shifted in the seat. Now that Liam had pointed it out, I couldn't escape the feeling of where I'd leaked. Really, it was bad enough he'd mentioned it, now I was intimately aware of it. As for the jerk in question, he still stared at me. The scrutiny didn't help at all, so I just took another long drink of the beer. I kind of hoped the more I had the better it would taste.

Sadly, no.

The silence stretched, and Jasper swore again then slammed back the rest of his beer. Then it was just the four of us with the thump of music vibrating the walls for company. I didn't sigh when Doc appeared, but I almost sagged. The last thing I needed was to incite Jasper, because the tension thrumming through him snapped him straight like someone had yanked a cord.

The scuff of Kestrel's shoe behind me was the only warning before his hand brushed my back where he braced it against the chair. He wasn't gripping me, he gripped the chair.

"Hey, little bit," Doc greeted me, ignoring the obvious tension in the other men present. Well, in Jasper and Kestrel.

Liam looked more intrigued than he did tense, and Vaughn's expression was hard to read. "Vaughn said you're having a bit of an issue."

There was no mistaking the assessment in his eyes as he looked me over or the way his mouth tightened when he got to my leg and then back up to my arm.

"I got my period," I explained. "And I didn't have any supplies. I used some toilet paper, but apparently, it's heavy this month."

He nodded. "That's normal for you?"

"For fuck's sake, man," Jasper snarled. "Really?"

Doc ignored him and focused on me. "Would you like to go somewhere more private?"

"Doc," Kestrel warned, and I didn't even have to look to know Jasper had stiffened further.

"It's fine," I said, not interested in getting Doc killed. "Prisoners don't get rights. This happens some months. I just lost track of time."

"Have you tried birth control to modify it?"

A faint smile pulled at my lips, because Liam actually looked a little ill and Vaughn shook his head in slow disbelief. I kind of wished I could see Kestrel and Jasper's faces right now, but I kept my attention on Doc. "Not specifically, no." I used birth control for the base purpose. Besides, I'd tried the pill, it wasn't as effective as I'd have liked.

Doc narrowed his eyes. "There's other options."

Fuck it. "I have an IUD. Sometimes the flow is just heavy. It is what it is. I really need pads or tampons if you have them. Or if you don't, could someone just get them for me?"

"IUDs usually help with the flow." He let it go, thank fuck. The IUD was still new, and I'd rather *not* have that discussion. "I have some. Since I'm here, let's get you cleaned up then I can look at that wrist and ankle."

Great, we weren't doing the physical exam in the kitchen,

and I needed to change. I guessed I was going back to my cell after all. When I stood, Kestrel moved the chair, and Vaughn scowled. The pants were sticky. Yeah, I was a mess.

Whatever.

I didn't ask to be here.

Snagging a bag from the floor, Doc looped the strap over his shoulder and headed out of the kitchen. I was right behind him, violently aware of four sets of eyes drilling into my back. The weird thing in all of that, I'd offered to pay the ransom and they hadn't even mentioned it.

They were so confusing.

A step next to me had me jerking slightly, and I glanced up to find Jasper moving next to me. Doc didn't slow until he got to the door I'd snuck out of earlier. The room had lights on, the bed was disheveled, and the comforter on the floor.

With a sigh, I walked into my room behind Doc while Jasper crowded up next to me.

Yay, it was just the three of us.

CHAPTER 12

JASPER

*D*oc cut a look in my direction as I closed the door to her room. A quick scan of it showed nothing out of place. After putting her clothes away, we'd removed the bags. She didn't need to be tripping over them, particularly when her ankle still gave her issues. I'd pulled all the books I'd saved over the years, the ones I would reread in here. We needed to get a television, but we didn't have anything wired to run something to it.

We would be correcting that this weekend. She needed something more to do in here. Her boredom wasn't lost on any of us, even if she hadn't displayed the slightest interest in talking. Vaughn had tried, but then, Vaughn was just thrilled to have her here. Freddie wanted in here, but I'd have to cut his balls off, so better he wasn't trapped in a room with a bed and her.

Arms folded, I leaned against the door as Doc set his bag on her bed after snapping the comforter up. Too much military was still in that man. I trusted Doc with her health. I didn't trust him with much else. Not after I'd found him giving her a bath. She'd been naked, vulnerable, and alone with him. Doc might be the closest thing we had to a friend outside of the Vandals, but no way in hell would I trust him with her after pulling shit like that.

He pulled out a couple of Ziploc bags filled with pads. Fuck me, he did actually keep them on him. Scrubbing a hand over my face, I waited for Emersyn to take them and get a change of clothes out before she disappeared into the bathroom. Once we were alone, I opened the door. "You can go now."

"I haven't checked her ankle or her wrist." Doc met my gaze without flinching. The blankness in his stare was a warning. I'd pulled a gun on him, and it broke one of his few rules. The fact he even showed up here had nothing to do with us and everything to do with the woman in that bathroom.

"Doc, she's not your concern."

"That's the problem with you, Hawk. You think you get to dictate what your people think and what they do." The barest hint of a smirk touched his lips. "You also think I give a shit about what you decide."

"Doc, you and Raptor go back..."

"We all go back," Doc reminded me.

"Yeah, we do. Don't put me in this position." Because if he kept up this campaign of disrespect, I was going to have to put him in his place. We had enough people who didn't know Raptor or the history. They would just see Doc, the guy who wasn't one of us, getting away with not following the rules.

That shit didn't fly.

It couldn't.

"You're the only one putting yourself in that position," Doc said. Fuck his cool under pressure. "You brought her to me. That makes her my patient and my concern. You've been playing this bullshit game of keep away, but Kestrel kept me in the loop."

The fuck?

"Yeah, he takes her health a little more seriously than your jealousy."

The door to the bathroom opened, and Doc turned, his expression gentling almost immediately. "Better?"

"Yeah," she said, folding her arms. The pants she'd had on earlier were in the sink. I frowned, but she rubbed her good hand against her upper arm. "Thank you. I don't suppose you have extras of the heavier pads?"

"I do," Doc said. "But I can also get you your own supplies." He turned back to his bag and pulled out two more sealed baggies. "Do you not want to use the tampons?"

Why the fuck were we having this conversation?

"It's a little awkward to insert it at the moment and not a good idea on the heavier days."

But she didn't miss a beat. Goddamn. It was almost impossible to not like her, even when she got all irritating and standoffish. She was tough as hell.

Tougher than I gave her credit for. Liam wasn't wrong about her not being a sparrow.

A sparrowhawk?

Much more likely.

Doc lowered his voice. "Well, then I'll make sure I get you both. Do you have a preferred brand?"

Were they really fucking talking about pads and tampons? I scrubbed a hand over my face. Of all the fucking conversations. She held onto her words, dribbling them out like they were precious gold. But this? This she talked about.

"No," she answered him, and her gaze cut to me. Those whiskey brown eyes held an almost malicious amusement, and one corner of her mouth curved faintly before it flattened again. She was enjoying this torment. "Beggars can't be choosers after all, and I doubt prisoners are allowed that much choice either."

"You're right," I said, agreeing with her, and some of the amusement faded. "Good thing you're neither. Tell the doc what you want. You might as well be comfortable."

"Comfort on a period isn't really possible."

I shrugged. "Then I'll bring you a bottle of whiskey. I'm sure after a few shots, you'll be comfortable enough to sleep."

"Well, don't go out of your way or anything."

The bite in her voice made me smile, and that just seemed to piss her off more. "You don't have to worry about that. I take care of my own."

Doc snorted softly. "Tell you what, you two lovebirds can go back to swiping at each other in a minute. Let me see that wrist, and I want to check your ribs while I'm here."

The heat of her glare abandoned me for Doc. Maybe she'd stop thinking he was gonna rescue her or some shit.

"How's the ankle? You seemed to be walking on it fine."

"It aches," she said with a shrug and moved to perch on the bed. "It's hard to rehab it stuck in this room."

"I'm going to check your ankle first, that means I'm going to handle your leg and manipulate your foot." He waited for her nod before he did as he described. Next, he moved to her wrist. Same thing. He told her everything he was going to do before he did it. The splint he'd used was kind of scuzzy looking as he removed it. That irked. If it was in that bad a shape, he should have told us we needed to change it.

"Have you been able to clean the skin here?"

"Didn't take it off," she answered, almost mechanically.

"Flex your hand for me."

At his order, she opened and closed her fist. If I hadn't been watching for it, I would have missed the twitch near her eye.

"Painful?" Doc asked.

She shrugged. "I've had worse." Still the flat tone.

"I'm going to put a fresh splint on this, but let's wash the skin. Then we can check it again in a week or two. I may want to do another set of X-rays in case it's setting incorrectly."

The flinch was barely perceptible but there, and it happened when he wasn't touching her.

"Let me check your ribs first," Doc said as if she hadn't reacted to the news her wrist might not be healing the way it should.

"If she needs X-rays to make sure it's setting correctly, then we should do those now," I said. Logistically, taking her out of the clubhouse was a bad idea. Her face was on the news, and so was the meat-sack down in the cooler. Though the fact we'd taken all of their things made it look like they'd run off together.

I hated it, but it worked for now.

Doc glanced at me. "We'd have to take her to the clinic." The reproach in his dark eyes held a warning for me. While he hadn't commented on her identity, he knew who she was. It was hard to miss. Even without the news showing her face.

"Tonight, after it closes." If she needed the care, we'd get it for her. We had just taken that haul, once we delivered the stash and picked up the fees, we could cover any extras she might need.

After a moment, Doc gave me a curt nod. "Okay, little bit," he murmured to Emersyn. That nickname needed to go. He wasn't going to be spending enough time with her to develop that affection. "I need to check your ribs, so I'm going to start at the bottom and work my way up. Just tell me if you experience even mild discomfort."

"A little difficult for that right now, Doc," she told him

with the first glimmer of a smile. "I'm nothing but discomfort."

"Fair enough."

For the next five minutes, Doc moved his hands up and down her ribs. More than once, his thumbs were awfully close to her breasts, but he kept from actually touching them. That was good, it meant I didn't have to break his hands. Doctor or not, Doc was pushing it here. She only let out one hissed breath toward the end, and Doc nodded as he backed up.

"They're healing, but you're still tender. I want you to continue taking it easy."

"Well, I'm pretty much stuck in this room," she said, sliding a defiant look toward me. That was better. I liked the fire in her eyes. That defeat she'd been wearing earlier rubbed me raw. "So I suppose rest it is."

Really? "What do you need to rehab the ankle?"

At my question, she frowned. "Out of this room, clearly."

"So your little sojourn downstairs to the warehouse was all you needed?" Bullshit. But I made it sound like that was reasonable. "Good, then you've rehabbed it."

"You are so full of crap."

Doc chuckled. "Hawk's an ass. But you can tell him what you need. If he can get it, he'll do it."

"Then let me go."

"Can't do that, Swan, you're going to have to choose something else."

"Why can't you? If it's a matter of ransom, I have the money. I can pay it. Better me than my family anyway."

I put that information in my back pocket. "I said no. Now what else do you need?"

Her shoulders dropped, but the heat in her eyes increased. That was better. Be fierce. After seeing the fear on her face that night and her pallor when she woke up at the clinic, I couldn't shake it. I'd taken it out of that asshole's hide a few times now. I'd do it a few more until I was satisfied he hurt as much as she had.

Doc ushered her into the bathroom to wash her wrist while I waited. I'd damn near put a bullet in him when I realized she was in that room and he was heading for her.

A huff of her laughter escaped the bathroom, and I frowned. They had to use the bathtub 'cause her sink had something in it. Why the fuck was she laughing with Doc?

"Are you done?" I demanded, and Doc gave me a look as he guided her out with a hand on her lower back. All the humor in her expression dried up.

"Almost," he told me, and then he dug out a clean splint and reset it in place on her wrist. He secured it with Velcro. "If we go to the clinic tonight and X-ray it, I may put a real cast on it, though I'm not an orthopedic surgeon."

"I understand. I suppose I should be grateful for medical care at all."

That little dig landed. "Did you come up with what you need for rehab?"

When she glared at me, some of my unease settled. I didn't want her attention on Doc. "I need a place to train. To dance. Every day I go without, I'm losing muscle tone and flexibility. I've been stretching in here, but this room is too small to do anything resembling a workout."

"You need to keep it light on that wrist," Doc said. "Your ribs may not be up for a punishing schedule."

"This is hardly the first time I've cracked them." The snotty tone she directed at Doc made me smile. "I'm not an idiot. I think I know my body better than any of you. Every day I stay in this room is going to cost me in weeks to get back up to full strength."

"So you need a dance studio?"

She eyed me briefly, then nodded.

"Like the stage you were using?" I had the full measurements and I knew the layout. "We can't set up ropes or the silks, not while your wrist is still hurt."

"I need equipment. Bars. Wooden floors. A mirror would be ideal, but I can do without. My toe shoes would also be good."

I made a mental list as Doc packed away his stuff. "Put on some socks before we go back down."

She froze at the words, and even Doc paused.

"Your food is coming," I said. "You also want out of here. You can come down and eat. You'll stay with us. Then when you're done, you can come back up here."

We needed to clear out the rats. That was fine, Kestrel was still ticked at them for some fucking reason. He'd given them every shit job he could think of the last week or so. Maybe he was just testy in general. Instead of working at the garage, he'd been bringing cars back here.

Probably to be close for her, even when it wasn't his shift. Rome, on the other hand, had been avoiding all of us more and more. I pinched the bridge of my nose. That was another issue I needed to take care of.

Him and Freddie both.

We had enough problems, I didn't need them creating more. Doc helped her put socks on and she gave me a wary look when I opened the door.

"What?"

Then she glanced over at the corner where there was a stack of dirty clothes. "What do I have to do to get my laundry done? Or at least access to a washer and dryer?"

A couple of smartass replies filtered through my brain, but I dismissed them both. At least for right now. I wanted the feisty, fire-breathing danger bird back. The graceful swan who took flight, not the wary and worried woman who kept looking at me like I was a monster.

"I'll take care of it," I told her curtly. "And if you need anything else, like the feminine supplies, make a list."

I should have thought of those. I mean, I knew women had them. But I'd never had to plan for it before. I'd take care of that now. I also made a note to change the sheets on her bed.

"Thank you," she said after a moment, and I nodded. Doc guided her downstairs, and I followed them, making a mental list of my own. Food waited for us in the kitchen, and most of the rats who'd been around earlier were scarce. Kestrel had a beer and was watching a game on television, but he left it to follow us. So not watching, just waiting.

Doc paused me after she walked into the kitchen and said, "You can't just keep her here, Hawk."

"We don't have a choice," I told him. "Don't overstep."

"What does Raptor have to say?"

I met his stare and kept my expression impassive. "I said stay out of it."

Not when her life was on the line.

I'd taken her for a reason, and until I was satisfied, she wasn't going anywhere.

CHAPTER 13

EMERSYN

To my shock, not only did Jasper take me back downstairs with them, but then he and the others ate with me too. There was so much food they'd brought back, most of it wouldn't fall into any classification of healthy, but then egg rolls were amazing and the moo goo gai pan was delicious, but when Vaughn offered me a bite of his General Tso's, I was pretty sure I'd fallen in love.

I ate until I was too full to eat anymore, but I worried about the leftovers. Vaughn wrote my name on them though and promised they'd be in the fridge for me. We all ended up in the little living room area sans Doc, who had left, and Liam, who'd just snorted at me before he disappeared upstairs. Maybe to sleep?

I didn't know.

It was Kestrel, Jasper, Vaughn, and me. There were others who came by, but one of them always got up to intercept. Apparently, they didn't want anyone to see me. The two times I tried to bring up Eric, Jasper changed the subject, and to be honest, I didn't care about Eric's safety that much. I figured they'd watch sports, but Vaughn went down a list of movies they had and I hadn't seen most of them. To be honest, beyond the occasional reality television show, there hadn't been much in the way of movies or books.

My life had been dance, dance, and more dance.

Part of the reason not dancing was making me crazy.

"Well, fuck that," Kestrel said when I explained it. "Sparrow, you need to watch a few more movies."

They picked pirates for the first binge watch, and it seemed strangely apropos for my kidnappers. At the end of the first one, Vaughn left because he had his *appointments* and Freddie arrived. Jasper glared at him when he went to sit with me and shifted to take Vaughn's spot on the sofa. Despite how entertaining Freddie's arrival was, Jasper's mood seemed to sour until I focused on the movie instead of him. Kestrel made popcorn and got more beer. I was ready to sleep by the end of the second movie, it was a fight to keep my eyes open.

After days of being with only one of them doing almost nothing, it was exhausting just hanging out and watching the movies. As it was, Jasper walked me up and we had to go through what I guessed was Rome's room, but Kestrel followed us and he stripped off his shirt as he headed for the bathroom in there, giving me an eyeful of the tattoo on his back with massive wings flowing off a bird's body, its talons outstretched. I couldn't make out more because he didn't turn on the light before he closed the door.

Jasper opened the door to my room and followed me in. I frowned at him, but it felt almost rude to chide him considering the afternoon. Well, day I supposed. I actually had no idea what time it was or whether it was day or night. That was...aggravating, but I bit back those complaints. At the dresser, I pulled out the last of my clean T-shirts and panties. I'd finish washing the ones I had soaking in the bathroom and hang them up.

Aware of him still in my room, I took my time changing for bed and washing out the stuff in my sink, then washing up before I let myself back into the bedroom. Jasper was absent, and I let out a breath. Of all of them, he seemed the most unpredictable.

It wasn't until I crawled into bed that I realized the stack of laundry in the corner was gone. Also, the sheets on the bed had been changed and there were fresh pillow cases. Huh. The door opened while I was still processing that, and Kestrel shuffled in wearing a pair of gray sweats and a T-shirt while carrying a sleeping bag and a pillow.

He shut the door, then dropped the stuff down in front of it. The dark hair on his face had begun to fill in the harder angles and softened his expression. He gave me a long look. "Do you need anything before you sleep? Meds? Water? Heating pad?"

Surprise flickered through me. "You have a heating pad?"

"I can get one. Do you need it?"

I opened my mouth. I should say no. I was pretty relaxed at the moment, and that was helping the cramps. In fact, I'd kind of forgotten about them over the last few hours of movies and beers and popcorn. Not to mention all the Chinese food. "Please? And I can get a cup of water."

"Just stay there, I'll get you a thermos. It'll keep the water colder, and you can fill it more than that puny cup." He shot me a quick smile, and then he was gone again. It took me a full minute to process the devastating effect that smile of his had on my system.

The flutter in my gut had nothing to do with cramps. I was still turning that over in my head when he came back in. The door hadn't locked either time. He plugged the heating pad in before he held it out to me, and I was careful of his fingers when I took it.

"Ice water in here." He set the screw-top reusable water bottle down. "And I got these." He held up a couple of different kinds of pain relievers. "Doc said you might need them if it gets too uncomfortable, and he's coming back tomorrow with different supplies for you."

"Thank you."

He nodded. "Get some sleep, Sparrow. I'll be down here." By down 'here,' he meant right in front of the door. I curled up into the pillows and hugged the heating pad against my stomach and turned it up.

"Do you need the light?" I asked.

"Nope, I'm good. Sleep, Sparrow. I'll be here if you need me."

I snapped off the light and lay there for a long time. His breathing never evened out. I kept waiting for him to go to sleep, but I finally drifted off before he did.

THE NEXT FEW DAYS FOLLOWED A NEW PATTERN. ONE OF THE guys was always in my room again, at night. Like Kestrel, they would sleep on the floor in front of the door. Apparently, they didn't want me taking any more sojourns out of the room without them.

One difference, however, was they let me out of the room itself. Every morning, I'd go down with whomever had slept in the room, and we'd have breakfast and coffee. The coffee was crap some days and better on others. I had a feeling it depended on who made it. It was coffee, I could drink tar if they had it.

Most of the time, the food came out of boxes. Sometimes one of the guys cooked. Freddie, as it turned out, was an amazing cook. There had to be other people around, I'd seen them that one day, but not as many showed up when I was out of the room.

Rome appeared again. At least I thought it was Rome, his silence spoke volumes. He didn't talk so much as sketch in one of his books. I was curious about it, but I didn't ask and he didn't show. Liam was there once or twice, but there was friction between him and Jasper. More than what was between Jasper and Freddie, and colder.

Most of the guys showed deference to Jasper. Figuring out the dynamics there took a little time. Kestrel and Vaughn deferred to him less. Vaughn didn't seem to argue with anyone, and when he was around, I relaxed more. Maybe it was because like Freddie, he made an effort to talk to me, but unlike everyone else, he didn't seem to act differently when I was there.

If anything, he just seemed to include me. I actually liked the nights he spent in my room more than the others because there was no discomfort. He talked in that soothing voice until I went to sleep. I swore he told the best stories too.

Jasper had taken my laundry that evening, and it was back the following day. Each week, the laundry would vanish and it would return the next day, usually by evening. Also after that first day, they took me to the clinic to get my wrist X-rayed, the one and only time I got to leave the clubhouse—their word for the huge warehouse.

Doc said it was healing properly, which was a relief, and to keep taking it easy, but he didn't think it needed a cast. The trip was a short one, but it was good to see Doc and he promised to see me later that week. He dropped by every couple of days, and it was always good to see him.

When we came back, I shot a look to the room I'd seen Eric in, but Jasper just led me back inside.

Two weeks of this new routine later, I'd watched more

movies than I had in my entire life, learned how to play pool, figured out one of the arcade games they had set up and beaten the pants off Vaughn, Freddie, and Kestrel at poker.

That was one game I did know.

Funnily enough, they assumed I didn't. They wanted to call it beginner's luck, and I let them.

But I was so fucking bored.

I did stretches every morning and evening. I'd taken to watching the movies on the floor doing the splits. It didn't matter, it was getting harder to sleep at night. I'd read every single book they'd brought me. Twice.

Jasper started bringing me new books on the nights he stayed in the room. Fuck, those nights were uncomfortable. I was aware of every breath he took, every time he shifted, and each time his gaze rested on me. Yet not once had any of them done anything threatening. If anything, they'd been solicitous and kind.

They still wouldn't tell me what they wanted or how long they planned on keeping me. I'd actually given up on asking.

One morning, Vaughn guided me down to breakfast, then leaned over and kissed the top of my head. "Be good today, Dove. I'm at the shop until late, but I'll bring you back a surprise." Then he was striding away.

The whole room froze, not just me. Rome and Liam were both at breakfast, and Liam just smirked as he poured white gravy over some biscuits. My heart thudded painfully at the ease of that motion and the fact I'd actually smiled. I couldn't fucking help it when he said he'd bring me back a surprise.

Vaughn was a tattoo artist. One evening, I'd finally asked him about all these appointments he had. I mean gang member, kidnapper, and living in this box with no windows, and he had appointments?

"I work in a tattoo shop," he told me. The smile curving his lips had my heart doing that weird flip thing again, as did the way he winked. "Where do you think I got all this ink?" I hadn't seen all of it yet, but I'd gotten a look at some. It was as eclectic as he was.

But after Vaughn left, Jasper slammed out of the room without a word. Kestrel had just sighed and made himself coffee to go. "Be good, Sparrow. I have a feeling today is gonna be a long day."

He took Freddie with him, despite Freddie's protests.

Then I was alone with Rome and Liam. Not that Liam stuck around. The twins never said a word to each other. It was kind of unnerving. Liam just bumped his fist to Rome's shoulder and left. When I followed him with my gaze, he paused at the door and shot me a wink, then he was gone and it was me and Rome.

Rome who never talked.

"You done?"

The two words surprised the hell out of me, and I glanced over to find him watching me, head cocked to the side. He was dressed like he always was—dark jeans and a gray hoodie half-zipped. Most of the time, he didn't have a shirt under it. Today he did. It was dark blue like his eyes.

I glanced at my empty plate and coffee cup, then nodded. I carried them over to the sink. As rundown as parts of the place was, at least they kept it mostly clean. The linoleum was probably thirty years old and the dirt so deeply ingrained it had become a part of it, but it always seemed swept.

"Leave it," Rome told me as he stood.

"I was just going to rinse them out."

"Leave it. The rats can clean up later." He jerked his head to the door. "C'mon." Then he headed out as if expecting me to just follow.

A part of me wanted to argue and be stubborn, but the rest of me was kind of curious. Rome had just said more words to me in the last five minutes than he had in the last three weeks.

Three weeks. Or that was how long I thought it had been. At least two since I'd made my abortive escape. A week or more prior to that I'd been here. Or was that two? It all seemed to run together. I hurried when I found Rome almost all the way down by the stairs going up. Usually, this was when we'd go watch movies or play games or whatever, but he took the steps two at a time.

"Do you have shoes?" he asked.

"Um…I guess. In my stuff." Not that I'd looked. "Why?"

"Go grab them and a jacket." He pushed open a different door. This one right on the other side of my room, and there was a door on the far side. One that looked like it went into the room I stayed in. The room itself was a wreckage. There were boxes and cans everywhere. The bed was also disheveled.

He glanced over his shoulder at me.

"Go on."

Okay.

I went to the next door that I thought went into Rome's room, but I guess it was Liam's? Maybe that was why he slept here? Then again…

Whatever, I went into my room and found shoes, they were in the very bottom of the dresser under some jeans. I put on some warmer leggings and then the shoes. It felt weird to tie on the sneakers, and it took a minute with my arm still in the splint. I couldn't find a jacket I could get over it, and when Rome appeared in the doorway, I held up the wrist.

He grunted, then disappeared again.

I managed to run a brush through my hair and brushed my teeth by the time he came back, this time holding a larger hoodie, darker colored than his. He zipped me into it, then pulled the hood up.

"Okay, let's go."

"Where are we going?"

"Do you really care?" He shot me a faint grin. "Or would you rather get out of this place and see some sunshine?"

Fuck it.

"Sold."

"Then come on."

CHAPTER 14

EMERSYN

When Rome said we were going to see sunlight, he hadn't been kidding. The air was brisk, but I savored the cold wash of it against my cheeks, even as I had to squint against the too bright light of the sun. I hesitated just outside the main doors. We'd passed the room where I'd seen Eric without slowing, and instead of the big rolling doors, Rome pushed open a smaller one I hadn't seen and it let us out into a dingy little alley.

The smell of exhaust tangled with dampness, oil, trash—my nose wrinkled at the last—then a breeze pushed chillier air down the street from where cars thrummed as they drove past. It was almost sensory overload after weeks of being inside. I tipped my head back to look at the building I'd been in. It definitely had the look of an old, well-used warehouse. The wood was dark and stained, the roof stretched higher easily two, maybe three stories.

Did they use that space?

"Come on, princess."

I clenched my teeth at that nickname. "Don't call me that." I loathed it with every fiber of my being. *He* called me that, and I didn't want to hear it from anyone.

Rome shot me a curious look, then shrugged. "Starling then, come along."

Irritation scraped under my skin. Now was my chance, I had on shoes and clothes. I could make a run for it. Rome wasn't even looking at me, he'd headed down the alley with a backpack over his shoulder. I could run.

But where would I go? I needed the lay of the land. I didn't know anything about the area. Following Rome, however, wasn't the right answer if I wanted to get away. I knew it, and when he glanced at me over his shoulder, I recognized that he knew it too. The corner of his mouth curved, and then he looked away again.

Stuffing my hands in the pockets of my borrowed hoodie, I hurried to keep up with him. Honestly, I was a little breathless after three blocks. Holy crap, a month of not working out was going to be the death of me. Focusing on my breath control, I refused to pant. Panting could flood the body with a quick fusion of oxygen, but deeper breaths worked better for longer, sustained performance.

The morning streets were crowded.

And it was morning because a local bank ahead had a digital clock that flashed nine-thirty in the morning, temperature forty-two degrees, and the date was...

I stopped in the middle of the sidewalk and waited for the date to flash up there again.

Time.

Temperature.

Date.

Someone bumped into me and jostled me. Then another person did.

"Move," a woman snapped when I stepped into her path, and I shifted to get closer to the curb. A car horn blasted at me, and then a hand gripped my upper arm and pulled me back from the road. I swung my head to find Rome staring at me. Unlike when I stood still on the sidewalk, no one bounced into him or me. They took a wide step around us both.

"You okay, Starling?"

"Has it really been almost six weeks?"

How many days had I lost? I knew it had been a month. But holy shit.

It was deep into winter now. No wonder it was so damn cold.

Rome glanced from me, then across the street and back. The blue of his eyes was like ice, gleaming and yet opaque. No emotion reflected in his expression as he looked me over. "Yeah."

That was it.

Nothing else.

Just 'yeah.'

"Come on," he said, and this time, he held onto my arm as he started walking again. All of the guys were tall, but right here on the street while he was holding my arm, he seemed even bigger. Lean where Vaughn was thicker in the shoulders and the chest, but I'd seen the ripple of muscle Rome sported. He might be skinnier than the other guys, but he was still wiry. Jasper and Kestrel were built similarly, tall, broad shoulders and thick arms, but narrower at the waist.

Vaughn was just big.

Weirdly, he was also the one I felt the most relaxed with.

Arguably, he was the most dangerous.

I tried to match Rome's pace, but his legs were a lot longer and I had to take two steps for every one of his. The thoughts pinged off each other. Six weeks. The guys—my kidnappers, arguably the men keeping me hostage—had become more familiar over the last few weeks, and I'd gotten comfortable. We even had routines. It was deep into winter. The show was probably in Florida now? There was a European leg coming for January and February, and then I was done.

I was free.

Except, I wasn't with the show and I was far from free.

It wasn't until Rome came to a stop that I glanced around. We'd walked a few blocks. It was busier here. There were shops up and down the street. A lot of them had holiday decorations in the windows. Christmas had to be coming. I guess it didn't snow here that much.

One window display showed a toy train chugging through the snow-capped 'mountains' with toys in the back. It was kind of cute. I hadn't spent a Christmas at home in a few years. They probably had the big tree up in the main hall, and they'd be getting ready for the winter formal they hosted each year for their friends.

"Starling, you want anything?" Rome nudged me again, and I blinked. We were standing in front of a really pretty black lady with gorgeous gold piercing through her left eyebrow and a second glittering diamond in the corner of her nose. Her full lips were shiny with gloss, but she had the most perfect complexion. Her hair was dyed a rich shade of purple, and she had it all piled up on her head like a crown.

"It's coffee, sugar. You look like you could use some. You tie one on with these assholes last night?" She thumped Rome, and I blinked again. "Don't ever try to keep up with them." She filled a huge cup with black coffee. The smell of it had my mouth watering. It was a dark roast, but I would swear it had to be like an expensive bean.

"I'm just…distracted. Thank you," I told her as she held out the cup.

"You want anything in it? I got some of those fancier creamers," she told me with a wink. "Flavored if you prefer. Even got peppermint mocha, but it's my own stash." A real smile lit her up and transformed her from pretty to downright beautiful.

I didn't even try to swallow my smile this time. "No, thank you for the offer though. Just black is fine."

"I got you, girl. You want something to eat? Rome here is buying. Get one of everything."

"Nikki," Rome said with a sigh, and she laughed, flicking her fingers at him dismissively.

"You dragging this poor child out with you for one of your days, she needs all the calories she can get. Besides, she's so tiny. I could put you in my pocket and keep you."

I burst out laughing at that. "I might be tiny, but I'm also mean."

"Oh I like you."

Rome stared at me like I'd grown a second head, and some of my humor dried up.

"I like you too, and the coffee is great. I'm not really hungry."

"All right then," Nikki responded with an aggrieved sigh. "If you gotta be that way. You bring her back to see me, Rome Cleary, you got it?"

"I hear you," he replied in a noncommittal tone. He stuffed a twenty-dollar bill into the jar on her counter and then lifted his own coffee before jerking his chin for me to walk. He didn't go as fast this time, and I kept up. The coffee helped.

Six weeks.

It seemed impossible that it had been that long. The world had just gone on without me. Insignificant to the end. My ankle ached, and more than half my coffee was gone before Rome turned a corner and led me along a narrow alleyway that angled downhill. The sunshine was absent from the alley, though a damp trickle of brackish water filled the center.

I wrinkled my nose at the smell and followed Rome as he reached the end, and when he hopped down, I paused. It was a broken basketball court, the tarmac that made up the center had cracked and fissured, buckling in places. There were metal poles leaning on opposite ends with no hoop baskets, and the white paint marking the zones was so faded, I didn't think I'd have noticed it if not for the rest of the layout. The alley we were in dead-ended at the upper lip of a crumbling cement wall.

Rome set his backpack down and turned to me. "Jump."

I stared at him as he held out his arms, then down at the wall and the six-foot drop.

The stubborn part of me wanted to just jump and land on my own. But the combination of uneven pavement and newly healed ankle coupled with the splint still on my arm, and I risked further injury. I had to heal up if I was supposed to get away. I moved to sit on the wall, then handed him my coffee cup. He put it to the side, then reached for me.

Pushing off the moment his hands touched my hips, I braced my good hand against his shoulder, and it was hard to miss how tense he was as I slid down the length of him until he put me on my feet. Heat penetrated the hoodie and seemed to roll off him in waves. Suddenly, I wasn't chilled anymore. He lingered for longer than a moment, and his gaze seemed riveted on me.

"Get your coffee," he said, releasing me and breaking the spell. I swayed as he turned away and grabbed his bag and his own coffee cup. As I picked up mine, I tried to regather my composure, but I seemed to have left it, along with my common sense, back up on the wall.

I was not attracted to the surly, silent twin with his penetrating stares and curt words.

I wasn't.

Kidnapper, I reminded myself. He was one of my kidnappers. Maybe he wasn't there that night, but he'd been one of my keepers since then.

"You coming?" He was halfway across the broken basketball court and heading to the far wall. Like the wall we'd climbed down, it was also cracked and crumbling. There was old and fading graffiti along different parts of the wall. Numbers. Names. But the section he was heading for was a lot different.

It was painted like a beach, right down to the way the water rippled in. It looked real.

Like really real.

He dropped his backpack and drained his coffee. Then he tugged off his hoodie and his shirt came next. I blinked. We were in the sun and it was great on my back, but the air was still freezing. He stuffed the shirt into his hoodie and then unzipped the bag. There were cans upon cans of paint in it, and he shot me a grin.

Then turned away. Two cans in hand, he moved to the next section of the wall next to the beach that looked so real, you could step out on it and so utterly incongruous to where we were. The dilapidated play-court with the broken pavement, listing poles, and surrounded by sad buildings with their broken windows covered over by cardboard and tape.

It was almost eerie. It was even harder to believe that there was a busy street just up that alley we'd walked down. We might as well have disappeared into some other place. At the first spray of the nozzle, I turned to find Rome focused on the wall. He was moving the can of spray paint in waves, and it wasn't long before the beach had been extended.

With not much else to do, I sat slowly, riveted by the

almost hypnotic motions as he worked from can to can. Beach. Shells. Ocean. Foam. Then sky. The sun moved overhead, and my coffee was gone and I had my arms crossed as I huddled in my hoodie. As long as the sun was on me, I wasn't too cold. A couple of times, I'd gotten up and moved around. Then I'd stretched, but I stayed where I could see Rome work.

I kind of thought he'd forgotten about me. The beach had covered maybe ten feet of wall, and he added another ten feet of it. Though he kept going back and forth. At first, I couldn't figure out why. Then there were seashells on the beach. An abandoned pail. A ball buried in the sand. It was…exquisite.

Rome had to have painted that picture on my wall, the one that didn't even have a frame and yet had the feeling of being three-dimensional.

He went through can after can of spray paint. His torso and fingers were splattered with it. I suddenly understood why he'd taken off his shirt. It also let me watch him move, the way his muscles rippled. He was wiry, built like a dancer in some ways—all long lines and lean strength. I'd say he moved like one, but his focus was too specific, all the grace was in his hands, everything else an afterthought.

I was on my third set of stretches when he finally took a step back and cocked his head to the side as he stared at the wall. The water had foamy caps where it rolled in. The sand was golden, a burnished shade that would be a little coarse under your feet and not as soft as say the white sands in some places, but it would still be sweet.

Everything about the painting that now took up about twenty-five feet of broken and crumbling concrete wall was an invitation to escape. He'd even incorporated some of the graffiti that had been present by making it shadows in the sand or in one place, a word that looked like it had been etched with a stick.

I had to step closer, but it said *starling*.

"You do really good work," I told him, and he jerked a little before turning to look at me. He blinked like he had to refocus his eyes, and I almost laughed.

"You're still here," he said, then gave me an almost heart-breaking smile. "But it's cold." The smile vanished, and he was packing up his stuff. The sun was already edging down in the west. We'd been here all day, and my stomach had started rumbling earlier, but I ignored it. Watching Rome work had been fascinating. "You should have told me it was getting colder."

"You were the one without a shirt," I reminded him. "Even your nipples are on point."

He paused to glance down at himself, then shrugged before he pulled the shirt on over his paint splattered chest. The hoodie was next, and he scooped up the bag with the mostly empty paint cans. They had to be mostly empty after what he'd done.

"I've survived worse," he told me.

"So have I."

Since we were done, I pivoted and headed for the wall we'd come down before, and I didn't wait for him to help. I just gripped the edge with my good hand and pulled, even as I used the broken bits in the wall to climb. At the top, I glanced back to find him staring at me.

"You coming?" I repeated his phrase from earlier, and the corners of his mouth curved. A bottle smashed behind me, and I turned in time to see three guys I didn't know heading toward me.

"Well, well, well, what have we here?"

CHAPTER 15

EMERSYN

The crash of the bottle and the splintered glass scattering wasn't my concern. The way the three moved, swaggering and spreading out like they wanted to cut me off from any avenues of escape worried me. I didn't recognize them, and in the half-light of the alley, I couldn't make out much of their features. Of the three, one moved with a faint limp, a second one had his jacket tied around his waist, and the third one wore his baseball cap backwards.

"Hey, pretty girl, you lost?" Backwards Baseball Cap asked, his lips curling into a less than friendly smile.

"She looks lost," Faint Limp suggested as he moved sideways with a shuffle step. He wasn't quite bending his left knee.

He'd be the way to go if I had to get past them.

"Nah, she's not lost," Jacket Around His Waist threw into the conversation as he strolled right up toward me. "We've got you. Don't we, pretty girl?"

They were all medium build to tall, most of them were skinny though. Not muscular. Didn't matter. Most guys started off stronger than girls. Biological bullshit rules. Mother Nature had a really vicious sense of humor if you asked me.

I shifted my weight to the balls of my feet. The splint would protect my wrist, but one thing weeks of inactivity had done for me—my bruises had healed. I could breathe better. My chest no longer constricted. My ankle was solid, tired and a little achy, but solid. Even the headache from the concussion no longer plagued me.

If I had been working out, I'd be more confident, but I had stretched and I was warmed up. I knew the distance between the top of the wall where I stood and the uneven ground below. If I jumped, I'd make it. Rome was down there too. I didn't turn to check. I didn't dare give these guys my back, and I sure as fuck didn't want to warn them I wasn't alone.

The smell wafting off Jacket Around His Waist hit me with eye watering force. Sweaty body odor, alcohol, and something like day old garbage rolled into me. I swore it had to be coming off him in waves.

He was within arm's reach when he grinned this vicious little smile, but a hand clamped down on his arm before he reached me. Rome had come up from behind me. One minute, he wasn't there, and the next, he just surged up next to and then in front of me. He moved like a wraith. No words. No warnings. No sound.

Well, the sound of Jacket Around His Waist's arm breaking echoed through the sudden plummet of silence. The man let out a shriek and there was a flash of a knife, but Rome was already moving, twisting the guy around and shoving him forward. A paint can flashed up in his hand, and he sprayed it at Backwards Baseball Cap, leaving the man clawing at his eyes, and then he grappled with the third one as he swung a knife.

I moved, giving Rome more room. The guy clawing at his eyes fumbled with something in his waistband. I didn't have anything to throw at him, so I just kicked him in the side of the head.

Fuck, that hurt my foot, but he went down and I turned to see another flash of silver vanish as it plunged into Rome. He grunted, but he was still eerily silent as he delivered several hard punches to the man's torso and face.

Something wet splattered against my cheek, and I grabbed one of the chunks of cement. It cut against my palm, but the guy with the broken arm was rising on unsteady feet. I didn't know if he had a weapon, I didn't want to know.

Rome had the guy he was fighting turned and his back was to me, so I swung that rock as hard as I could. There was a sickening crunch of sound as it hit, and Rome's next blow knocked the guy right off the wall. He didn't pause to see what happened to him, just turned and went after the last guy.

Dropping the rock, I grabbed Rome's backpack. It was a lot heavier than it looked, and the cans inside made the weight uneven. Rome pummeled the last guy and slammed his head against the ground until he stopped moving. But even after the guy had gone limp, Rome kept hitting him.

"Rome," I called to him. The setting sun had accelerated, taking what heat there had been in the chilly day. Rome glanced up at me. With half his face in shadows, the other half was a frozen mask of fury. The color of his eyes seemed to stand out in stark relief against the contrast. "We have to go."

"They were going to hurt you." The deadly calm in his voice sent a shiver down my spine.

"They were never going to hurt me," I told him. "I knew you were there."

And I'd known he wouldn't let them.

Rome glanced down at the man whose arm he'd broken and whose face resembled so much ground meat. He wasn't getting up anytime soon.

If at all…

Then there was the guy I'd hit and Rome knocked off the wall.

"We need to go," I said again. We needed to call the police, but they would lock Rome up. One guy against three, no one would believe it. Even if I told them…

If I told them…

They'd lock him up for kidnapping me.

"We need to go," I repeated a third time, and Rome finally stood. A part of me wondered if he wanted to make sure they were dead before we left. He glanced toward Backwards Baseball Cap. "I kicked him in the head."

I didn't really know why I volunteered that information. Rome's chest rose and fell rapidly, but he was so still otherwise. I dragged his backpack onto my shoulder and moved closer to him.

"Are you okay?"

He turned slightly and nodded. "Yeah. I have to call Hawk."

Oh.

"We're leaving right?"

But he already had his phone out, and I cast a look down the dark alley to where I could see headlights passing on the street. We were mere yards from others. Anyone could walk up on us. That was how these guys had gotten there.

I could still get away.

Rome had his back to me, but he glanced at me more than

once as if to make sure I hadn't disappeared. "Hawk," he said. "Trouble. I need cleanup."

Silence, and I swallowed as I glanced around at the still bodies. I wasn't even sure if they were still breathing, and I didn't want to check. My stomach clenched as I edged closer to Rome before I glanced over the edge of the broken and cracked wall. There was a figure lying at the base. Not moving.

I swallowed.

"Old community court, down near seventieth."

I glanced back at Rome, and he stared at me.

"Yeah. I have her."

I swore I heard the growl, even though I wasn't right next to him. He lowered the phone and stared at it a minute, then put it back in his pocket.

"They're coming."

"Okay."

He glanced at the bodies again, then moved to me abruptly and took the bag off my shoulder. A minute later, he pulled out a cloth and a bottle of water. He damped the cloth and then reached for my face. I backed up a step and teetered on the broken wall, and he tugged me back to him with a scowl.

"You have blood on your face."

Oh.

Then with extreme care, he dabbed at my cheekbone and then above my eye.

"They didn't touch you?"

"Well, the one guy kind of touched my foot, but more like I touched his head with my foot."

A grin split his solemn expression, and a single muddy lamp came on, casting us in this eerie glow in the darkness. The cold grew even more biting as a breeze whipped across the court. The smell of the ocean had me turning my head.

Were we close to the bay? The last city we'd been in had been a city on the coast. Maybe?

I really should have paid more attention, but I'd been so tired.

When he finished wiping my face, he let go and then washed his knuckles carefully. I would have offered to help, but he turned away. Lights pierced the darkness below on the court, headlights, accompanied by the rumbling growl of a vehicle.

Fear spiked through me as the headlights illuminated the body below and the unnatural angle it lay at.

I'd seen falls before.

The guy hadn't been able to stop himself or catch himself. I'd hit him with that rock. Car doors slammed.

"Let me talk," Rome said as he pulled me back away from the edge again. The hardness of his chest framed my back, and his head bent as he spoke right against my ear. "Don't worry about Hawk. Just let me tell them what happened."

I nodded because someone suddenly climbed up the wall. They were utterly backlit by the headlights, then almost as suddenly, the lights cut off.

"Are you all right, Dove?"

Vaughn.

Relief sagged through me. He grasped my face in his hands and tilted my head back as he studied me. Then he turned a hard look on Rome. I tried to turn because Jasper appeared from behind him every bit the wraith Rome had been earlier. His dark eyes bored into me, but he didn't pause as he greeted Rome with a hard fist. I flinched, but Vaughn tugged me to him.

"Don't look at them," he ordered in that soothing voice. "Look at me. Are you hurt? Did they do anything?"

"No, Rome never let them touch me."

There was another hard grunt behind me and the sound of flesh slamming into flesh, and I winced.

"Good," Vaughn said, rubbing his thumb along my jaw in a gentle motion. "We're going back to the car now."

I shivered.

"What the fuck were you thinking?" Jasper demanded.

"I was thinking she needed a break from the asylum and some sunshine. It was a good day."

"A good day?"

Vaughn tugged me up against him and wrapped arms around me. I froze, not only at the close contact, but at the sheer heat coming off of him. He wasn't even wearing a hoodie, and his sleeveless shirt left his colorful arms on display. "Guys, settle this later. She's freezing, and we still need to clean up."

"Starling's okay, aren't you?" Rome's voice carried a twinge of pain in it, but try as I might, Vaughn would not let me turn around. Being pressed right up to him made me want to rub my nose against his shirt. There was something deeply clean and spicy about his nearness. Coupled with the chilly air, it erased the sour stench of the guys on the ground.

A shudder went through me. What the hell was I doing? I might have helped kill someone.

"We were done and heading back. They tried to surround Starling, and I took care of it." Rome's flat delivery pulled another frown from me. Vaughn had cupped the back of my head, and the soft stroke of his fingers against my scalp eased some of the tension.

"I want Dove gone before the rats get here." An inflexible steel entered his tone. My eyes drifted half shut, both from the comforting way he held me and the soft touches. Nothing got too personal, and yet it sheared away the jagged edges of nervous energy.

"Go," Jasper said. "We'll clean this up. Make sure she isn't hurt." Then Jasper stunned me when he put a soft hand against my back and pressed his lips to the side of my head where Vaughn's hand didn't cover it. "You'll be okay."

It was a promise.

"What the hell were the 19 Diamonds doing down here, and are any of them alive to answer questions?"

I didn't catch Rome's response. Vaughn kept me tucked up against him as he turned, and then he picked me up and lowered me like I couldn't do it on my own. Kestrel was waiting at the bottom, and I blinked up at his impassive face. Like Vaughn before him, he looked me over closely, then shrugged off his leather jacket and pulled it over my shoulders. It enveloped me in warmth.

Between them, they moved me over to the idling car and around the unmoving body. When I tried to look at it, Vaughn blocked me. They tucked me into the backseat, and Vaughn slid in with me.

A minute later, Kestrel was behind the wheel and the growl of the engine vibrated through me. I glanced forward as he turned on the lights and stared at the body lying there. The scarlet of blood on his slack face was unmistakable.

As were the open eyes.

Oh fuck.

I had killed him.

Or helped.

"Look at me," Vaughn said as he cupped my face, and I turned to stare up at him as Kestrel backed up with his arm braced on the passenger seat. I could almost feel them both studying me in the dark. Then the car spun and we were leaving the court, Rome's painting on the crumbling wall, and the bodies behind. "There she is. How you doing, Dove? Hungry?"

I swallowed and shook my head. Whatever appetite I'd had earlier fled.

"Damn, I was going to offer to get us some pizza with the mushrooms and olives that you like so much."

I grimaced. "I can't stand olives."

"That's right," he said with a chuckle, stroking my cheek. He kept touching me, and I kept leaning into the contact. Without meaning, I turned my face into his palm. The scent of coconut oil and soap filled my nostrils. "Dove, they didn't touch you right? That's what Rome said."

"They didn't."

"Good," Kestrel snapped from the front. "What the hell were you doing out there anyway?"

"Ignore the grump." Vaughn chuckled. "He's just pissy 'cause he didn't get to spend the day with you."

"Fuck off." There was such a disgruntled snarl in his voice that I almost laughed.

"He had work, and so did you. Rome took me for a walk and got me coffee. It was wonderful."

It had been.

"Yeah?" Vaughn's smile shone at me as the streetlights rolled past, making the shadows jump. "Did he paint for you?"

"He did." The image of the beach. "It's amazing. He did the painting in my room, didn't he?"

"Yeah," Kestrel said with a sigh. "He did."

"I love it."

"Good." Vaughn ran his nose along my hairline, and an entirely different shudder went through me. "Still cold, Dove? Turn up the heat, Kestrel."

Then he tugged me over into his lap, and of all the places I could have been, this was not where I imagined. The warmth of him seeped into my bones. I wasn't remotely chilled. In fact, I was cooking, and worse, my nipples tightened at his nearness. When he ran his nose along my throat, I let out a sigh and turned.

This close, his eyes were just darkness and stars and his breath was a whisper against my lips. He smelled like peppermint. Had he come straight from showering and cleaning up after work? I flicked my tongue out to wet my lips and Vaughn gave the slightest pull, but just as my lips brushed his, Kestrel slammed on the brakes and we jolted.

"We're here," he growled over his shoulder, and I pulled back.

Belatedly, I realized we were back in the warehouse as Kestrel slammed out of the car and then yanked open the backdoor. He didn't wait for Vaughn to move before he hauled me out and against him.

"Walk it off," he snapped to the other man and then all but marched me past the others and to the door.

My last sight of Vaughn was him glaring after us.

Holy shit, I'd almost kissed Vaughn. Wanted to kiss him, and my core clenched so tight, I ached for the feel of him against me.

What the hell was I doing?

CHAPTER 16

KELLAN

I got Emersyn up to her room with one hand firmly against her lower back. "Are you still not hungry?"

She'd been shocky at the playground. It would have been hard to miss the enormous size of her pupils or how they swallowed the sweet brown of her eyes, even if I hadn't been looking for it. We'd been looking for her for hours. Fucking Rome hadn't answered his phone.

It had taken Jasper an hour to call me in. Vaughn left work early to help us search. Freddie and some of the others were still out. I'd have to call them back. Liam had been conspicuous in ignoring his phone too.

The twins were gonna tap dance on Jasper's last nerve, and considering how hard Jasper just punched Rome, that was going to get dangerous.

"No," she said, her soft voice had gained in strength, and she frowned when she realized we were at the door to my room. I opened it to let her in and then walked her to her door. "I mean, I suppose I should be. We were out there all day, but I'm just not. I…"

She glanced at her hands as she stood in the center of the bedroom.

"You?"

Concern rippled through me as I reached over and turned on the light, then closed her bedroom door and then opened the one to her bathroom and flip on the light in there. Emersyn glanced up at me with those fathomless dark eyes, and I wanted to swear. She was so pale and there was the faintest tremble to her lip, but she kept stilling it like she could make it all go away.

Goddammit.

I'd watched this girl steel herself every time she'd walked into that theatre and seen the exhaustion on her as she collapsed in the car after rehearsals and shows. Always watchful. Always wary. Then that damn attack.

God. Fucking. Dammit.

Why the fuck had Rome taken her out there?

"Come here, Sparrow," I said as I crossed to where she was. I thought she'd ignore me or push me away again. I'd been a bastard to her, but I needed to keep my distance. She was already getting too comfortable here, and she shouldn't have been here in the first place.

Now, this happened.

She stared at me for a long moment and then folded forward until I could wrap my arms around her. I picked her right up. She was so damn tiny. Sparrows were delicate little birds, but they were also fierce and fast. She was all of those things. And damn if she couldn't fly.

It took me a minute to recognize it, but she was wearing my hoodie under my jacket. I didn't know who gave it to her, but I didn't care. I just lifted her as I moved over to sit on the bed and then pulled her into my lap as she curled into me. My cock stirred at the first brush of her ass, but I shifted her weight and my leg.

"You want to tell me what happened?" I'd caught some of Rome's story, and I could probably fill in the blanks. But I needed to know what she'd seen. What had happened specifically. Then I could work on fixing it.

"Not really," she answered quietly. "Rome was right—they…they just showed up when we were leaving. I was showing off that I could climb the wall on my own, and then they were right there. I didn't know who they were." She gave a little shrug and started to sit forward, but I tightened my arms.

"You're good here unless you really want to get up." We were already holding her against her will. I wouldn't force anything else on her.

"It's not that…" She shot me a look and then settled back against me again. "I don't even know what I'm doing here. Today was… I liked today, until that last part."

"Well, I'm glad you liked today." I wouldn't lie to her. I wished Rome had used his fucking brain and *told* someone he was taking her out of the clubhouse instead of just disappearing with her. Jasper might kill him.

Or at least make him wish he were dead. I hadn't seen Jasper that close to fucking losing it in a long time. I didn't think any of them realized just how on the edge he was. I sighed and reached up to tuck some of her hair behind her ear.

"What happened when the guys showed up?"

"Rome took care of it." But there was the barest hesitation before she said that. "No, they didn't touch me. Everyone keeps making a big deal about that."

"Well, yeah," I told her bluntly. "You're under our protection. Anyone touches you, they die."

Maybe I should have chosen better words, because those swollen pupils seemed to grow even larger as she stared at me. "But why?"

"Because you're under our protection." Maybe she didn't understand what that meant. But she'd been hurt on our watch. It had driven Jasper to make a reckless fucking choice, but here we were.

Her throat convulsed as she swallowed. "I don't get that. I don't or I didn't know you guys."

"You knew me a little." Not even sure why that was important. Not that she hadn't looked at me with betrayal since we got here.

"I didn't know you though. Who you were was a lie."

And with that, she wiggled to stand up, and I helped her rather than have that gorgeous ass grind against my dick. Vaughn couldn't keep his hands off her. Jasper couldn't stand not seeing her. Rome was hooked, or he'd never have tested Jasper's patience. Particularly after the incident with Doc. Even fucking Freddy adored her.

One of us needed to keep our head. She paced away.

"Do you want me to call Doc?" I'd run interference with Jasper if Doc was who she needed. Her trust in him wasn't lost on me. Not after finding her completely naked with him helping her bathe. The fact Jasper pulled a gun had left a bad taste in my mouth. The blow up they had in here and then later downstairs had been fucking ugly.

He did not want Doc alone with her.

Too fucking bad.

"Jasper will just get mad," she said, and that defeated tone pissed me off.

"Who gives a fuck? He's a big boy. He can take it. You

need Doc, I'll call him." With that, I stood and pulled out my phone.

She moved toward the bathroom again and shrugged out of my jacket and then my hoodie. I kind of liked her wearing them. "I don't want to cause more problems." With that, she closed the door and shut me out.

Cause. More. Problems.

What the actual fuck?

I texted Doc.

Me: *You ever get out of her what happened?*

I stared at the closed door. The sound of water turning on in the shower told me what she decided to do.

The second message I sent to Hawk.

Me: *Cleanup?*

Hawk: *Done. Two for the station. One for the show.*

One of them was still alive.

Good. I had questions.

Me: *I'll make room on the stage.*

Hawk: *Call Doc in.*

I frowned and read that twice.

Me: *You know he doesn't like patching up ragdolls.*

If we weren't planning on them living, Doc wasn't prolonging their suffering. He had lines, and he wouldn't cross them. Not even for us.

Hawk: *Rome caught a knife. Be back in thirty.*

Fuck.

I glanced at the bathroom again, then switched to Doc's messages. He hadn't answered me, but he had read it.

Me: *Rome needs stitches. Clubhouse in twenty-five.*

Three dots appeared on the screen.

Doc: *How bad?*

Me: *He's still walking.*

Which was true. If it was going to be thirty before they got back here, then he wasn't in danger of bleeding out.

Was that what had Emersyn all tied up in knots? She said those guys didn't lay a finger on her. I could get that answer out of our survivor. I hadn't taken my next turn with our other guest. Maybe it was time he answered some questions.

Not that Hawk had bothered to ask him anything. We didn't need to know the why to know what he'd done. At this point, we'd just taken our pound of flesh for her over and over. Every single injury she'd suffered had been inflicted on him.

Repeatedly.

I tapped the phone against my chin, and it buzzed again.

Doc: *What's wrong with Little Bit?*

I debated answering that, particularly after he didn't answer me earlier. But fuck it. She needed to talk to someone, and she trusted Doc.

Me: *She got caught between Rome and some 19 Diamonds. Wrong time. Wrong place.*

Then, because I wasn't a dick, I clarified.

Me: *She doesn't appear to be hurt.*

Doc: *On my way.*

The shower cut off, and I moved over and knocked on the door once. "Sparrow, I'm going down. You can join in the kitchen or the playroom, but stay inside the clubhouse, yeah?"

"I might just stay up here."

I clenched my fist. "If that's what you need. Food will be down there though, and Doc is on his way. If you don't come down, I'll send him up."

She sighed. "I don't want Jasper to shoot him."

"I'll take care of Jasper, Sparrow. Trust me." I winced on the last two words, but she rewarded them by opening the door and letting a wall of steam out. Her skin was reddened all along her arms and shoulders like she'd stood in the scalding water, and there was only a towel wrapped around her.

At least the mottling of bruises she'd had from the beginning had all but faded. But this was new.

"I want to trust you," she whispered. "I did before. But I thought you were just this really nice guy that treated me well, and I thought...you could be fun to escape with."

"Well, I'm not a nice guy." Facts were facts. "But you can trust me. I will treat you well."

"And if I ask you to let me go?"

"If I could Sparrow, I would." Then I touched her chin gently when she looked away. I wanted her eyes on me. "I mean it. Get dressed. Come eat. Talk to Doc."

"I'll think about it."

Unwilling to push her further, I forced myself to leave the room. I was halfway down the hall when I spotted Freddie. Perfect.

"I didn't do it," Freddie said, holding his hands up. "It wasn't me."

"Uh huh. Then why are you declaring your innocence?"

"'Cause you're wearing the *you're fucked* face."

Right. "Get cleaned up. Then go wait for Emersyn to come out of her room. Hang out with her, get her something to eat. Keep the rats away." I paused and looked him over. He smelled like two-day old hot dogs, and there was vomit on his shoe. "Definitely clean up first."

"I thought I wasn't allowed near the pretty little princess?"

"Freddie, you try to touch her with any part of your anatomy, just be prepared to lose it." I smiled, and he snapped his mouth shut. I didn't make threats. "Keep her happy. She's had a shock. Doc is on his way. Rome got stabbed and needs stitches. *Don't* tell her that part."

"Got it."

"And Freddie…"

"I got it—I won't touch her. Just entertain her and keep the rats away. Then make sure I leave her alone with Doc, which means then Hawk kills me. You guys…I swear. You're the worst brothers ever."

He was bemoaning his fate as he trudged down the hall to his door, which was at the very far end.

"Go to work, Freddie. Get a new job, Freddie. Don't fuck the waitress at the kiddie circus, Freddie. Babysit the hot dancer with the pretty pussy, Freddie. But don't forget, don't touch. Assholes. All of you."

"Wait," I said as I reached the stairs, and he paused at his door. "You fucked Daniella down at Circus Pizza?" She was what, in her forties? And a *mom*?

Freddie shrugged. "She's hot. Good ass. Really likes it in the ass too." He saluted me and then vanished into his room.

Fucking Freddie.

Jesus.

There were rats waiting out in the garage when I got out there. They had a van open, and Jasper was already climbing out of it. He yanked one of the 19 Diamonds out, staggering. The guy was bleeding from his forehead, and one of his eyes was swollen shut. Shoving the walking corpse at one of the rats, Jasper jerked his head toward the fridge.

"Park him."

The guys didn't ask questions. They just moved. They weren't gentle about it either. Rome came out next. He was still on his feet, and he had his hoodie packed around the knife, holding it steady where it rested in his side.

"You good?" I asked.

The guy laughed. "Hawk's just worried 'cause he punched me before he realized I took a knife."

"I'll fucking punch you again if you don't get your ass in gear. Office. Emersyn doesn't need to see this shit."

"I didn't let her see it there," Rome told him bluntly. "Won't let her see it here. Where is she?"

"Showering. Why is she so upset?"

Rome stilled as Jasper pivoted midstep, turning away from heading to the clubhouse and facing Rome with me.

"They didn't touch her." Fierceness entered his eyes, and he glared at me. "I got there before they touched her."

"So she said. So you said. Why is she shutting down again?" Because she was. It was like after she first woke up here, for real. She'd retreated into herself.

"Maybe because some 19 Diamond fucks acted like they were gonna mess with her?" Rome shrugged, then grimaced. "I don't know. She was with me. She trusted me to protect her, and I did. Hell, she even…" He paused.

"She even what?" Liam asked. When the hell had he gotten here? Rome's twin aggravated Jasper on a good day.

Surprisingly, Jasper ignored him as he focused on Rome. "Answer him."

Rome leaned back against the van. "Do you mind if I go park my ass in the office before you interrogate me?"

"I do," I said, mostly because I had places to be. But I wanted this answer. "What happened?"

He sighed. "She backed me up. She kicked that asshole in the head. The one in the fridge. Kept him down. Got the other one with a rock. The one who went over the wall."

The dead guy.

"She killed someone?" Liam asked the question pinging around inside of me and Jasper swore, but I shook my head and just turned my attention to Hawk.

"Take care of your brother," I told Liam.

After the twins headed for the office on the far side of the warehouse where we had a clinic set up that would work for minor injuries, I faced off with Hawk. "She's killed someone. You happy now?"

"Fuck off, Kellan." He pinched the bridge of his nose, then raked a hand through his hair. "No, I'm not fucking happy. I'd be less happy if she hadn't defended him and had gotten hurt. Rome getting stabbed is bad enough."

"We can't keep her here."

"She's been fine the last few weeks."

Was he for real? "She's losing her mind being stuck here. This isn't her life. This…" I stuck my hand out. "None of this is her life."

"Yeah well, the one she had wasn't doing her any favors." He rubbed at his jaw.

"Have you even told Raptor yet?"

Jasper not answering was an answer.

"He's going to kill you."

"He'll understand."

I tilted my head back and looked up at the rafters.

"He will." There was more confidence in Jasper's voice. "She's not safe with her people. Look at how they are even dealing with her disappearance."

They'd treated it like she and that shitstain had run off together. Half the tabloids made it out to be some romantic escapade, and the rest chided her for being a spoiled rich kid. The cops weren't looking. A couple of our guys had done some asking around, and there was no report of her being missing.

The show had moved on.

They even had a new headliner.

A door at the far end of the warehouse opened, letting Doc in. Jasper's aggrieved expression washed away, and he shot the other man a look. "I'm going to deal with the Diamond and find out why the fuck they were up this far. You get Doc in and then out."

"Sparrow needs to see him."

Jasper whirled on me. "I thought you said she wasn't hurt."

"Physically? No, she isn't. Mentally and emotionally? Different story. She trusts Doc. Trusts him like she can't trust us. She needs to see him."

Fists clenching until his knuckles went white, Jasper glared at me. I didn't flinch or look away. She needed this. If he could get his head out of his ass for five minutes, he'd see it. Doc had gotten her through some of the worst of those injuries.

"I don't want him around her."

"She's not ours."

"The fuck she isn't," Jasper ground out.

"Hawk, she doesn't belong here." How many times did I have to say it before he'd hear me?

"Give me one reason why I don't just fucking shoot you right now." Despite his words, there was no heat.

"Because I'm your brother and I've never lied to you. I know you want her. But you can't have her." None of us could.

"Shut up." Jasper shoved past me. "Let him talk to her. Give her what she needs. But she stays."

I sighed.

He didn't slow down, and the door to the fridge slammed as he disappeared inside.

We were all fucking dead if someone didn't tell Raptor what was going on. I could do it, but that would mean going around Jasper and I wasn't ready to take that step yet. Doc slowed when he reached me, and the man's unflinching attention to detail meant he hadn't missed any of that.

"Rome's in the office. Sparrow's inside. Freddie's keeping an eye on her, so don't take too long."

Doc nodded.

"And, Doc?" I didn't look at him, and he didn't turn. "Take care of her."

"That was always my plan."

I debated heading into the fridge for my own answers or hunting down Vaughn. I'd told him to walk it off, and apparently, he'd taken the words to heart. Still, I hesitated and glanced back at the clubhouse door.

When the hell had this all gotten so fucked?

CHAPTER 17

EMERSYN

*a*s promised, Kestrel sent Doc to see me that night. Freddie had shown up at my door to harass me into coming down to eat. I went more because I hadn't had the energy to dissuade him. It wasn't like I had to talk, he chatted enough for both of us. It was also hard to not laugh at Freddie's outrageous statements.

Even if he did call me Boo-Boo.

What a name. At least it wasn't a bird.

Doc called me Little Bit. That wasn't a bird either.

So I was two for two.

Freddie left when Doc came in and I answered his questions, but mostly, I wanted to go to sleep. So when he asked to check my wrist and ribs, I let him and kept my gaze fixed on the wall when he checked them. There was almost no ache at all.

"Little Bit, do you want to talk about it?"

"No," I told him. "I really don't. Goodnight, Doc."

I'd left him downstairs and returned to my room on my own, aware of his gaze following me. The next few days, I didn't want to leave my room. That one little taste of freedom, and not only did I not take it and run, I'd helped to kill someone.

One part of my brain said self-defense. The rest of it though? I kept replaying the crunch of when I'd struck with the rock. The meaty *thunk* of it. Then Rome knocking him over. The body had been so still.

And those eyes had been open.

Lifeless.

I couldn't close mine without seeing them.

The first night, I pretended to be asleep when Kestrel came in. He slept on the floor in front of the door. The next night it was Jasper. He actually tried to talk to me, but after a few monosyllabic answers, he left it alone. The third night it was Kestrel again, instead of Rome or Vaughn, but I didn't say anything and neither did he.

I hadn't seen Vaughn since the night we came back. Weirdly, I hadn't seen Rome either. On day four, Jasper woke me early, or I guessed it was early.

"Get dressed," he said. "Doc's here, and he's taking the splint off today."

A part of me wanted to be excited, but the rest of me just wasn't. What did it matter? I was still going to be stuck in this building.

I'd still killed someone.

Self-defense.

Didn't matter. Someone was dead. I'd struck him like I'd been struck over the years.

I helped kill someone.

If I ever met the angel and devil on my shoulders, I'd punch them both in the mouth.

Jasper opened the drawers on the dresser and pulled out a couple of items and passed them to me. One was a leotard. The other was capri dance pants.

I stared at them for a moment.

You know, it wasn't worth the effort.

He turned away as I went into the bathroom and began stripping my bed. I paused in the doorway and watched. In all the time I'd been here, Jasper had done some odd things, but this was weird, even for him.

"Get changed," he said without looking at me.

I closed the door and stared at myself in the mirror. I barely recognized myself anymore. More, I hated what I saw when I looked at the dark hair that needed to be washed, the wan face that hadn't seen enough sunlight—not that I ever did, but I didn't recall ever being quite this pale.

I stripped off the nightshirt I'd been wearing, which probably belonged to one of the guys, and the panties and dropped them on the side. I had become an expert at wrapping a plastic bag that taped closed over my brace before I got in the shower.

Icy water on, I stepped right under the spray and stayed there until my teeth chattered, then I flipped it over to hot and washed my hair. The chill knocked some of the cobwebs away, and I finished the shower as efficiently as I could.

Hair toweled and combed, I dressed in the leotard and squeezed into the dance pants. It was weird. They were form-fitting, but they were looser than normal.

The loss of muscle tone had my gut dropping all over again. Maybe that was why my face looked so hollowed out in the mirror.

Jasper was not only *not* in my bedroom when I came out, but the door between my room and the room next door was wide open. I still hadn't figured out who slept in here, but it couldn't be Rome. Even if Liam had slept in here that day. As far as I could tell, Rome was never in here, or maybe he just hadn't been back. The guys had said something about a cleanup.

I should ask.

I made it all the way downstairs before I found people.

"There she is," Vaughn greeted me. Surprise fluttered through me. I hadn't seen him in days, and I hadn't even realized I missed him. "You look a little lost, Dove."

"Where have you been?" The words escaped before I could haul them back inside and barricade them behind a door locked with common sense. He wasn't my friend. None of them were my friends. Granted, they were better than my family...

That uncharitable thought ignited guilt in the pit of my stomach, and I drew back a step. Why had I come down here again?

Tugging the knit cap he often wore off his head, Vaughn stepped farther out of the kitchen and into the hall. The conversation in the other room was just a din of masculine voices. It sounded almost like an argument, but I withdrew another step.

"Hey," Vaughn said, and the soft, melodious nature of his voice beckoned to me. "What's wrong?"

"Are you really asking me that question?" I quirked a brow. Because seriously? "Did you forget why I'm here?"

"No," he answered, his tone cautious, but his eyes... Fuck, they just stared right inside me like he could see all the way to my soul. Nothing about Vaughn said gentle, trustworthy, or safe.

So why the fuck did he make me feel that way?

From his colorful tattoos to his bulging muscles to his blunt expressions and huge hands, he was the picture of a gang member. He was one of my kidnappers. He was...

He was someone I wished was my friend.

And I knew better.

God, did I know better.

Lifting my chin, I forced myself to meet and hold his gaze. "I just haven't seen you in a few days. But I don't suppose you have to check in with me. It's kind of the other way around." Clearing my throat, I nodded more to myself. "Speaking of which…"

I walked past him, but I didn't even make a full step before he clasped my upper arm in a gentle grasp and pulled me closer, even as he moved us farther from the kitchen. "You're mad at me."

The hint of wonder in his voice made me frown. "Don't pretend with me."

"What?"

I blew out a breath. "Look, you were great the other night. Got me back here and kept me compliant and cooperative. You're like the good cop to Jasper's bad cop."

Honestly, the fact that he blinked and then started laughing at me annoyed me more than the rest. I tugged my arm. It took two times before he finally let me go.

"Dove…"

"I have a name, and that's not it." Folding my arms, I walked away from him and headed into the kitchen. He was right behind me though, still chuckling. Glad I could provide some amusement.

The kitchen was full.

Fuller, I thought, than I'd ever seen it. Rome and Liam were both present, so apparently, like Vaughn, they'd crawled out of wherever they'd gone to hide. Jasper stood by the counter, his own arms folded and facing Kestrel, who glared at him. Doc was also there, sitting at the table with a cup of coffee in hand, while Freddie gestured wildly.

"You guys are blowing this all out of proportion," Freddie said, flicking a look at me. "Back me up here, Boo-Boo. If a woman tells you she needs your cock, it would be rude to tell her no, right?"

I stared at him a beat, and the corner of my mouth curled almost involuntarily. It was really hard not to laugh at just how outrageous Freddie could be. I honestly never knew what would come out of his mouth. "If a woman told me she needed my cock, I'd have to apologize because I don't have a strap-on."

He opened his mouth, then closed it with a pop that the sudden silence made audible. Behind me, Vaughn's soft chuckles turned into very real laughter. Kestrel crossed the kitchen and slapped Freddie right upside the head. I flinched.

I tried to suppress it, but it happened anyway. Freddie didn't seem remotely disturbed as he laughed. Liam just gave him a baleful look as Rome groaned. Rome seemed paler than the last time I'd seen him, and I tried to look anywhere but at Kestrel hauling Freddie up out of his chair.

"You have got to learn to think with something that isn't your dick," Kestrel scolded him. "Now move so Sparrow can sit."

"That's not her name," Vaughn announced from right behind me. "She has one."

Kestrel pivoted to stare past me, and Jasper raised his brows. In my attempt to find somewhere else to look, I locked gazes with Doc. The thoughtful patience in his eyes trapped me until he nodded to the chair. "Join us?"

Arms still folded, I moved over to the chair and sat down.

"What crawled up your ass and died, princess?" Liam asked a moment before Rome jabbed him in the ribs with his elbow.

"She doesn't want to be called princess."

"Sounds to me like she doesn't want to be called a lot of things—"

"Shut up, Liam," Jasper and Kestrel said in the same breath, with Vaughn only a quarter syllable behind them.

"Yes," Freddie chortled with a fist pump. "Suck it, you Irish bastard. For once, it's not me."

"He's not a bastard," Rome said with a smirk. "That's still you."

"Enough, Freddie," Doc said with this quiet snap that silenced the lean jokester with the quick smiles and easy humor. "Rome, don't provoke him."

"He's a prick," Rome retorted as if that were a defense, but raised his hands before glancing at me with a frown.

"Emersyn," Doc said as he sat forward.

"If you ask me what's wrong, I'll throw this cup at you." The cup in question being the one that Kestrel slid onto the table in front of me. Black coffee, just the way I'd drunk it pretty much every day.

"Thanks for the warning," Doc said as he covered my hand on the mug and locked it down. "What's wrong?"

Liam snorted a soft laugh, but it ended as abruptly as it started. I stared at where Doc held my hand on the cup and shook my head. "I came down because Jasper said you wanted to take the splint off."

"That doesn't answer the question."

"You're right," I agreed and met his gaze. "But it's the only one I have." I wiggled my hand some, and he lifted his grip. The silence splintered the room as he drew his hand back, and I debated whether I should reach for the coffee or just wait. As it was, Kestrel and Jasper were glaring at each other. Vaughn stood so close behind my chair, I could feel the heat rolling off him, and I swore Doc and Rome both stared at me like they could see through my skin.

The only two ignoring me were Freddie and Liam. The former was rooting around in the fridge, and the latter slathered butter on some toast. It was the first time the scent of food registered. Including pancakes. There was even maple syrup.

Doc downed his coffee and stood.

"Let's go ahead and get that splint off."

Fine by me. I left the coffee behind and rose. I nearly collided with Vaughn as I stood, but he steadied me with a hand on my waist. The contact sizzled, even through the leotard. I might as well have been wearing nothing.

With care, he pulled my chair out of the way and then stepped aside to let me follow Doc. We went to the little living room area. I wasn't sure why we had to do this in here rather than the kitchen. He was just taking the splint off, right?

"She doesn't need an audience, boys," Doc said without glancing back.

I did.

Jasper was at the doorway to the kitchen where Kestrel seemed to be blocking him, but Vaughn prowled right behind me.

"I'm her friend," Vaughn announced. "Not an audience."

I stopped dead and turned to face him.

"You're my *what?*"

"I'm your friend, Dove. You may not think so, bad communication on my part. Don't worry, I'll fix it."

The flutter that hit me at that promise sent heat pulsing through my system. Even my chest seemed to lock up against taking another breath.

Grinning, he touched my shoulders lightly, then turned me around before whispering against my ear, "Whatever is going on, we'll figure it out. Okay?"

I wanted to believe him so badly.

It was actually kind of pathetic how much I wanted to believe him.

"You don't have to believe me," Vaughn murmured, even as my gaze locked on Doc's where he watched us almost impassively. The silken velvet of Vaughn's voice smoothed out the roughness in my system, sanded down the jagged bits, and even broke up lumps of fear that kept trying to collect in my throat. "I'll earn that belief from you. I promise." Then, raising his voice, he continued, "Now let's get this splint off and get Doc to tell us you're all healed."

Then what?

What happened when Doc pronounced me one hundred percent healed? Did I end up in that room where Eric was? That seemed pretty farfetched. They'd been looking after me. I had my own room.

And my own keepers.

Still, it was like chasing my own tail as I tried to solve this riddle. I didn't have all the pieces to the puzzle.

Doc motioned for me to take a seat on the sofa, and he took a seat next to me. Vaughn actually kept his distance, arms folded as he leaned against the doorframe to the room.

None of the others showed up.

Not even Jasper.

Another puzzle piece.

Except I didn't even know what picture I was supposed to be making.

I didn't even know if it was a picture.

"Little Bit," Doc said as he reached for my wrist. "I'm going to take the splint off, then we're going to test your mobility and the stress on it. If it even twinges, I need you to tell me."

I nodded.

"Now, I expect there to be some weakness, probably

muscle tone loss in this forearm. We'll work out something to help build that back up."

Vaughn's phone rang, and he ducked out of the door to answer it.

"And if you want to get out of here," Doc continued as the splint came free. "Just tell me. I'll find a way to get you out."

CHAPTER 18

EMERSYN

I had no way to follow up Doc's surprising offer because Vaughn walked back in. "How's she looking?"

"We're just getting started," Doc told him without looking at him. "And friend or not, you don't get to ask the questions."

I bit back a smile, but not before Doc noticed it. The corner of his mouth kicked up a little higher, and then his warm hand wrapped around my wrist. It felt weird to have the splint off. Even as he flattened my palm to his free hand, I schooled myself for the inevitable discomfort.

His hand was warm and calloused against mine. They were also scarred, like the rest of him. He had tatted over the worst of it, the tale of what happened to him etched into his flesh. Not that he'd told me what happened, just shown that like me, he also had his scars.

With the heel of my palm against his, it was easy to see how his fingers dwarfed mine.

"You really are a little bit," Doc said with a grin. "Now I'm going to manipulate your wrist. Relax and let me do the work."

I nodded, not quite trusting my voice when my mouth went dry. He began to rotate it slowly, first clockwise, then counter-clockwise. There were faint twinges, more protests from neglected muscles infuriated by the action after so much forced passiveness. The stretch along my forearm offered its own complaint, but there was no sharp pain. No grind of bones.

Weakness could be trained away. Broken bones healed stronger.

That was the old saying, right?

I should be a woman of steel then.

"Good?" He gave me an assessing look.

"Achy, but that's to be expected. It's not my first break."

"Oh, that I know. You're going to want to get right back to work on that, I suppose. But we're going to focus on stretching and strengthening first. Too much stress could re-injure it."

I shrugged. "That depends. It wasn't broken from my work."

Not that I could dance or perform at the moment anyway. It would be nice to shower without having to wrap the wrist. Or maybe even just soak in a bath without my arm up or propped at some weird angle.

"Let's check the ribs."

I raised both brows. My ribs were fine. We both knew it. Most of the bruising had faded. What few yellowish-green marks remained weren't even painful. It was just the body being sluggish to clear it all. I stood and Doc rose with me. Like all of them, he towered over me.

"Starting at the bottom," he told me, telegraphing and announcing every move he intended before he did them. He took his time, moving rib by rib up my sides, and I stretched my arms out as he brushed the sides of my breasts, then down again. "No discomfort?"

I shrugged. "Not really. I'm sure there will be when…if I ever train again." If I ever trained again. "I'm fine, Doc. I'm pretty sure you've fixed all the broken bits and put me back together."

Whatever that meant for me now that I was healed.

"Pretty sure I haven't done that," he said in a low tone that I nearly missed when Vaughn surrounded me from behind in an unexpected hug. Even knowing he was there, I wasn't ready for that embrace. Fortunately, the minute I stiffened, he loosened his hold.

"Sorry, Dove. Just excited about the good news."

Doc packed up his stuff. "We still need to talk about rehabbing that wrist and doing more for the ankle."

"I actually know what I need to do. I've rehabbed after a lot of injuries." I lifted one shoulder, hoping that Vaughn would get the hint and let me go. Despite the initial surprise, it was kind of nice to have his warm arms around me. Too nice. Rather than let me go, Vaughn settled his hands down on my hips and tugged me back a couple of steps as Doc finished packing up.

"How many injuries is a lot?" Vaughn asked.

I shrugged again. "Dancing is pain. I'd really rather not discuss this."

"I'm just asking a question, Dove."

Stepping away from him, I pivoted to face him. Sure, it put my back to Doc, but for the most part, he'd seemed to be on my side. Granted, he'd left me here, but after Jasper pulled a gun on him, I couldn't really blame him for that.

And I'd seen what they'd done to Eric.

"I've asked a lot of questions. I'll answer yours when you start answering mine."

The pale brown, almost topaz eyes remained guarded as he frowned. "Dove, there's some things you're better off not knowing."

"Right back atcha then." I folded my arms, and it felt weird to not have that brace on anymore. Not that I was complaining.

"What's the final verdict?" Jasper asked from the doorway before Vaughn could respond with whatever he planned to say.

"She's good," Doc said. "She will need to rehab the wrist and the ankle. I have stuff at the center she can use—"

"That won't be necessary." Dark gray eyes arrested me as Jasper cut off Doc and stared at me. "Come on, fierce dancer, I have something to show you."

Fierce Dancer?

"Do you guys have an actual problem with people's names?" All of them came up with some kind of nickname for me, and they were all different. Some were sweet, some were cute, and some were just downright funny.

I possessed a dark enough sense of humor to appreciate Freddie's Boo-Boo. At least he'd nicknamed me after my bruises rather than my pussy. Though, I supposed that could have been funny in some twisted way.

Jasper smirked. "We tend to call people how we see them."

"And you see me as a fierce dancer?"

"I do," he agreed, extending his hand and curling his fingers in a beckoning gesture. It was the first time I got a good look at him today. He was dressed in slacks instead of jeans, and a dark gray button-down shirt rolled up to his elbows on both sides. The top button at his collar was undone, but the rest of it was neatly pressed. His hair, while a little on the longish side, brushed the collar, and his beard had been groomed. He was even wearing dress shoes.

He looked...good.

Curiosity burned through me as I side-stepped Vaughn and headed toward Jasper. I didn't take his hand, I just nodded to the door. Despite all other appearances, we did need some boundaries. "The best part of being healed is I can manage on my own."

Instead of irritation, amusement filled his eyes. "Good point." So he shifted and motioned to the door, arms wide to allow me to pass. It shouldn't have surprised me to find the hallway filled with Kestrel, Rome, Liam, and Freddie.

"Clean bill of health, Boo-Boo?" Freddie demanded as I exited. He didn't wait for my answer as he stared at my newly-bared wrist and fist pumped. "Yes! I need a new partner in crime." He slung his arm around my shoulders. "I nominate you. First of all, you're prettier than the rest of these assholes and you smell better too. Notice, I'm not discussing how pretty your pussy is, though that was pretty damn spectacular too."

Kestrel glared at him, but I cracked up. I couldn't help it. Despite the word vomit flowing out of Freddie's mouth, he seemed genuine, and even the arm around me was light and almost affectionate. There was none of that crowding sensation. No matter how obnoxious and crass his statements were, there was zero threat in them.

He reminded me of some of the dancers I'd worked with during my first professional show. They talked about everything from pussies to breasts to asses and dicks. I had a lot of information on all of that from those very vivid discussions, but like Freddie, there was never anything invasive or even sexual about it.

They talked about bodies because bodies were our business.

Tears pricked the backs of my eyes, even as I laughed, but I blinked them away. That first tour had been the best one.

Before everything changed.

"You know," Freddie continued, tugging me along at his side as we headed away from the kitchen and the living room down a hallway I hadn't walked before. I mean, I'd known it was here. It was a mirror of the second floor above. But there'd been no reason to go down here. "We should totally show you the new addition before the guys take my head off. You know I'm harmless, right?"

"I'm not a forty-year-old mom who likes it in the ass," I told him glibly. "Pretty sure I'm safe."

Freddie threw his head back and laughed. "I'd never say no to your ass, Boo-Boo. I promise. But I can already tell you're going to be my favorite. We're going to have so much fun."

Before we made it another two steps, Jasper was in front of us and Kestrel peeled Freddie right off me, then Vaughn replaced him. When I glanced back to make sure Kestrel wasn't throttling Freddie, I caught Rome's wince and Liam blocking Kestrel and Freddie from bumping into him again.

Was Rome all right?

I didn't get a chance to ask because Jasper caught my hand and tugged me from Vaughn.

"Guys," Doc said with an almost aggrieved sigh. "She's not a damn bone for you all to fight over and play tug of war with." Until he spoke, I hadn't even realized he'd followed along.

The scuffling around me ceased and Jasper's grip gentled, but he still threaded his fingers with mine. When I glanced down at it and then up at him, he raised his eyebrows. "Is this all right? Freddie might be an irritating shit, but he is right— we have something to show you. I have something for you."

"Okay." I mean, that seemed easy enough to say. "You all are officially the strangest kidnappers ever."

Because either they had lost their minds, or I was losing mine. Nothing about this made sense. Why would he have something to show me? I'd be worried it was Eric in that room, broken and bloody, but this wasn't even in the same direction.

The nervous flutters hit my stomach again as Jasper waited, my hand still firmly in his. At least it wasn't the one I'd just gotten out of the splint. It was even weirder though because he seemed genuinely excited, and after weeks of surly attitude, monosyllabic responses, gun pulling—let's not forget the gun pulling—and scowls, he seemed almost happy.

So. Fucking. Weird.

"Show me?" It was the best I could do. A real smile softened his features, and holy crap did it change everything about him. Even his eyes gentled and reminded me of a wintry sky right before a heavy snowstorm came in to blanket everything in gorgeous silence.

I didn't resist in the slightest as he led me down the hall, measuring his strides so he matched mine. They all had longer legs than me. A fact I'd already filed under irritating.

While there were doors on this hall, they were all two doors wide and spaced much farther apart. The very last set of two doors were the ones he opened, and I swore we had to be out in the warehouse and we kind of were except…it had walls, mirrors, a wooden floor. There was even a dance barre at one end, and strung to the ceiling were silks on a pulley, though they were up higher than I could reach at the moment without leaping.

The pulley went all the way to the ceiling of the warehouse, and the walls extended pretty high.

I tried to take it all in but it was…it was so much. The

flooring was even right. It was a little too polished though. Regular movement on it would scuff it up.

Suddenly, the reason for the leotard and dance pants registered.

"You built me a studio."

"You said this was what you needed to rehab," Jasper said as if it was the most reasonable thing ever and they hadn't transformed an entire section of their space in order to accommodate me.

Wait... Why had they?

"You're not planning to let me go."

His humor seemed to dry up.

A sigh echoed from someone behind me, but I didn't look.

"This is safer for you," Jasper said, all trace of the softness gone from his voice. "If we missed something, tell us. We can move the silks when you're ready, but we need to add some safeties down here."

I wasn't really listening anymore because he'd also let go of my hand.

"Do you need music? We have a shitty stereo system for right now." He fired every word like a bullet.

"It's not that shitty," Kestrel said. "But it's also not high-end. Vaughn has a list of the music you were using for the warmups, and I have the stuff from the school where you were training."

Right. Because Vaughn had been one of the stagehands. Jasper had been on the crew. Kestrel drove me around.

I licked my lips.

"I might need shoes. But I don't have to have them." I could make do without. The calluses on my feet probably needed toughening up.

"You mentioned ballet, right?" Jasper asked as he walked over to a crate I hadn't even seen tucked against the wall just inside the door. We'd kind of sailed right past it. "Toe shoes."

He popped it open, and there were all kinds of dance shoes in there. He looked at them, then at me.

"We had to guess on the sizes. Freddie did some research." He shot a skeptical look at Freddie, but the smartass kept his mouth shut. He even made a show of zipping his lips, locking them, and throwing away the imaginary key.

"We had the pair from your room," Kestrel offered. "But far as we could tell, all shoe sizing is different."

They'd done research on dance shoes.

"But you prefer the Capezio Hanami," Rome said, and I couldn't help it, my jaw fell open. "It was in that article about you in the paper. Those were your ballet shoes of choice."

The article in the paper.

Dance shoes.

Research.

A dance studio just for me.

"If it's not enough," Jasper said, slamming the crate shut and making me jump. "Tell us. You can use this room to rehab."

I literally had no words.

"Everyone out."

"I thought we were gonna get to watch," Freddie protested, abandoning his vow of silence. "Not all of us got to go and see her at the theatre."

"Yeah," Kestrel told him, gripping his shoulder and hauling him backward. "That would be because someone got pinched, or you would have been there too."

Liam laughed, but Rome actually looked pained. But they also tracked out behind Kestrel and Freddie. Doc hadn't moved from the door, and I was grateful for the steadiness of his presence. Vaughn folded his arms and leaned back against the wall. Jasper glared at both of them.

"What part of 'everyone out' did you think didn't apply to either of you?"

"I worked all the backstage stuff. If she wants the silks down, she'll need someone to tie it back off." Vaughn didn't even blink. "Doc probably wants to make sure she doesn't hurt herself, and he had some ideas about her rehab."

With a snort, Jasper shook his head. "I can work the pulleys fine. And Doc's job is done here."

"Don't make him leave," I asked quietly. "Please?"

Doc had offered to get me out of here, and clearly, these guys had zero intention of letting me go. As wonderful as this whole set-up seemed on the surface, they were building me a very pretty cage.

Still scowling, Jasper glared at me, and a muscle ticked in his jaw.

Be smarter, Emersyn.

"Thank you for doing all of this." The words tasted like ash, but I was accomplished at thanking people for things, even if it was the last thing I wanted to do. Maybe he was a bit psycho, but he had gone to a lot of trouble to do something because I'd said this was what I needed.

Don't fall for it.

"I really do appreciate it, I just…didn't know what to say. I had no idea you would do this." The last part was the absolute truth.

Some of his scowl eased, and a hint of the earlier softness returned. "I want you to be comfortable. You didn't like having people in your rehearsal space."

Surprise flickered through me. "How do you know that?"

I never said that. Sometimes, I simply didn't have a choice.

He lifted one shoulder. "You always timed your rehearsals when everyone else was done. You trained for several days at a private facility away from the theatre while they were all there."

"And some of the other dancers talked," Vaughn supplied. "But Jasper's right. If you need privacy, we'll go."

Did I need it?

No.

Did I want it?

I wasn't sure.

I glanced around the room and then back to the chest. "Um…maybe let me warm up on my own and come back? I don't know how weak my ankle is going to be, and I need some time to stretch."

"Do you need to eat first?" Jasper asked. "You haven't even had coffee. You know what… I'll go get you some water."

He was gone before I could answer him, and Vaughn chuckled and muttered something under his breath as he followed him, and for just a few seconds, I was alone with Doc.

"Remember what I said," he told me. "I'll give you a few minutes to warm up."

"Yes," I told him. "I do."

He paused, gaze fixed on mine, and goosebumps rioted over my skin. He gave me a single nod.

"Be patient. It might take a while to get everything where it used to be."

I let out a shuddering breath as he exited, leaving me alone.

He'd help me.

I just had to be patient.

CHAPTER 19

EMERSYN

I stared at the mirrors on the far side of the room for several long seconds after the door closed behind Doc. The racing of my heart left me lightheaded and more than a little dizzy. Worse, I was so tempted to run out behind him and beg him to get me out of here now.

Not only would that be stupid, it would also be ineffective. Jasper wasn't likely to let me go anywhere with Doc. The overzealous leader of my self-appointed guardians had a real hard-on where Doc was concerned. Fine, I just had to assuage Jasper's worries so he would loosen his grip.

I could do that.

Closing my eyes, I worked on getting my breathing under control then turned to where the stereo was. There was a stack of homemade CDs. The one on top bore the label, *Emersyn's Weird Warmup Shit.*

The next one bore the strokes of a black Sharpie and the title *Happy shit.*

The one below it was *Depressing as fuck.*

The corner of my mouth twitched. There had be a dozen CDs. They even had one with the show's title on it. A cold feeling inched up my spine. It had begun growing when Rome detailed what my favorite shoes were. My clothes. My preferred shampoo. My preferred soap. Sure, they could have gotten all of that from my hotel room.

Now these CDs with music they'd apparently put together from what I liked or used. The apprehension wound tighter in me. How long had they been planning this? Stalking me? I used to muse I'd been living in a cage for years. So what did it say about me that I was putting their CD into the player and hitting play before I took a few steps back into the studio they'd set up for me?

Gilded cage?

No.

But this cage didn't scare me to death.

The first bars of the music washed over me, and I tilted my head back and closed my eyes as I began to stretch.

Arms up, I stretched them. Oh, it felt so good to reach for the sky with both arms free. The air was so cool against my wrist and forearm. The muscles protested the stretch, but I ignored them. The first song was slow on purpose as I rolled through each set of steps. Lunges that got deeper and deeper. Back bends. Loosening the IT bands. Rotating the shoulders. Flexing the wrists.

While I'd made sure to stretch every day, this was different. I descended into a slow split, controlling the descent with only my muscles in my inner thighs, all of which screamed at the intensity. Stretching each day wasn't pushing myself. I pointed my toes to increase the stress on my calves and lower back as I leaned over my right leg and then my left.

I repeated it until there was no pull left and everything

was loose. Back straightening, I planted my hands on the floor. The music was a slow descant, a remix of something, but I barely heard it. The beat was absent and it remained slow, all mournful horns and harmonic counter melodies from the piano, as though the two instruments warred over who controlled the song.

My arm was weaker and the bone newly healed, but even if pain waited at the other end of this move, pain could be compartmentalized. It was a slow, punishing process to roll all of my weight upward as I balanced on my hands. Upward and over my shoulders until I was completely inverted, legs stretched out to either side of me, still in the split.

Balanced.

Even.

The protest in my muscles was profound.

But I could do it.

I could still do it.

The tremble in my muscles warned me so I rolled out of the hand stand and onto my feet. The rush of blood from my head took a moment, and then I did a cartwheel, and another, and another. Bare feet flexing against the floor as my blood seemed to pump harder as the music segued from concertos to rock, I grinned.

This was home.

The place between music and movement.

Serene, despite the exertion, I repeated the cartwheels, rolling my whole body all the way across the studio then back. The spin coupled with being upside down sent all the blood pounding into my skull. If dancers and performers weren't used to it, it could disorient even the most capable.

And I hadn't been capable of much the last few weeks.

I came out of the last cartwheel in an arabesque. I hadn't bothered with pointe shoes. I'd need to smash the boxes. And I could dance barefoot. Today it was just about the music.

The music segued to another familiar tune, and I went through a whole series of positions, riding the grace of the music. The suite was perfect for warming up, building control and then letting loose.

Every step elongated the stretches I'd already done. Every motion reasserted my control. The constant hum in the back of my mind silenced as I flowed with the music. No bruises to stiffen my movements, and there was an odd elation that struck when that thought eddied to the surface. The music shifted again, this time to something more rock opera, and my mind relaxed as my body took over.

Riding the razor edge between performance and exertion, I surrendered to the motion. This wasn't some rehearsed moves, but just letting my body move to the music. I wanted to go up en pointe, but without shoes, my toes would have to do. Pirouette. Arabesque. Step in. Step out. Back to center. Around. I spun with the dance, and when the music changed to something much more pulse pounding, I just let go.

The rush of it and the motion. The silks weren't too far above me, and I did a series of flips then caught them, suspending as I held there and flexed as I began to roll them and up I went. The peace I'd found in the music and the motion couldn't compare to the elation flooding me as I began to work my way up.

Roll, twist, weave, and catch the foot, then tumble and swing and back up again. I flew up and then down. Each sinuous motion would allow me to climb as I rolled with them. There was a moment when I was suspended only by the weight of my feet balanced in the folds of the silks, my arms outstretched, that everything fell away.

Eric.

The company.

The bruises.

The bones.

The terror.

The kidnapping.

Even my erstwhile guardians, who despite their rough, tatted exteriors and dangerous air, didn't frighten me.

Well, not much.

"Hey, pretty girl, you lost?"

"She looks lost."

I slipped a little but caught on the swing and then twisted up and rolled down until I hung just from the two edges and dropped. I didn't land as I expected though, hard arms closed around me as someone caught me.

My eyes flicked open, and I found Jasper staring at me with the most unexpected openness and wonder in his dark gray eyes. The hammer of my heart thudded against my ribs. Rather than just set me down, Jasper curled his arms up until he almost had me in a bridal carry. Panting, I fought to find words. They weren't always easy to reach when I was lost to the music. The next song clicked over, and it was a slower tempo, something to cool down with, and I needed to…

"Can you put me down?" I managed to push those five words out, and Jasper shifted his grip and slowly let me stand. It involved me sliding down the front of him, but he didn't brush my ass or catch the side of a breast. More, he moved almost subtly so I didn't hit his groin. I swallowed around a suddenly dry mouth because I wanted to see if he was turned on.

Sweat slicked my skin, and the air had turned humid around me. Though I was breathing far harder than I should be for the workout. Jasper didn't withdraw once I was on my feet. If anything, he seemed to be studying me intently like he wanted to dig inside my brain or something.

I took a step back, and his hands loosened before they fell away from me. A quick sweep of the room showed me we were alone, and I turned away and began to move again to the music. Longer motions, stretching again. I'd pushed and I could feel twinges, especially in my arms, but I didn't care.

Pain was life.

Living was pain.

For the first time in forever, I'd danced without having to fight through the pain to breathe. Despite weeks of inaction, muscle memory proved to be my greatest asset, and I reached for the peace I'd found in the dance and the silks. It was harder with an audience.

It shouldn't be.

"Hey pretty girl, you lost?"

"She looks lost."

The crunch of the rock hitting jarred me as the music faded between songs, and I just stopped moving. Hands on my hips, I dropped my chin and tried to slow my breathing. I didn't want to think about the boys or the park.

Or the beautiful painting Rome made before there was blood on the cement.

A click had me opening my eyes again. Jasper stood at the CD player, and he'd turned it off. "Talk to me," he said quietly.

"What do you want me to say?"

"Tell me what's wrong."

I laughed, and the sound came out muddied with tears I refused to shed. I'd given up crying a long time ago, and I wasn't about to start now. "That's a stupid question, and you're not a stupid man."

Surprise flickered across his face.

Moving to walk in a slow circle, I worked on cooling off.

"I want to help you," he said in a voice so soft, I thought I had to have imagined it, but whenever I faced him, he tracked me with that storm-kissed gaze.

"Then let me go."

"I can't do that. Ask me for anything else."

I laughed again and shook my head. "You built me a dance studio." That I could appreciate.

"You said you needed it."

"But if I say I need you to let me go, that's off the table."

"It's safer for you here."

I spun to face him. "What the hell does that mean?"

He stalked toward me. "That's a stupid question," he parroted back at me. "And you're not a stupid woman."

Woman.

Not girl.

I didn't understand why that registered with me. "Why do you want to keep me safe?"

Lifting a single finger, he raised his eyebrows but didn't touch me until I nodded slowly. With care, he stroked that finger down my cheek. I was sweaty and gross, but it didn't seem to bother him in the slightest. "You're perfect."

Of all the things he could have said, that never even ventured in the direction of a list I would have made. The breath I'd been trying to regulate backed up into my lungs. He drew a heart against my cheek.

"You're a work of art in motion," Jasper continued, and I couldn't look away from his eyes as he seemed to bore his gaze into mine. "There is nothing I won't do for you."

That should scare the shit out of me.

"Eric?"

"Nothing," he repeated. "He'll never touch you again. You can forget him."

Fear shivered through me, and something a lot darker. "Is he still alive?"

He trailed the finger down to my throat, and my heart grew a bit more frantic at the contact. "Do you really care?"

"Maybe," I said. "He blames me for being here."

"Fuck him."

"I'd really rather not," I retorted, and a smile curved

Jasper's lips. It was the first real grin I thought I'd ever seen from him. It softened his entire expression and transformed it. I clenched as liquid heat pooled between my thighs, and fuck me, wanting any of these guys was the worst idea.

Wrapping his hand around my nape, Jasper stroked his thumb against the base of my skull, and my pulse began to rabbit. "He hurt you."

I didn't answer. I didn't have to answer.

"We know about the bones. The bruises. The violence."

I still didn't respond.

"Did he do anything else?"

"Why?" I was so proud of my voice for not coming out tremulous or weak.

"Because every fucking thing he's ever done to you, I'm going to visit on him three-fold. He's going to suffer for hurting you."

Holy.

Shit.

"You're torturing him?" My nipples tightened, and I swore I had to keep still or I'd have rubbed my thighs together.

Jasper studied me for a long moment, then he gave the barest pressure and I tilted my head back, well aware I was baring my throat. Everything about this was wrong. I should take a step back. Put more distance between us. But I didn't fucking want to.

"The idea of me torturing him turns you on," Jasper murmured. "Doesn't it?"

I licked my dry lips, and his gaze seemed riveted to the action. Fuck it, what could a little truth hurt? "I hate him."

"What did he do to you, baby?" The soft croon of his voice seeped in to me and prodded more truths loose from the gnarled knot I kept hidden away, but they wouldn't part so easily. Some were glued. Some were stuck with rubber bands. Others were plastered and soaked in blood.

"It doesn't matter… If you're serious that he'll never leave here alive."

His nostrils flared. No, he hadn't told me he was going to kill him. I just…

"He won't be."

Fuck.

I closed my eyes at the very real sense of relief flooding through me. Never having to worry about him grabbing me. Banging on my door. Forcing his way inside.

Never having to put on a happy face or smile as he touched me.

Breath feathered over my lips, and the faint notes of tobacco, coffee, and, of all things, maple syrup teased my senses, along with the very distinct scent of Jasper. "What did he do to you, baby?"

The words clawed at the back of my throat, and I shook my head. The snap of the band pulled them back, and I opened my eyes to find Jasper staring down at me, barely a breath between us. The heat coming off him competed with the fire burning inside of me.

"I don't want to talk about him." I couldn't. "Please don't make me."

My voice cracked on that last part, and Jasper's whole expression grew fierce and furious. Dammit. I pulled away from him, or tried to, but I barely made it a step before he yanked me back around and I collided with his chest. A moment later, his mouth was on mine, and the hot demand of his tongue sliding between my lips exploded through the sadness, the confusion, and the pain.

Hard and firm, he moved his lips like it was a massage. His beard tickled my face, and his hands were hot where they rested on me. Seemingly of their own accord, my arms wrapped around his neck. For a moment, one long moment, Jasper broke the contact and lifted his head. I couldn't read his expression. The intensity of it and the rawness of emotion in his eyes—the anger. It was…it was like someone had lit a match.

Then his mouth claimed mine again, and there was no room for thought as he slid his hands to my ass and dragged me upward so my face was level with his and my breasts crushed against his chest. Hot laving strokes of his tongue interspersed with nibbling bites on my lips. The pressure and the pace changed second to second.

I was fucking dizzy from the contact as he kneaded my ass with his firm, hot fingers, and I locked my thighs to his hips and ground against the very thick erection straining his jeans. A moan tore out of my throat as he pushed me back against the wall, and then he had a hand on my chest, teasing and tweaking the nipple through my leotard. I raked my fingers through his hair. I swore he sought to devour me as he demanded more and more in the kiss.

And fuck me if I wasn't giving it to him.

A moment later, I was on my feet and leaning against the wall as Jasper backed up and glared at me, blazing hot daggers in his eyes.

What the fuck?

A fist slammed against the door in a hard cadence of knocking. "Open the fucking door, Hawk," Kestrel called. "We have a problem."

Jaw clenched, Jasper suddenly thrust a water bottle at me. His tone was almost as scathing as his eyes as he raked his gaze over me. All at once, I was too exposed, too…vulnerable

"Go back to your room and take a shower. Stay there until someone comes for you." Then he was walking away and jerking the door open. I didn't hear what was said as he exited, only caught Freddie's wince as he peeked inside.

"Come on, Boo-Boo," he murmured in an almost sympathetic voice. "I'll walk you up. Don't mind Jasper. I swear he tested anal out with real wood at some point and it left splinters behind."

The joke should have been funny, but I couldn't laugh.

What the fuck just happened?

I'd climbed him like a pole, but he'd kissed me first.

Right?

CHAPTER 20

KELLAN

"What?" Jasper demanded as he stalked out of the studio. Rage radiated off him, and I spared a look at Emersyn's profile and curled my fingers into a fist. She had her face away from us, but her shoulders rolled forward. Freddie leaned against the wall, and I jerked my head back toward the room. While he was not our first pick for babysitting duty, we didn't have much choice. We were running thin on people we could leave her with, and right now, we would need our heavy hitters out there.

"19 Diamonds," I told Jasper as I pushed open the door to the main warehouse. The layout put several layers of protection between the possibility of drive-bys and where we slept. Right now, it also put several layers between Emersyn and the people trying to hurt her. Something we were supposed to be working on and had done absolutely nothing about.

As much as I hated to admit it, that was tomorrow's problem. Today's waited for us, armed, furious, and barely restrained.

He was also not alone.

"What the fuck do they want?" The question required no answer. We still had their boy in the fridge. He wouldn't be leaving either. First, he'd been planning to hurt Emersyn, that alone was enough to earn him a bullet, but he and his crew had been in our territory. That meant we needed to know what else they were planning.

Wallace Meeks was an enforcer for the 19 Diamonds, their third-in-command. Sending him made sense. At six foot two, two hundred and twenty-five pounds, he was nothing but solid muscle and stubborn strength. He was good with knives and guns. I had more than one scar from that fucker. At one point, he'd had ash blond hair, but he started shaving his head and we hadn't seen his hair in a while. The tattoos crawling up his neck were starting to find purchase on his bare scalp.

"What the fuck are you doing here, Deuce?" Jasper's tone was five different kinds of unfriendly, and not for the first time, I was glad for the Glock tucked into the holster at the small of my back. The brass knuckles in my pocket would come in handy too.

Jasper always had a gun on him. Always. Even when I couldn't see his weapons, he had them tucked away. He strode across to where the enforcer waited with two guys to back him up. Rome and Liam were there, both stoic with unreadable expressions, but Vaughn squared up, toe-to-toe with Meeks. He was bigger than Meeks by maybe five pounds. Didn't matter, I'd seen Vaughn take down bigger guys.

"Get your pet dog off me," Meeks warned.

"I asked you a question," Jasper stated, ignoring Meeks' comment. He didn't repeat it, just stared at the other man, flat-eyed and expressionless. While Meeks was in my line of sight, I kept my focus on the two punks he'd brought with him. I didn't know either one.

While that didn't mean much, my job wasn't tracking 19 Diamonds recruitment, the fact they had a lot of new blood like the assholes who went after Emersyn and these guys didn't bode well for us.

"Where are my boys?" Meeks demanded.

Jasper shrugged. "Do I look like their keeper?" He didn't ask who or even affect any kind of interest in who he was discussing.

"Don't get that attitude with me," Meeks snarled as he went to step forward and got bodychecked by Vaughn. I didn't go for my gun, though the two lumps with Meeks twitched like they were reaching. Lump number one with the scar over his eye was carrying on his left. Lump number two, who looked like he should be in science class or some shit at the high school rather than here, had his in the front of his pants.

Dumbass needed to learn you didn't put a gun where your dick lay. That was a fast way to lose it. Course, the kid wasn't long for this world, dickless or not, running with Meeks. The fucker burned through fresh blood like a player at a virgin prom.

"My guys headed down here yesterday, and they didn't come back."

"If your boys got lost in our territory, that's not my problem. The fact you sent them into our territory is about to be your problem." Jasper sounded almost bored.

Dickless and Lumpy twitched. They really did want to go for their guns. The air reeked of violence, along with the hint of marijuana and liquor. Drugs were a no fly for the Vandals. Not even the rats touched the stuff. Not if they wanted to stay. Some rules were hard and fast, set in blood.

We controlled the distribution in our area and monitored who brought what in as a way to make sure it stayed out of the hands of kids, and it also gave us a line on the junkies who were a little too liberal with their violence. That was a no go here too.

Dickless shifted his weight, and then his hazy gaze snagged on mine. Sweat beaded along his forehead, and he kept licking his lips like they were too dry. Lumpy wasn't doing much better. They were both a little strung out, and Dickless was coming down.

Idiots.

Liam stretched.

Fucking stretched.

And all hell broke loose.

Vaughn had Meeks down in two seconds. He and Jasper could handle the fuck no issues, but Rome startled because wound or no wound, he pounced on Lumpy like a man on a mission.

There were cleaner ways to do this, but Rome was a flurry of hits and wild violence. They'd come here looking for a fight, and he was all about giving it to them. Narrowing the gap between me and Dickless, I got my hand on his where he grasped the gun. Pain escaped his mouth as I gripped his fingers. One of them ground on that hand, and if he slipped his finger a little lower, he'd be on the trigger.

The gun barrel though? It was firmly against his dick. His back slammed into the wall, and my fingers bit into his shoulder before the knowledge fully registered. Rome was still kicking the absolute fuck out of Lumpy. At the rate he was going, Lumpy was going to be un-fucking-recognizable.

Vaughn wrenched Meeks to the ground with Jasper, so they were no help. I cut a look to Liam, who stood there with a faint smirk on his face as Rome all but curb stomped the guy.

226

The rats present weren't gonna intervene, even if a couple of them already had guns out. Goddammit, when did those two start carrying pieces?

"Liam," I snarled, and the other man glanced from his twin to me. Blankness rapidly overtook his more blood-thirsty expression, and he let out a sigh like I was asking for a lot. But he caught his brother's arm as Rome lifted his foot to stomp on the guy's leg. Lumpy wasn't moving anymore, and fuck if I knew whether he was still breathing. Gripping Rome's arm, he dragged his blood-spattered twin away from the body.

"Fuck, if you guys killed him—" Dickless didn't finish the thought, because I had my finger between the trigger and the guard so he couldn't pull it and shoot himself in the groin. As funny as it would be to see the idiot get what he deserved, I didn't feel like cleaning up *another* body.

I slammed my knee right into the gun, which drove the metal into his dick. The 19 Diamond let out a whimpering gasp of sound that I cut off by yanking the gun out of his pants then backhanding him with it.

The rats scrambled when I pointed to the downed man as I turned to face Meeks. He was on the ground, his arm locked back into a painful position as Vaughn kept him pinned in place, one knee between his shoulder blades.

Jasper squatted in front of him. "You used to be smart," he told him.

"I didn't fucking tell him to make a move," Meeks grunted out.

"Not my problem," Jasper informed him in an ice-cold voice he reserved purely for business. "Or it wasn't, until you made it mine. We have rules, Deuce. Rules that you don't break unless you want us to retaliate."

"I'm telling you, I didn't tell him to make a move. I'm here for my guys, nothing else."

I checked the weapon. One in the chamber. Clip with sixteen shots. They came armed for a fight. The rats on Dickless pulled another gun off him and a couple more knives. The second gun was smaller, but also loaded. The ankle holster made it a bitch to pull, so just a backup weapon.

Liam had gone back to the blood stain his brother had made and removed weapons from him. At my look, Liam pressed two fingers to the guy's neck, then nodded.

Thank fuck. One less body to get rid of.

"Jasper—" Meeks cut off on a pained snarl as Vaughn tightened the arm bar. Any second, there was going to be a crack of a bone or a tear in the other man's shoulder. Our bodies weren't meant to contort like that.

All of a sudden, an image of Emersyn rolled through my head. She bent and twisted as she wound her way up the silks. The dancing had been one thing, but the moment she'd dropped from the ceiling, suspended only by her skill and a pair of silk that could tear at any second, my breath had been lodged in my throat.

I couldn't count the number of videos I'd watched of her performing in the last few years. She'd always been something else, but she'd also been a kid. A beautiful, talented kid.

The woman suspended above me caught not only my eyes, but my imagination. I'd been with her for days, looking after her. Right there at my fingertips was everything I never thought about before. We'd come to look after a kid, but she wasn't a child. She was everything I thought she'd be and nothing like I'd dreamed. Real. Raw. Visceral.

Hot.

Passion incarnate.

Fucking beautiful.

"Hawk…" Meeks' strained voice drove the sexy image out of my head, and I blew out a breath. The last thing I needed was a fucking hard-on dealing with these assholes. Especially when the little sparrow was right there and a thousand miles away at the same time. "You have my word, we didn't come here for a fight. I just wanted to pick up my boys. They were talking shit, and I didn't hear about it until too late."

"So you come here making demands?" Jasper asked him, still squatted in front of the other man. He had his hunting knife out. We'd seen one of those blades in a movie when we were kids, and it was all Jasper talked about for three months until Raptor stole one for him.

We'd cut our fingers and sealed our blood pact the same night with that knife.

"I just want my boys."

"You know the penalty for breaking the treaty. You gonna pay the price?"

"Blood for blood," Meeks answered.

"That's right," Jasper sounded almost pleased. "Your boys are done. You need to forget about them."

Because the one who had survived wouldn't be long for this world. They tried to attack Emersyn. Bad enough they'd wandered into our territory. Touching her signed their death warrants.

Even if Rome made sure their hands hadn't landed on her.

The experience had left another mark on her. She already carried far too many.

"They were acting on their own," Meeks said as Vaughn relaxed the pained hook of his arm, but he didn't release him. "They weren't under orders."

"Fine," Jasper said with a faint smile that held far more malice than it did friendship or acceptance. "But you coming here, orders or not, that does violate our agreements."

Meeks exhaled raggedly, but he didn't argue.

"I'm willing to work with you, but not without compensation. You made a mess in here, interrupted my day, and generally pissed me off." Jasper ticked the items off like he dictated a shopping list. Meeks had to hear it. Whatever was going to happen would happen, the level of pain would be determined by how cooperative he was.

The last thing we needed was a street fight with the 19 Diamonds. We could take them, but it would be a bloody, costly fight.

Jasper lifted his chin, and Vaughn released the other man, muscles tensing and flexing in his arms as he straightened. Tempers were running high across the board. Rome might be still, but he had his gaze pinned to the downed Lumpy like he was still picturing taking him apart. Liam stood between his twin and the other man's death.

Dickless was still out, but the rats holding him weren't being gentle, and he was going to wake up with more bruises than he'd had when I knocked his ass out. Meeks' face was ruddy from pain and exertion, sweat slicked his skin, and even without Vaughn holding him, he had the sense to not rise off the ground.

Still playing with the knife, Jasper studied Meeks. I'd give Deuce credit, he didn't beg.

"Blood for blood," Meeks said finally, agreeing to the penalty.

"Spread your hands out on the floor."

At Jasper's command, the other man swallowed and extended one arm, and then with some effort and more than a little pain, he did the other. It took him a minute, but Jasper was patient while he spread his palms against the floor.

"I'm going to do you a favor," Jasper said, all reasonable and shit. "Your guys are out, so no one is going to hear you scream. We're getting you some ice so if you're fast about it, you might be able to fix the problem. That seems fair, right?"

Fuck, this was going to be messy. I jerked my head at one of the rats, and they went to get some ice.

Meeks' expression tightened and his lips thinned, but all he said was, "Fair."

"Probably should thank me," Jasper suggested thinly. "Because I don't have to do you a solid."

The malice in his glare when he looked at Jasper promised all kinds of retribution. Goddammit. Just fucking do it and get it over with. One would think he'd learned to not play with his prey.

"Thank you, Hawk," Meeks ground out between his teeth like the bitter words poisoned him, even as he gave them air.

"You're very welcome," Jasper told him a split second before the knife came down and severed his trigger finger.

I'd give Meeks credit.

He didn't scream.

Much.

CHAPTER 21

EMERSYN

"*Y*ou don't have to stay with me," I told Freddie as he walked me up the stairs, and he grasped his chest with both hands.

"Boo-Boo, you're gonna hurt my feelings." The melodramatic note made me roll my eyes. "Besides, do you know how long I've waited to get alone with you and your perfect pussy again?"

We were in the hallway, and I paused to look at him. "You've never been alone with my perfect pussy."

"So now would be the time to start, right?" He leered so playfully, I couldn't help laughing. It was the most ridiculous expression. "Besides, I've got excellent conversational skills and more—I can cook."

"Really?" The flip from playful leering to just plain playful was refreshing. Everyone else was so stoic. Like Kestrel. He was supposed to be my ally. I'd trusted him, and I still wanted to trust him. When he said if he could let me go, he would, I believed him.

Yet, here we were.

Then there was Vaughn. My whole body heated at the thought of him. He flirted and soothed. His voice could melt me, even when I wanted to punch him for laughing at me. Rome was…a mystery. His art though, that took my breath away. Jasper was so damn controlling. The image of his kiss seared through me. Then there was Liam—he was more of a mystery than Rome.

Beyond all of them? Doc.

I didn't understand any of them. At the door to my room, I put a hand on Freddie's chest so he wouldn't follow me inside. "I'll be out after I shower."

"Awww, no free looks at that pretty pussy? I promise, I won't touch."

I snorted. "Keep asking like that, and you'll never see it."

Just as I closed the door, he said "Yes!" with great vehemence.

I pulled the door open again and eyed him. "Why are you so happy?"

He grinned, arms folded and looking cocky as hell as he leaned against the doorframe. "Because you just told me how I could get to see it again. I just have to stop asking."

My mouth opened, but he seemed so damn pleased with himself, that I didn't have it in me to burst his bubble. With a shake of my head, I closed the door and headed for the bathroom. I paused only long enough to take a change of clothes in with me. I was soaked through with sweat, and I needed a shower.

Fifteen minutes later with my wet hair pulled into a braid and dressed in clean clothes, I found Freddie sprawled on Kestrel's bed, studying his phone. He glanced over at me as I opened the door and then sat up.

"Damn, I was hoping for a little towel and flash." He winked as if to let me know he wasn't remotely serious, which I appreciated. Still, I shook my head and padded for the door. I'd left off shoes and put on thick socks.

I didn't expect a chance to blow out of here yet. I didn't even know when Doc would manage it, but I planned to trust him as much as I could trust anyone in this place. I was halfway down the hall before Freddie caught up to me.

"Maybe we should hang out up here?" he suggested, and I hesitated.

Did he want to stay here because he didn't want to let me go downstairs? Was something wrong? Jasper had taken off like a bat out of hell the moment Kestrel knocked on the door. One minute, he was burning me alive with his kiss, and the next, he was glaring at me like I'd committed a crime.

"I'm hungry," I said. "And I want to go watch something on the television."

"Oh." Freddie scratched at his smooth jaw like he had scruff. "Yeah, and you don't have a TV in your room. I do, but my room looks like shit. Not to mention I'm not in the mood for having my balls chopped off. Jasper has one in his. Tell you what, come on." He caught my hand in his and half pulled me down the hall.

"I don't want to go to Jasper's room," I argued. My body protested the lie. I wanted more than Jasper's room, but I had zero intention of chasing him down after his reaction in the studio.

"Trust me, I don't either," Freddie assured me as he guided me down the hall. "I don't feel like having him wring my neck. Though that's a step up from having my balls removed." He checked a door, then pulled a slender case out of his back pocket and knelt down at the door with a pair of picks.

That's what they were. Lockpicks.

He slid them in, and a moment later, the tumblers gave.

The door opened to another bedroom, this one as neat as Kestrel's, as colorful as mine, but with darker woods and heavier blues. There was a huge desk with tools scattered over it and slouchy chairs, as well as a video game system and a huge television.

The door had been locked.

"Here," Freddie said, thrusting a remote control at me. "Make yourself comfortable and stay here, okay? I'm gonna run down and get you food." He was halfway out the door before he slid to a stop and looked at me. "What do you want?"

I needed to carb up after that dance, but right now, I didn't want anything fancy. "Whose room is this?"

"Tell me what you want to eat, and I'll tell you whose room it is." Freddie waggled his eyebrows at me, and I sighed. Glancing over the room, I paused on a familiar T-shirt.

"It's Vaughn's."

"Wow, you're amazing. How did you even guess that? Or did you guess? You know, never mind. I forgot, never play poker with you. Um...food?" Freddie sounded more disgruntled than impressed.

"I really don't need to eat." Yes, I'd said I was hungry, but I wasn't starving. Eating after a workout was just an old habit. I'd only been here a few weeks, and my real life seemed so far away.

Freddie squinted at me. "Yeah, that doesn't work for me. You're not some weirdo herbivore or anything, right?"

I picked up Vaughn's shirt. It smelled like him. "You don't know?" That was curious. "Rome knows my favorite dance shoe."

"Rome's got champion stalker tendencies and he likes art. Dance is art, you know? He used to hit some of the magazine stands over on 20th, they had the best one. The artsier ones. Me, I was more into the tabloids and skin rags." A faint rush of pink touched his ears as he rubbed the back of his neck. "You never posed for any of those, right?"

"No," I said and sank down into the soft bean bag chair. It was huge, kind of like a nest, and I sank into it.

"Damn."

"I'm not an herbivore," I clarified. "So as long as it's not spoiled or made out of something I can't identify, I'll eat it."

He gave a little half nod and closed the door behind him. The lock tumblers secured, and I leaned back in the chair, pressing Vaughn's shirt to my nose. It took a minute longer than I expected, but the thump of Freddie hitting a wall made me laugh. He was probably asking himself if I had posed for a magazine.

I probably shouldn't tease him. I couldn't help it. Freddie was funny. I pointed the remote at the television and turned it on, then skimmed the channel for the news.

They never turned the news on downstairs.

I WAS HALF ASLEEP WHEN THE DOOR OPENED AND LIGHT spilled in the room. I smothered a yawn and tried to sit up. I hadn't meant to go to sleep, but this floofy chair was the most comfortable thing I'd ever sat in before. It was like a ginormous body pillow that hugged.

And smelled like Vaughn. Not that the latter had anything to do with my interest or why I was still holding his shirt.

"Did you have to kill the cow or something yourself?" The flippant question was meant for Freddie, because not only had he not come back, it had easily been a couple of hours. The news channels had offered me glimpses of the outside world, but it had been far too early in the day for anything local. I had watched a gameshow and then found reruns of *Law and Order*.

It was one of the staples of road life. No matter what town we were in, someone had it on, and the shows from the beginning cracked me up 'cause they were still using pagers. There was an episode still playing, but I forgot all about it when Vaughn half turned toward me and then suddenly whipped his shirt off and rubbed at his face.

I'd turned off the light switch when I'd decided Freddie had forgotten about me. The light from the television still played over the ripple of muscle Vaughn bared. Since he was half turned away, I was free to ogle. Not that I should've been, but he had this habit of losing his shirts around me.

"I didn't know you were in here," he said in that melodious, panty-melting voice of his, and I sighed. Right. Not my room. Not invited.

"Freddie was gonna get me food, but I wanted to go down and watch television, but I'm assuming whatever dragged Jasper away meant that I shouldn't be down there 'cause he stashed me in here."

He cut a look over his shoulder at me. It was a quick one, and the flickering light seemed to turn his eyes into twin shadows. "The door was locked." Before I could comment or defend that, he shook his head. "Fucking Freddie. It's fine, Dove. You make yourself comfortable. I'm going to shower, and then I'm going to get you food."

"I don't have to intrude…"

He waved me back to my seat as he strode past me, but the distinct smell of copper and sweat rolled off him as he passed. The sweat I'd expect, but the copper was almost too thick. I twisted in the seat and caught sight of his arm just as the door closed.

His blood-streaked arm.

Heart clenching, I faced the television again.

The swift way he'd removed his shirt. How he'd turned his back—kept it to me. That didn't mean he'd done something, but maybe something had been done to him. I worried at a bit of a hangnail on my thumb and glanced at the television as the water cut on in the bathroom.

The rumble through the pipes reminded me of my room. It came out cold and took a minute to get warmer. The show had segued to commercials, and I glanced at the bathroom again. If it were me and I was bleeding and hurt, Vaughn would help. But he also hadn't asked for any help.

I twisted his shirt in my hands and then tried to focus on the advertisement for sinus medication. The list of things that it could cause included a stroke. Yeah, that was comforting.

"Just go knock on the door," I told myself. If he was really hurt, I could go get one of the others or Doc.

A little kernel of hope burst inside of me. Doc had been there earlier. Before I danced. He'd said he would help, then they'd all left. But it seemed ages ago. The next commercial was for dog food, and I shoved out of the comfy pillow chair. My muscles protested. I'd stiffened up in the time since I'd just lounged in here.

I was probably dehydrated too. That was a problem for later Emersyn. I was capable of going down to get stuff for Vaughn if he needed it too. I knocked on the door.

It was a timid as fuck little knock, and I rolled my eyes at myself. How was he supposed to hear it over the sound of the water in the shower?

Blowing out a breath, I raised my hand for a second knock and then...

You know what? Fuck it. They'd all marched in and out of my bathroom, bedroom, and everything else. At this point, they'd probably all seen me naked at one point or another. I'd been wearing Vaughn's shirt, for fuck's sake.

Turnabout was fair play.

I'd take that truth to my grave. Twisting the knob, I opened the door. The light made me squint, and the wash of steamy air hit me. The first thing I saw were his discarded clothes on the back of the toilet. The yellow, sleeveless tank top poking out from beneath his jeans was streaked in orange. The coppery scent was still there, but faded beneath the scent of rich musky soap that was intensely familiar.

The water splashing drew my attention, and it was the first time I realized that Vaughn's shower curtain was clear vinyl and the full outline of his back tapering down to his bare ass was visible where he leaned with one hand against the tile wall as the water spilled over him. All the moisture dried up in my mouth.

Holy shit.

I mean, I'd known he was cut. That much had been obvious every time he took his shirt off, but this was something else altogether. Muscles bunched and moved in his legs as he rolled his head around. Tracking my gaze up to where his hand was visible against the white tile, I froze.

The red around his hands and staining along the back of them had me jerking my attention back to the shirt. He pulled his hand away, and a bloody handprint remained.

"Are you hurt?"

Vaughn twisted and stared over his shoulder at me as he raked that bloodied hand through his hair. The streaks on his face had my heart twisting. "What are you doing in here, Dove?"

Shifting my weight from one foot to the other, I forced myself to meet his gaze. "You were bleeding, or someone was."

I glanced over at his discarded clothes again. The way he'd abruptly ripped off his shirt and turned away from me.

He hadn't expected to find me in his room. The rush to the shower.

When I returned my gaze to him, he'd turned to face me fully, and no matter how hard I tried not to glance down, the semi-hard cock jutting out from between his thighs was unmistakable.

The fact it had silver studs piercing it riveted me when I damn well knew better than to stare. Fuck. I'd seen naked people before. Nudity and dancing went hand in hand. Staring was rude, but when I looked up, Vaughn just grinned at me. The ruddy flush of color to his cheeks from the heated water just added to the appeal of that smile.

He certainly wasn't ashamed of his body. Not that he had any reason to be. His deep red hair was plastered to his skull and seemed darker still in the bright light. The pale brown, nearly topaz eyes of his gleamed. "See something you like, Dove?"

I could lie.

But really, what was the point? My nipples were pin points of hardness beneath the oversized shirt I was wearing, and my panties were damp from far more than the humidity in the air. I licked my lips as I locked my gaze on him again.

"You're a beautiful man."

Surprise flickered across his features as if he hadn't expected my answer, but it didn't diminish his delight in the slightest. Then because he dragged the curtain to the side, allowing me an unimpeded view, I drank in the sight of the tattoos all over him. His thighs were nearly as colorful as his arms. Each time he raised a hand to his hair, the shield on his biceps flexed. More and more, the rivulets of water began to run clear as the ruddy brownish stain from the blood washed away.

"The water's hot if you want to join me."

That offer tempted me way more than it should. But

instead of backing down, I pushed deeper into the room and then closed the bathroom door and leaned against it. Arms folded, I watched as he filled one palm of his hand with a couple of pumps of shampoo. Then he worked it into his hair.

The bloody handprint on the wall had already begun to rinse away as water splashed off him. Some of it spattered the floor, but he made no move to close the curtain or obstruct my view.

What the hell was I doing?

A part of me tried to tell myself I was searching for injuries, but I really wasn't a big fan of lying to myself.

To others? Sure.

To me? Not so much.

Only a few hours ago, I'd been making out with one of his friends, and my lips tingled at the memory. I'd been climbing Jasper like a pole, and now I was considering a repeat experience, only with significant less clothing and a new pole.

Though to be fair, Vaughn would probably be the thickest pole I'd ever worked. As if he could read my mind, his dick grew thicker and harder. Fuck me.

I closed my eyes and forced my head to lean back against the door. "I'll go."

"You don't have to leave," he said. "I don't mind you watching me, Dove. Just promise to let me do the same sometime."

I snorted. "You guys watch me all the time."

"True."

I really did love the way the smooth, sensuous nature of his voice rolled over me like a caress, wearing away all the brittle, broken edges. A part of me could listen to him all day long.

"Open your eyes, Dove," he beckoned, and I didn't argue or even try to resist the compulsion. He ran soapy hands over his broad chest and then to his dick. Every stroke had my attention. He watched me with an intensity that seared into me as I watched him, and when I met his gaze again, I almost said fuck it. "You ever had a man with a piercing, Dove?"

"No," I told him honestly. Not that I really wanted to discuss prior lovers.

Just, no.

A shiver went through me.

He let out a sigh. "So I'd be your first?"

There was something about the way he said 'first' that had my toes curling. Firsts didn't have a lot of meaning for me.

But the more he washed his dick, the harder it grew, and I kind of wondered how that would feel pushing into me.

"Yes," I admitted. "Though it remains to be seen if I'm even interested in trying it."

He laughed softly and rinsed off, then shut the water off. Free of all the soap, his whole body gleamed. The word beautiful did not do him justice.

"You're interested," he said, and I didn't even try to retreat as he dripped his way over to me. When he settled his wet hands on the door, one on each side of me, I had to tilt my head to meet his gaze. Heat hit me in waves.

"I came to make sure you weren't hurt."

"Would you care if I was, Dove?" Wonder reappeared in those eyes of his, and I almost forgot how to breathe.

I licked my lips and considered my answer as he leaned in a little closer. Warm water from his hair dripped against my cheek like a forgotten tear. The moment I opened to admit that yes, I would care, he swallowed the sound as his mouth claimed mine.

Fuck the water. I wrapped my arms around him, and then his banded against me as he picked me right up off the ground. Everything faded away except the feeling of his body crushing mine and the heavy weight of that pierced dick pressing against my stomach.

"Yes," I managed in between breaths as he tilted my head to the side and nudged my mouth open wider. The sweep of his tongue stroking mine provoked a rush of need to boiling in my system. I clenched my thighs against his hips.

The yoga pants I had on were not remotely thick enough to do more than provide the suggestion of impediment.

"Yes what, Dove?" He kissed away from my mouth and tracked a path of biting kisses along my jaw to my ear. I shuddered with every connect as I dug my fingers into the hard, tense muscles of his shoulders.

"Yes," I whispered, the single syllable strained.

With sharp teeth, he tugged at my earlobe, and then a wide hand slid under the waistband of my pants, and I swore my panties fucking disintegrated.

CHAPTER 22

EMERSYN

*V*aughn dug his fingers into the muscle of my ass, and I hitched my thighs a little higher on his hips. The water still sluicing off him soaked my shirt in seconds. But I was already twisting to find his lips with my own. He rocked his hips into me as I sucked his tongue in to play with my own. There was a hint of mint on his breath and the notes of coffee.

Three thoughts collided as the seam on my yoga pants tore. The first was I'd had time to nap and get a little recovery for my sore muscles. The second that I'd showered. And the third…?

"Fuck," he muttered as he pulled me away from the door. "Dove, do you really want this?"

His pupils were huge, and his chest heaved with his panting breaths. I licked the taste of him on my lips, savoring it. Wiggling against him, I asked him almost word-lessly to put me down. Despite the raging need demonstrated by his thick, red crowned cock with the mushroom shaped head flushing an almost painful crimson, he released me.

Almost instantly, I missed the bite of his fingers against my ass and the heat of him crushing my breasts. My nipples were particularly needy, but they'd been trapped behind cloth, so I yanked the shirt up and over my head. The sports bra I'd tugged on went next.

The humid air was almost a cool caress on my flesh.

"Holy shit, Dove." He exhaled the words with a kind of reverence that turned my cunt slick with need. I stripped off what was left of the yoga pants, and despite the way his fingers twitched, he didn't reach for me. The sense of control was heady as fuck, but I'd take it.

Right now, we were trapped in this bubble of expectation and desire. Nothing else mattered in this steamy bathroom. Just me. Just him.

When my panties hit the floor, I followed them down to my knees and ran my hands up the bunching and flexing muscles of his thighs. At eye level, his cock was even more impressive and kind of pretty in a heavy, blunt way. There was just the hint of a curve to it that had my core clenching.

He was going to hurt me in all the best ways. I traced my tongue against the slit where pre-cum gathered, and his dick fucking twitched. I wrapped my hand around the girth of it, and he slammed his palms against the door again.

Stealing a look upward, I found his hot eyes on me, and I smiled as I traced my tongue over his tip, exploring each of the bits of metal jutting out in the form of a cross. I had no idea why he'd pierced himself like this or how much it had to have hurt when he'd done it, but I wanted to know what it felt like. Everywhere.

I gave his cock a slow pump, not once losing the focus of his gaze. "Are we really doing this, Vaughn?" It was as close to asking permission as I could get at that moment. We were playing with fire, and I wanted to burn.

"Dove, you can have every fucking thing from me you want," he promised. "But be sure, sweet girl. 'Cause I have a feeling once I'm in that pussy of yours, I'm not going to want to be anywhere else."

"Then let's start here," I suggested before I closed my mouth over the hot tip of his dick, and he released a litany of curse words that just made me clench everywhere. The weight of his cock on my tongue was a drug, and I worked the base with my hand as I sucked him as deep as I could. There was no way I was getting him to my throat, but I could damn well try.

A flash of darkness filled my eyes, but I flung it away. I traced the piercings on his cock, grounding myself against their presence. A heavy hand came down on my hair, but it was so light and tentative.

Another slow suck and pump, then I pulled off, aware of the string of spit still connecting us as I gazed up at him. The rawness in his expression turned me inside out. I wanted more of that. I was here with him.

"You can pull my hair," I told him. "You can fuck my mouth." A shudder went through me as he bared his teeth in an expression that fell somewhere between a grin and a grimace. "You can do anything you want to me."

"Yeah?" he asked, his breath coming in shallower breaths, and I swore his cock pulsed in my grip. I licked the head again, sucking away the salty drops of pre-cum. They were his, and I wanted them.

Nothing mattered right now.

Except him.

Except this.

"Yeah."

He closed his eyes for a moment, a hint of rapture in his

face. "Dove...hold on for me, because I am going to eat you fucking alive."

The silkiness of his voice punctuated by the raw promise had my thighs turning damp. I was this fucking turned on, and we'd barely done more than kiss. In a move so quick and smooth, he had me up from the ground before I even realized what he was doing.

He yanked open the bedroom door, and the light from the bathroom spilt across the room, highlighting his bed like a guidepost. But he shut off the light, and with only the flickering light from the television playing over him, he carried me to the bed. The band of his arm around me was steel, but the brush of his skin against my nipples had me squirming. His cock nudged at my cunt, and he let out a growl of breath as he dropped me onto the soft fucking cover.

The contrast of sensation against my overheated skin had me squirming. I started to move, but he caught my calves and pulled me toward him. Then my knees were over his shoulders as he knelt onto the bed. The angle pushed me up onto my shoulders, but I could handle the bend.

Then his mouth closed over my cunt like he planned to kiss it as deeply as he had my mouth. The pure liquid heat coursing through my veins caught fire at the first thrust of his tongue. His nose moved in slow circles on my clit. It was swollen and needy, no doubt, because even the gentlest of brushes sent electricity to sizzle over my nerves.

Every time he pressed his tongue into me though, I wanted to clamp down on it. Not enough pressure. Fuck, I needed more. Hands flattening on the bed, I wrapped my thighs tighter so I could grind upward.

His wicked chuckle sent a ripple of want straight through me, and then he locked his lips over my clit and sucked it against his teeth until the pressure made my vision white out and a sharp sting had me gushing.

The orgasm detonated in my system and ripped a cry from my throat that startled me. Holy shit, that felt so fucking good, and he didn't let up. It was like he'd found the pleasure trigger and kept squeezing it. I bucked my hips, but he held me in place, one arm over my hips as he kept sucking, nipping, licking, and thrusting. He spread his free hand over my torso and then slid it over a breast.

I found myself laying my hand over his as he reached for a nipple. The calluses on his fingers were the perfect roughness against the pebbled flesh. He teased them, gentle tugs and twists.

A mewling sound tore out of my throat as I covered my free breast with my other hand. "Harder, Vaughn. Fuck me everywhere..." I wanted to feel nothing but him. As if to illustrate my point, I pinched the nipple until pain sparked through the white heat he kept stroking with his mouth.

I swore even the noises he made, slurping and sucking, added fresh kindling to the fire consuming me. "Come for me, Dove," he whispered against my flesh. "Fucking come, I want to taste you again."

Back to back orgasms were not my thing. The fact he'd already wrung one out of me was amazing enough, but my body bowed obediently and he matched the twist of my fingers with his own, and when he scraped his teeth over my clit, he twisted the nipple almost painfully and I fucking screamed.

The sound was raw, and it exploded out of me as pleasure flooded every part of me. I didn't know if I blacked out or floated, but one moment, his mouth was feasting on my cunt, and the next, he was kissing me. The taste of my release was all over him. His whole damn face had been painted slick.

Thrusting my fingers into his hair, I gripped and tugged as I rocked him between my thighs. Between us, we lined him up and he wrapped a hand around my throat. No pressure at all, just the barest of tension.

"Slow," he commanded, and I swore my body melted into the sheets. I was not obedient by nature, and he made me want so much more. My limbs tingled and my lips burned from his kisses. My nipples ached beautifully, but the clenching of my cunt had become a real need.

"I want you," I confessed without an ounce of shame.

"And you're going to have me, Dove, but you're a little thing, and even as bendy as you are, I don't want to hurt you."

"I want that hurt," I argued. I wanted every-fucking-thing.

"No more pain," he whispered before claiming my lips to silence my objections, and then he nudged at my entrance. The first push was shallow, just barely breeching past the mouth. The rub of his piercing lit me up, the sensations almost alien and in competition for the hot heat of his erection.

When was the last time I wanted to ride a dick? I'd forgotten, but even as I arched my hips, he kept his hand firm on my throat and I kept my upper body still for him as he worked his way in.

Huge.

Bendy was right, and I had my legs up and wrapped around him to deepen the angle of his thrusts. Each time, he pressed a little deeper, and I wanted to weep for how fucking good it felt.

"Hold onto me, Dove," he ordered, and his voice held a lot more strain. A vein throbbed in his forehead, barely visible from the flickering television light, but I gripped his arms. The roll of his muscles as they bunched and gave under my fingers just added another level of excitement.

With every roll of his hips, he pressed deeper into me and

I arched up to meet him. His rough breathing began to echo my own pants. I wanted more.

"I'll give it to you," he promised. "It's coming. But you first..." Then he slammed into me, and I swore I saw stars. I screamed at the stretch and burn of him. The piercing just lit up more nerves, and I could feel him everywhere.

When he pulled out, I sobbed from the pleasure of it. When he thrust in, I keened. Then he was rocking into me and I was clinging to him, desperate to not be shoved away. He kissed me again, sucking away my air until he was all the oxygen I breathed, and when I came apart this time, real tears splashed onto my cheeks. The spasms started deep in my cunt and radiated out until I shook from head to toe.

I was still trembling when he pulled out, and before I could reach for him, he flipped me onto my stomach and pulled me up onto my hands and knees.

Oh.

Fuck.

Yes.

"My turn, Dove," he whispered, then lined himself up and pushed back into me. Fuck. I threw my head back, and he wrapped my hair around his hand and gripped my hip. I dug my fingers into the sheets and braced for it.

"Yes," I begged.

Fucking begged.

I didn't have to ask twice. Vaughn began to drive into me with pounding thrusts that left my cunt shaking and convulsing around his dick. He rotated his hips as if shifting the angle, and every strike just sent me higher.

Flying. I knew flying, and fuck me, this was flying. I whimpered and moaned out his name, over and over again, as he kept rocking into me. The rhythm he set was a punishing pace, and I swore he'd listened to me when I said I wanted the hurt because it was there, stretching me to the point of pain with every drive home, and then I was fucking coming again.

I'd lost count as I shook apart, and he let out a shout as hot seed jetted into me. It was like a chemical reaction that had me clamping down on him desperately. I wanted him inside me. I wanted him exploding like I was. Sweat dripped down my face, and at some point, we collapsed together. His huge body covered mine, and I reveled in the feel of it.

The world out there was a dark, dangerous place. They'd tried to make my prison pretty, but until this moment, I'd been unable to forget that it was a cage. First the studio where I could dance and fly, now this…

I never wanted to move again.

I dozed almost sluggishly, half aware of him moving as he eased out of me. I groaned, the sound escaping without any effort. He smoothed a hand over my hip and then along my back. The soft, silken croon of his voice in my ear said, "Sleep, sweet Dove, I have you."

He did, and for the moment, I was so willing to believe him. The bed shifted with his absence, and then he was back with a warm, damp cloth. He stroked it between my thighs, and I whimpered at the touch on my sensitive flesh. But he kissed one nipple, then drew it against his lips, laving it with his tongue in a soothing motion that had less to do with exciting me than easing me.

I drifted again, and then he was back on the bed and his arms wrapped around me as I snuggled close.

Whatever happened next was tomorrow Emersyn's problem. Today…

"I want to do that again," I whispered. "Can I fuck you again, Vaughn?"

His warm chuckle sounded almost sad for a moment, and a shiver of apprehension wound up my spine, but he eased it with a gentle stroke of his hand. "Anything you want, beautiful Dove. But sleep right now and let me hold you."

I could do that.

So I did.

Sleep claimed me, even as the news came on in the background with an update on the story of a missing heiress, but I was too comfortable and too full of the feeling of him to watch.

I could deal with it tomorrow.

CHAPTER 23

EMERSYN

*H*eat surrounded me, my eyelids were heavy, and all I wanted to do was burrow deeper. But I couldn't afford to sleep so deeply. The last time I'd been this comfortable…

My eyes snapped open to the dark room with the faint flickers from the television. The soreness in my body combined with the press of a hard body against mine and a very awake dick nestled against my ass filled in all the sleepy blank spots. I let out a little groan, and my bladder gave a protest.

With care, I wiggled out from under the arm. Even with the distinct ache between my thighs declaring my very thorough and deep fucking, I felt better than I had in days. I'd scraped back a little bit of power for myself. I'd danced. Flown. Then this beautiful man had played with my body and let me play with his.

In the annals of Emersyn Sharpe, we called that *winning*.

Thankfully, there was enough light from the television to make it into the bathroom. I flicked the light on and almost laughed at myself when I got past the squinting to see the crown of crazy hair I was sporting. Bed head had nothing on me. There was a bruise just below one nipple, the shape a perfect hickey, and a beautiful handprint on my hip.

The thrill skating through me should worry me. In fact, as I made myself turn away from the mirror, it definitely did worry me. I wasn't staying here. Doc was going to help me get out. Just the thought of Doc had my thighs clenching again. I peed, emptying my bladder, and then cleaned up.

Despite the soreness, I vaguely recalled Vaughn pressing a warm, damp washcloth between my thighs and cleaning me up too. The thoughtfulness in that action made me smile. I put some toothpaste on my finger and used that to clean my teeth. Despite my attempts to swallow his tongue—and ride it—I couldn't use his toothbrush.

I found a comb and worked it through my hair. Fortunately, I had washed it before so it detangled pretty well, but there was no smoothing out the lift. I studied my appearance in the mirror when the movement of the door caught my attention. It swung inward quietly, and the mass of beautifully painted muscle filled my vision. His sleepy expression and faint frown arrested me.

Turning, I leaned against the sink and met his hooded gaze. A genuine smile pulled at that sensuous mouth, and I swore my cunt fucking tingled in anticipation, even as my nipples tightened. The jut to his cock promised me there was equal interest there.

"Thought I'd had a dream," he murmured in that satiny voice as he closed the distance and boxed me up against the chilly counter. The contrast between his hot body and the cold marble just heightened my awareness of him. Vaughn filled the whole bathroom, and the brush of his overheated skin against my nipples had me straining upward.

He didn't make me wait for long.

The kiss had my toes curling, even as I wrapped my arms around his neck. Palming my ass, he lifted me until I ground against the hard length of his cock. Slick dampness coated my thighs, and the fact his cock slid right between them had us both groaning, but he didn't let up on the kiss. If anything, he fisted my hair and tilted my head back to deepen it.

Mouth open to his ravaging claim, I dug my fingers into his neck. All I could taste was him. Somehow, it seemed unfair that he didn't even have morning breath, and at the same time, I was so grateful for it. The rub of my breasts to his chest sent a wave of pure lust through me.

I might regret my next move later because I hadn't stretched, but I wrapped my legs around his hips and arched my own. At the first brush of his cock to my cunt, I swiveled and then sank down on him.

"Fuck." He growled the word into the kiss, and I swore his fingers tightened in my hair. The rush of power that accompanied the thickness of him filling my sensitive flesh lit me up.

Still gripping my hair, he pulled back enough to look at me, even as I rotated and rocked my hips, riding him slow and steady so I could savor the feel of that piercing and every nerve it stroked.

"You're a goddamn dream," he told me in a voice so thick with emotion, it threatened to wrest control away from me, but I dug my nails into his shoulders as I moved. The curl and tightening of my abs let me writhe up before I sank back down. Each thrust pushed him a little deeper.

A vein throbbed in his forehead, and his topaz eyes darkened. He never once released my hair as he began to work his palm up and down my back. When he reached my ass and squeezed one cheek, I replied in kind by clamping down on his dick until we both hissed.

"You want to fuck me, Dove?"

A throaty laugh escaped me at the temptation in his voice. Or maybe it was the temptation of his voice. Every syllable that escaped him was like liquid sex, and it just made me want him all that much more. Rocking my hips, I controlled the pace of his thrusts. It was a hell of a workout, but I was here for it, even if it left me shaking and trembling.

Who knew when I'd get another chance like this? Honestly, I was surprised it had lasted this long. Not that I had any idea how long we slept, but maybe my other keepers knew where I was and didn't care.

Based on Jasper's behavior around Doc, I doubted it. The thought of both of them had me clenching down around Vaughn even tighter. His grunt matched my own moan. "I thought I already was," I whispered, this time teasing my nails against his scalp. I loved how he hadn't let go of my hair and how his fingers dug into my ass. The tease of one finger against the rim of my anus suggested he had other ideas in mind.

What would those piercings feel like in my ass?

That sent another gush of warmth through me, and I began to add a full twist to every thrust. A muscle in his jaw ticked, and then he gave me a ferocious grin before he turned and walked us out of the bathroom. Every step he took just drove him deeper into me, and then he set me down on the bed. The pull of his hand forced my body to arch, only instead of following me down, he remained upright.

Oh fuck, someone wanted control.

"I can do this upside down, you know," I taunted as I let go of him to press my hands over my head to the covers. Pushing upward, I elongated my body, but I kept my legs wrapped around his hips.

"Fuck me," he whispered in a ragged breath.

"I want to," I promised, and I made good on my word. It was a little like the flexing of my hips and abs that I needed to do to climb the silks. The blood rushed to my head as I kept control of our pace, and every deep brush of his piercing seemed to only heighten the sensation.

I was right there—riding the edge. I could come so easily, but I wanted to make him lose it.

"So fucking beautiful," he whispered and spread one of those huge, colorful hands over my abdomen and then down to my breasts.

He palmed one, then the other. The touches rough, yet infinitely gentle. The first pinch proved a stark bite against the easier motions, and the shock of it radiated through my system.

"You said I could do whatever I wanted to you," he said, this time covering both breasts, one with each hand. The only thing connecting us and keeping up the rhythm was my legs and hips. The burn added an edge to the pleasure that the sharp twists of his fingers on my nipples only heightened. Fuck, the sting. I wanted the sting. I wanted the punishing force of his cock.

"Yes," I confirmed. "How do you want me?"

It was like I took some kind of leash off of him, one I hadn't even been aware he had. My shoulders hit the bed, and he unlocked my legs only to push my feet up to either side of me. I folded almost perfectly in half. The stretch on my hamstrings added a delicious flare to the fire already consuming me.

"Oh, fuck me, Dove." He pushed out each word like a bullet. One hand firm against one of my calves, he braced the other next to the bed and took over the punishing pace of his thrusts. At this angle, there was no escape, I felt him fucking everywhere.

I twisted back and forth, almost desperate to escape, and at the same time, I wanted more. I swore I screamed his name at one point, and that only had him adjusting his angle as he dragged my ass right to the edge of the bed. The cool air brushed against my bruised and swollen cunt, then he pushed back in with a firm thrust, and I came apart.

The cries left my throat sore as I bucked and twisted to the brutal rhythm he set, and at the same time, I fought to match it, even in this wildly vulnerable position.

"More," I begged. What was it about him that reduced me to begging every single time? I didn't have to ask more than once. He released my legs and straightened. When he pulled out of me, I wanted to whimper at the loss.

The angry flush to his cock just made it all that much more attractive as it glistened.

"Turn over," he ordered, and I all but scrambled to flip over onto my hands and knees. "This foot forward."

The challenge of sliding my right leg forward until my foot was parallel with my hand and side by side added a fresh burn to the stretch of my body.

"Have you ever had your ass fucked before, Dove?" His thumb teased the rim as I held my position. My breath came in explosive pants, even as I fought to calm it. Breath control meant I could last longer.

We could.

"You can if you want, but I don't know how easy those piercings will go in."

"That wasn't my question," he scolded, and the heavy slap of his hand landing against one ass cheek sent flames to consume me. "I know my piercing is your first. Have you ever had your ass fucked?"

He was killing the mood. I didn't want to discuss this. "Yes," I told him. "Can we get back to the rest of the fucking please?" I tacked the please as an afterthought. Then he rubbed the sting from my ass and lined up his cock with my cunt.

"Dove, yes, you can have anything you want. Just don't lie to me. If someone hurt you, we'll go slow. I promised you no more pain and I meant it." The words sparked traitorous tears. One escaped while the others clogged up my throat. He fucked into me like a man on a mission, and the orgasms he'd been edging struck me like an avalanche.

I swore I squirted a little as he pounded my cunt. The world darkened around the edges, and then I came harder than I ever had, my body straining back to him as I clamped down. He came with me on that one, the hot release turning my system molten.

It wasn't until he eased my leg down and rolled me over, cradling me to his chest, that I realized I was crying. Thank fuck he couldn't see my face. It was bad enough he could feel my trembling. The shakes seemed to come from my very core. He wrapped those strong arms around me and pressed his lips right to my ear.

I barely understood a word coming out of his mouth, only that soft croon that made me want to trust him. That beckoned to me to hold onto him, and I did. I dug my nails into his forearms. From my bruised and quaking cunt to my swollen nipples, to my mind rocking under the weight of letting him in.

What the hell was I doing? Fucking was fine, getting some release after all these weeks, I deserved that. But he was getting in too deep. The fact he'd gotten the negative relationship to anal. That conjured a loneliness I kept locked away, barricaded behind a dozen locked doors.

The press of his lips to my throat comforted me. So did the strength in his arms and the gentle sweep of his hands. Even as he eased out of me, I shuddered. When I tried to turn my face away, he rolled on top of me and cradled my face in his huge hands. "Dove, did I hurt you?"

"No," I said, and it came out a little more jagged and snotty than I liked. I sucked in a breath and then swallowed the tears. "You felt good."

With only the light from the bathroom and the television, his face was a contrast of light and dark. Shadows and lines. Fierce and devoted.

Devoted.

Where the fuck had that word come from?

Kidnapper, remember, Emersyn?

Right.

I sniffed and then ran my foot up the back of his thigh, wresting my control back to where it belonged. Years of discipline, breath control, and need dried up the tears and chased away the shaking.

Confusion flashed across Vaughn's face.

"Don't flatter yourself too much, *Falcon,*" I teased, using his predatory bird name. I needed that emotional distance. "You fuck real well and I'm going to feel you for days. But don't confuse fucking for a key to me."

His frown deepened, and then he kissed me. It was every bit the punishment I craved. Even the flash of copper where one of us cut our lip on our teeth, and I honestly couldn't have said who it was.

"Don't talk about yourself or this like it meant nothing," he warned in a low voice. "You can wrestle with it and try to lock it away. You can even be private and not want to discuss it. But don't dismiss me and don't *ever* dismiss yourself." Then he levered himself off me and vanished into the bathroom so abruptly, the loss was profound.

Regret left an acrid and bitter aftertaste in my mouth.

Rolling onto my side and away from the bathroom, I stared almost sightlessly at the television.

I was working my way through what I should say when the news came back from commercial, and I stared at myself on the screen with the headline *Missing Heiress* below the picture.

All the blood drained from my face when *he* came on the screen to declare how much my family missed me and how they were now offering a reward in the hundreds of thousands for any leads that would bring me home safely.

I'd sooner die.

The door to Vaughn's room burst open a split second later, and I scrambled backward like it was the cops coming for me.

No. No.

They couldn't have found me that fast.

CHAPTER 24

VAUGHN

BEFORE...

"Where are you going?" Jasper demanded as I headed for the fridge. I'd tell him, but that might involve an actual conversation with the dictatorial jackass, and in my current mood, that wouldn't end well.

For either of us.

So I pretended I didn't hear him and stalked inside. Dove should never have seen the interior of this place. She shouldn't have seen the bastard we had stashed in here. She shouldn't have been anywhere those fucks could have attacked her.

The 19 Diamond we had sitting on ice wasn't even a fully-blooded member. He wouldn't be either. No, he and his friends had been on their way to make their cut by ambushing someone on our territory. Get in. Get out.

What unfortunate fucking luck for them they'd chosen our Dove.

Meeks showing up here was just the icing on the fucking cake. Liam and Rome would make sure their guys left. Not sure what the fuck Liam was doing here anyway, other than trying to piss Jasper off. The door didn't slam behind me as I stepped inside the shithole. It fucking reeked. They didn't make enough bleach to get rid of this smell. We might very well have to torch the interior, not that it would do us much good.

It'd probably burn the whole warehouse down.

I didn't make it to the second door before Jasper gripped my shoulder.

"Hawk," Kellan damn near sighed, and I shook off Jasper's grip before I faced him. He'd just cut Meeks' fucking finger off and sent them out of here, tail between their legs. "Let it go."

"No, I want to know what the fuck he's doing."

Locking gazes with Kellan, I read the plea in his eyes. He wanted me to let this go and let him handle it. Do what he'd always been doing which was de-escalate, redirect, or run interference. I cut a look to where Jasper glared at me. There was a crescent-shaped impression in his neck.

Crescent-shaped like a fingernail.

I narrowed my eyes. He'd kicked everyone out of the studio we'd all fucking helped put together. Then he'd gone in there to watch her. She was right.

He was never letting her go.

"Jasper, for fuck's sake," Kellan dragged out. "Come on. We have enough problems, we do not need to be fighting each other."

"When are you telling Raptor?" Yeah, I was done with this particular discussion, and Kellan's gaze jumped from Jasper to me. I ignored the demand in them. He didn't want this fight. He'd been avoiding it for fucking weeks now, and we'd all let him.

I had let him.

"Leave him out of this," Jasper said, his heated tone cooling rapidly. The flashfire in his eyes went to ice, and his jaw tensed. "I've got this handled."

"Oh," I said slowly. "Do you? Because from where I'm standing, you're making this shit up as you go along. Let's see, we've got Eric fucking Arlington strung up to a wall in there, bleeding and healing up another set of broken ribs. Not sure if he's still shitting himself. But I do know if you bring Doc in to patch him up again, he's probably going to go postal on your ass."

Kellan groaned.

"Then let's talk about the little 19 Diamond fuck we're wasting time with. He has no answers. You know it. I know it. We're not bothering Eric with questions because we're taking a pound or ten of flesh. Fine. But the 19 Diamond, cut him loose or cut his throat, I don't care which. We do not need more trouble from them. Oh, and let's not forget fucking Meeks out there. 'Cause that's trouble just waiting to come at us again. He is not going to let that finger go."

Arms folded and eyes hooded, Jasper didn't back down. "He'll live, and if they move fast enough, they'll be able to reattach it. Killing him would have taken us right to a full-scale war."

"Bloody skirmishes are so much better when Dove's involved though, right? Something else to keep her locked down from."

I felt more than heard Kellan's deep sigh. Jasper took a swing. We were always a half-step away from violence. It wasn't the first time one of us went for the other, and it wouldn't be the last. I caught his fist, absorbing the impact as it crashed into my palm. There'd been just enough force behind the blow to tell me he was more annoyed than he was furious. But the fury was there.

He hated to be questioned.

And normally, I wouldn't question.

I locked my hand around his fist and caught the second fist as he let it fly. In pure strength, I had him. He knew it. I knew it. Still, he tried to bum rush it, and his knee crashed into the side of my thigh. If I hadn't twisted at the right moment, he'd have slammed my balls into my throat.

"Bad move," I scolded him and wrenched his arms outward. He hissed. He had a bad elbow from an injury when we were kids. It had taken me and Raptor weeks to get even for Jasper. For the longest time, we didn't think it would heal right. It had fucked up his idea of a baseball career.

Broken kneecaps had been delivered in warning and to extract the price in blood. You hurt us. We would hurt you back twice as hard. Eventually, we didn't just stop at wounds.

Taking advantage of Jasper's wince, I seized his throat and slammed him back into the desk. A minute later, Kellan's gun was pressed against my shoulder. At that angle, he wouldn't hurt Jasper. He'd fuck me up for a while though.

"Let him go, Vaughn."

"We need to talk this shit out," I countered. "And I didn't fucking start it."

"I know you didn't," he agreed. "But this isn't how we're ending it. We have enough problems. The three of us cannot be fucking fighting."

Jasper didn't say a word and neither of us looked away. The coldness in his eyes reminded me just how fucking dead my soul was. "When are you sending her home?" Because that was what it came down to.

"I'll decide when."

"When?" I snapped, because that answer wasn't going to fucking fly with me.

"When she's safe."

"We have that fucker right in there…"

Jasper slid a look at Kellan, and I growled. Letting him go, I withdrew a couple of steps. A fist slammed into my jaw and rocked my head to the side. Blood filled my mouth, but I didn't hesitate. I just reacted. My fist crashed into Jasper's face, and his ass went down. I caught him before he slammed into the ground. This time, I wrenched his good arm behind him and slammed him face down into the table.

"Are you fucking kidding me right now?" Kellan's aggravated growl bounced off the walls.

"I decide," Jasper snarled, undeterred by his position. "Not you. Not Kellan. Not fucking Rome or Freddie. *Me*. Her safety comes before everything else."

There was one person's decision he didn't get to bypass. Except he had been. Ever since we got her here, he'd avoided talking to Raptor. I contemplated just knocking Jasper's ass out. "You come for me again," I warned a heartbeat before I released him, "make it count, because you won't get another chance."

Kellan shot me a look as I headed for the door to the storage room.

"Vaughn…"

"No," I told him. "He can clean up his own fucking messes. He's got her here, pinned in a cage, and she had her hands on his neck."

The minute the words left my lips, Kellan focused his whole attention on Jasper, who was straightening. Blood flowed from his nose and his lip. Not waiting, Kellan fisted part of Jasper's shirt and looked at his neck. "What the fuck…?"

"Stay out of it." Jasper shoved him off, and for the first time in years, the three of us stood on our own sides, at odds. Kellan's gun rested in his hand next to his thigh and pointed at the floor. Jasper swiped at the blood on his face with a pair of takeout napkins from the desk, and I cracked my knuckles. There was blood on my shirt.

Not that I cared.

There was about to be a lot more.

Except the blood was Jasper's. We bled for each other. We didn't make each other bleed.

"We can't leave it like this," Kellan said after the moment elongated painfully.

"That's up to him," I told him. "He's been making a lot of calls lately, but this isn't just his to make."

"Since when do you think you get a say?" Jasper argued, pushing away from the desk and taking a couple of steps toward me.

"Because you weren't the only one there," I reminded him. It had been all of us. It had always been all of us. We'd been a family before we understood the word. "Now, I'm going to deal with the diamond and clean that shit up. Then you're going to deal with that Arlington fuck, and we're taking all the trash out."

The longer we sat on him, the more of a threat there might be. The search for Dove had quieted, but it was a mistake to think it ended. Rumors and tabloids suggested she and Eric had run away together, but that story wouldn't hold together long.

Not when two weeks earlier, they'd finally reported him missing. It hadn't come from the dance company but Arlington's family. Rumor held they'd hired a private investigator too. That meant there was every chance the search would narrow back to Braxton Harbor. If they started pushing, there was a chance it would put them on Kellan's trail since he'd been her driver, or they'd start looking for crew local to the city.

All roads could lead back to us.

Neither man said anything as I stalked into the room. Arlington had been gagged and chained in his corner. The smell in here made my eyes water. I didn't slow on my way over to the recruit. He hadn't known anything other than they'd been told to dip their wicks here and get blooded.

All they'd seen when they saw Dove was a bit of fun. A bit of fun they'd have torn apart like wild dogs and then left on our doorstep.

Fuckers.

Jasper and Kellan had followed me inside but said nothing as I snapped the diamond's neck. Arlington let out a series of screams as the other hit the floor. All three of us turned to look at him. Funnily enough, the last few weeks, it had been getting harder to make him scream. Jasper's look when he focused on him was positively murderous, and Kellan's wasn't much better.

"Fine," Jasper said after a moment. A single syllable. A harsh exhale.

But it was agreement. A knife found its way into his hand, and Kellan's gun vanished. I had a knife, but I preferred my bare hands. The diamond could stay there on the floor. We converged on Arlington, and the blond behemoth struggled as if he could escape us before we got there. The whimpers spilling out from behind the gag were pathetic.

Fisting his hair, Jasper dragged his head back until he couldn't look in any direction and not see us. The blade pressed right up against his throat. A drop of blood began to well up from the nick he'd pressed into the flesh

It reminded me for a second that Dove had dug her nails into Jasper's neck. Anger flamed from slow burn to conflagration, but I kept my focus on the prick who'd fucking hurt her.

He'd had his hands on Dove.

He'd dragged her out of the theatre.

There had been real fear in her eyes.

Then he'd knocked her into the wall.

On my watch.

The anger kindling in me at Jasper and Arlington split a third way to point back at myself.

It had been as much my fault that she'd gotten hurt in the first place. The idiot started to struggle, and his hand broke when I slammed it against the wall. Blood sprayed as the nick on his throat turned into a slice.

"I have a question," Kellan said in an icy tone. "Just one." Eyes rolling, Arlington shot a look to him. Pain and fear illuminated his face. "Tell me the truth. Don't lie, 'cause I will know."

Jasper and I said nothing. Of all of us, Kellan hadn't taken that many turns at the fucker. If anything, Jasper had been hogging him.

"Maybe you'll get out of here intact," Kellan suggested, and I didn't laugh. I didn't even crack a smile.

If anything, Jasper's expression was deader than mine felt. Arlington was only leaving here one way.

"Did you rape her?"

Panic turned Arlington's eyes even wilder, and he made a noise of protest in his throat. But it wasn't denial.

It was fear.

The blade in Jasper's hand slammed into the man's shoulder. Right into the meaty part. Blood sprayed my shirt, but I didn't let him go.

"How many times?" I asked.

Because it had been the one question I hadn't wanted to ask. The bruises on her were hard to deny. We'd all seen them.

Abuse.

Physical.

Mental.

Emotional.

Jasper twisted the knife. The ragged scream coming out of his throat wasn't enough.

Not near enough.

"Don't kill him yet," Kellan said as he rolled up his sleeves.

"No," I agreed. "First we cut off everything that ever touched her."

"Then we kill him," Jasper added.

At some point, he stopped screaming.

It was still way too soon in my opinion.

JUST NOW...

Coming back to my room after dealing with Arlington, the last thing I'd expected was to find Dove there. All I'd wanted to do was erase every bad memory. I wanted that bastard's blood off me before I touched her. Now that I had?

Fuck, I was never going to get enough.

I splashed water on my face. Of course, she didn't want to act like any of this was real. She was still looking for a way out. A way away from us.

Goddammit.

I needed a shower, and I wanted to take it with her. A panicked sound from the bedroom had me spinning, and I pulled open the door to the bedroom in time for the door to my room to swing inward.

CHAPTER 25

EMERSYN

The door burst open in front of me, even as the bathroom door swung open behind me. With only the sheet to cover up, I swallowed the sound of panic as Kestrel filled the doorway. He stared at me for a second, relief flitting across his face, and his shoulders sagged before his gaze jerked toward Vaughn.

"She's been in here all night?"

I barely heard the question over the wild hammer of my heart. There was some solace in it being Kestrel, but the fact I was naked and my face was on television, even as Kestrel stared at Vaughn with that unreadable expression, threatened to turn me inside out.

"Yeah," Vaughn answered with the kind of certainty that should have made me excited. Like he was daring Kestrel to question it. "Problem?" It wasn't cocky or smug, just unequivocal, as if the idea I'd be anywhere else would be ridiculous.

"Freddie was supposed to be watching her and he's missing."

"What?" I straightened. "He went to get food last night, but he didn't come back…" Now that I thought about it. He really hadn't come back. I'd thought maybe he got distracted.

"We're going to need you," Kestrel said to Vaughn, then he flicked a look to me. "You should probably stay in here for now."

"I want to help," I said before I slid off the bed. I almost lost the sheet.

"No," Vaughn and Kestrel said in the same breath, and I glanced from one to the other.

"No?" I dropped the damn sheet because fighting with it was making me awkward. Kestrel's eyebrows climbed, and Vaughn snagged something from behind him and then he tugged a shirt over my head.

Oh for fuck's sake… I yanked my hair out of the way and stared at him. "Really? You're naked."

"He doesn't care about my junk," Vaughn told me flatly.

I rolled my eyes and turned toward Kestrel, who stared at me with a kind of burning intensity. The blue-green color of his eyes wasn't visible in the half-light cast by the television. It took me a moment to realize he'd even stepped all the way in and closed the door behind him. "The door was locked."

Not that it had anything to do with anything.

"Freddie had to pick it to let us in here."

Vaughn snorted behind me, and a drawer closed. The thump of wood on wood pulled my attention from Kestrel, and I glanced behind me to find Vaughn dragging on a pair of jeans over his naked ass. A shiver went up my spine as the denim covered the flex of muscle.

"I wanted to watch television," I explained. This time, I didn't look at the television. I'd been on it a minute ago, but it would probably be better if I wasn't on it this time. If I was, let's not draw attention to it. "I'd planned to go back down-stairs—why am I explaining this? It's not like you minded finding me in here."

The curve of a hand wrapped around my nape, and I shifted my weight as Vaughn tugged me around to face him. "And you won't hear me complaining, Dove. I *snorted* because Freddie knows better than to go sniffing around in our rooms. But he never could resist a locked door."

"No one else seems to lock their doors," I argued, inti-mately aware of how warm he was pressed right up against me and the fact we had an audience.

"We do when you're behind them," Kestrel answered for him. "And I have keys to everyone's rooms. So does Vaughn."

"And Jasper," Vaughn added.

Oh.

A shiver raced over my skin, and I swore every nerve stood on point. Freddie. We needed to think about Freddie and not the way Kestrel's gaze seemed to be licking over my skin. Even if I couldn't see where he looked, I swore I could feel him. At the same time, Vaughn kept me pinned in place between the way his green eyes held me hostage and the soft wrap of his hand against my nape. I could move.

I could.

I just didn't.

"What time did he let you in here?" Vaughn asked.

I frowned. I'd kind of lost track of time. "It was after Kestrel came to get Jasper. Freddie walked me up from the studio to my room, and I took a shower…"

They both growled.

Actually fucking growled.

"Are you for real right now?" I demanded first of Vaughn then of Kestrel.

"He better not have fucking watched you shower," Kestrel snarled, and I groaned. Curling my toes, I ducked my head and pulled away from Vaughn. The magnetic hotness and all that beautiful and colorful muscle offered way too much distraction.

"You know what, if I want Freddie to watch me shower, he can watch me shower."

And they growled again.

I threw my hands up. "Fuck off." Surprise flitted across Kestrel's face. "I mean it. You can fuck off with that attitude right to fucksville. My body. I'll do with it what I want. No one tells me what I can or can't do with it or who I can do it with." If they thought kidnapping me gave them that right...

There was a beat of silence, and a second later, Vaughn snickered.

Fucking. Snickered.

I slammed my elbow into the wall of muscle and winced. He *oofed*. Probably more out of politeness and sympathy than because I did any damage. I rubbed my funny bone and glared over my shoulder at him. "It's not funny."

"No," he agreed with me, all solemn and sexy. The fucker. All at once, my cunt clenched and I refused to react, no matter how tempting he was or the fact that he had more than one hickey on his neck from where I'd been kissing him.

Shit. I forced my gaze away and back to Kestrel.

"It's fine, Sparrow. You're right—you decide who gets to do what to your body," Kestrel said with a straight face. "But not Freddie. We know where he's been."

Arms folded. "He also talks to me like a person and answers my questions." Not all of them, but whatever. "And we're wasting time when we could be looking for him."

"We'll find him, Dove," Vaughn said almost quietly as he rested his hands on my hips. There was a hesitance in the touch. It took a moment for it to sink in that he was giving me the option of moving away. When I didn't, he said, "Kel—give us a minute?"

Kel?

I frowned. "Kestrel's not your name."

"It is," he told me. "Just one of them. The other is Kellan."

Oh.

"Don't take long," he continued, flicking a look past me to Vaughn. "Jasper does not need to see her in here."

"Where does he think she is?"

Kestrel sighed, then raked a hand through his hair. "Her room. I told him she was asleep and to leave her alone." While he answered Vaughn, he looked at me. "I know we owe you a lot, Sparrow. And I also know we're asking for a lot in telling you to trust us…but I need you to do that right now. Stay here. The only people coming through that door will be one of us, and anyone coming to look for you…" He hesitated. "Not that they are. But even if they were, they wouldn't look in here."

He'd just lied to me. I had no idea why I knew that, but it was there in that brief moment where his eyes cut away.

"Five minutes, Falcon." Then he was gone.

The hands on my hips tightened, and Vaughn stepped closer to me. "This is not how I wanted to start our morning after…"

"It isn't how we started our morning after," I admitted and then sighed as I leaned back into him. I shouldn't give in to the need, but when he wrapped an arm around my chest and hugged me, I closed my eyes. "We kind of had sex and, you know, aerobic sex at that."

He chuckled softly. "We did."

"And now Freddie is missing."

"He's probably fine," Vaughn said in a careful tone. "But he shouldn't have left the clubhouse without telling someone."

"There are others," I suggested. "Maybe he told one of them."

"Maybe," Vaughn agreed, but the doubt was clear in his tone. "Still, it's not safe right now for any of us to be running alone. Too much shit going down."

I frowned. "Those guys from the other night…"

"Yeah. Those guys from the other night." He pressed his lips to the back of my head. "Thank you for last night and this morning."

Warmth bloomed through me at the quiet words in that silky voice of his.

"I want you to stay in here," he admitted. "But I can take you back to your room if you want."

The television was in here. That meant there might be other stuff here too. I bit my lip. I didn't want to use him or his trust. To be honest… "Are you sure I can't help find Freddie?" I turned in his grip and tilted my head so I could meet his gaze. "He went to find me food." And if I hadn't gotten so distracted with Vaughn coming in, maybe I would have noticed he was missing sooner. Or they would have.

"I'm sure," Vaughn told me, but instead of certainty, there was hesitancy in his answer. Sex never answered questions, even when it made empty promises of intimacy. I was no closer to understanding him than I was Jasper or any of the others who'd served as both jailers and companions the last few weeks.

I wanted to trust him.

Like I wanted to trust Kestrel or even Jasper.

The simple truth was I couldn't.

"Dove, if you went with us, we'd spend all our time making sure you were okay when we should be looking for Freddie. And to be honest…this isn't the world for you." He traced a finger against my cheek. "Promise me you'll stay here? Either in my room or yours?"

I studied him. Was he for real right now? "Why would you believe my promise?"

"I have my reasons."

"You all have reasons." I pulled back, and his hand fell away. I could almost sense the sadness in him, even after I turned back to his bed. "Reasons no one wants to share. Reasons why you took me." I dropped to sit on the edge of the bed. Reasons like Jasper swearing they were going to protect me. That was all he wanted.

None of this made sense.

"Dove…"

"You should go," I told him. "Hopefully, Freddie's not in trouble. I'd hate it if something happened to him when he was doing something for me."

"Whatever happened, I promise it's not your fault." He offered me a small smile that didn't quite reach his eyes. He snagged another shirt and then narrowed the distance between us. I should have expected the move, and yet when he pulled me up and then tilted his head as he claimed my lips, shock still rioted in my system.

Shock.

Want.

Need.

All of it twisting together. Almost as fast as the kiss began, it ended, and he stroked his thumb over my bottom lip. "I'll bring food back if you're hungry, but there's also a small fridge over on the other side of the bed. It's hidden under that sheet." I glanced over my shoulder to where he pointed. "It looks like a nightstand, but there's protein shakes, iced water, and some snacks in it."

I traced my finger along the Celtic cross on his right pec and the leafy vines twined around it. "Be careful?"

"Always," he promised, and this time, he really did smile.

"Stay here? Get some more sleep? Eat? I'll be back as soon as I can."

"Okay." It was neither agreement nor disagreement. Not really. Call it splitting hairs, but it served as an acknowledgment on my part. He gave me one more look I couldn't interpret before he stuffed his feet into his shoes, and then he was gone.

The light in the hallway made my eyes sting as the door opened, and I was blinking away spots as it closed behind him. The silence in the room seemed almost too thick, like it had a texture of its own. The news wasn't on the television anymore. It was some early morning talk show. I lost all track of time in this windowless existence.

I debated just crawling back into bed and burying my face in the scent of Vaughn on the sheets and in the pillow. Hell, the scent of him clung to the shirt he'd pulled over my head. I could do that. I could crawl in like the obedient little prisoner and kidnap victim, or did I go see just how many of them had left?

I had a reason to go downstairs.

The studio was down there.

The mental debate lasted all of a minute before I slid into his bathroom where my clothes were now folded neatly on the back of the toilet, but the blood-stained ones were gone. *Yeah, don't look too closely for those, Emersyn.*

Because they hadn't slowed my choice last night when I decided to scratch that itch or this morning, and if I were honest with myself, if Vaughn were here right now?

Yeah, I wouldn't be thinking about them.

The water heated up fast, and I threw myself through a sketchy shower. My hair was a mess, but I pulled it up and tied it into a bit of a bun. I needed to wash off the sex and the feel of his hands, his lips, his fingers—fuck me, his piercing.

Not that I had a hope in hell of erasing those sensations.

The soap reminded me of him, and I might have taken my time in washing down with it. After, I toweled off and pulled on my abandoned clothes. I left the television on and straightened the disheveled bedsheets. I had no idea why I even bothered. At the door, I paused, then backtracked to the little fridge.

Sure enough, there were protein shakes in there. I downed two in rapid succession. The pinching feeling in the hollow of my stomach vanished, and the water I washed down after it helped too. I debated taking some more, but once I got out of the warehouse, I needed to keep moving.

I left Vaughn's room and headed to my own for shoes. I wanted to take a bag or something, but I didn't dare. Instead, I went for running shoes, and if they asked about them, I could tell them I needed to run to warm up my muscles.

There was a slim chance some of them would buy it.

Besides, what was the worst they were going to do?

Lock me in my room again?

I paused only long enough to grab a hair tie. I pony-tailed my hair on my way down the steps. Every movement reminded me of the ache between my thighs. Fuck, I was gonna feel him for days. The quiet on the first floor was unnerving, but I swung into the kitchen anyway.

No one.

Licking my lips, I headed down the hall toward the studio. A rat poked his head out of the living room.

I really shouldn't call them that, but that was what the guys called them. He stared at me, but didn't say a word. Thankfully, he couldn't see my pulse racing. Once I was in the studio, I leaned against the door. There was no lock.

The way they'd built it, the ceiling climbed all the way up to the warehouse roof. The walls were there, blocking me from the outside, but they'd worked the harness for the silks into the struts of the ceiling supports. The scrape of a shoe on the other side of the door had me stilling. I crossed over and pulled out one of the marked CDs.

I put *Happy Shit* on to play and Bruno Mars filled the room. I turned it all the way up until the beat thumped. Then I began stretching. I had my reasons.

Going out through the main warehouse would automatically earn me attention from anyone out there, and I really didn't want to go past the room where they were holding Eric. I gave him all of point-three seconds of thought before I moved toward the silks.

Honestly, if they found Eric floating somewhere after this, I'd never point a finger at them.

Never.

The climb to the top didn't take long. My body only protested when I had to roll, but even then, it was more the phantom feeling of Vaughn's fingers on my body. The way he kissed me. I was almost to the top when doubt struck.

They hadn't been cruel to me.

Not at all.

If anything, they'd been kind and thoughtful.

What the hell, Emersyn? They still kidnapped you.

I needed to get out of here. I needed to get away from all of it. The theatre company. The Vandals. My parents.

All of it.

I reached the first strut and gripped it, then pulled myself up before letting the silks uncoil and fall back to hang like they had before.

Head tipped back, I studied the ceiling and then had to bite back a real grin. The walls didn't reach *all* the way up. So I worked my way over the wall and stuck to the struts. There were rats moving below.

Someone was hauling a body out of the room where Eric had been. I froze and stuffed a hand against my mouth. I didn't recognize anyone down there, and thankfully, I couldn't see the body. Hopefully it was Eric and not Freddie.

And if that meant I was going to hell, well then so fucking be it.

Still shivering, I forced myself to move, and I made it to the corner where a ladder ascended to a small portal to the roof.

In the shadows, I hung there, waiting. Sooner or later, they would… One of them started up a car, and the roar filled the space. I shoved the hatch open and trusted the vehicle to mask the sound. Twenty seconds later, I was outside and sucking in fresh air as the sun rose in the distance.

CHAPTER 26

EMERSYN

 crouched in the sunshine for several long moments as I tried to get my bearings. While the warehouse might be in the more industrial part of town, we weren't that far from the busier streets. I had to trust that knowledge earned from Rome taking me for a walk the other day. As it was, I moved to the edge to get my bearings.

Speak of the devil—and his brother—Rome and Liam were below talking to some of the rats, so I crept away from that edge. That wasn't the way we'd gone out before, anyway. A twinge of guilt panged against my insides. Rome had gotten hurt to help me, and now I was sneaking away.

No sooner did that thought register than I shook it off. In the last few weeks, I'd started to care about my *kidnappers* way more than I should. Too much of what they'd done and said didn't add up to what I thought kidnappers would be. What they'd done to Eric? Sure. But I was *glad* for that, and

I'd never feel a moment's regret for being happy he was gone from my life.

Enough.

I shook off the wimbling sensation. They weren't my friends. They were a gang. Kestrel said it himself in the very beginning. I shouldn't be here. I don't know what their plan *had* been or *why* it changed beyond Eric coming after me that night. It wasn't like it was even the first time Eric and I had gone round for round. Still...

It was time for me to go.

I really hadn't escaped one trap to land in this one. As it was, there was some kind of search going on for me. If it had just been a matter of ransom, I could have paid it for myself. Too much longer, and those assets were going to disappear. Even Doc offering to help—I couldn't afford to wait for him to get the time.

As it was, I'd already kissed Jasper or he'd kissed me, then I'd spent the night in Vaughn's bed. A shiver went through me. The part of me that craved that contact didn't want to leave, and that made it all the more important I get out of here before I was in so deep, I forgot I wasn't supposed to be here in the first place.

The next edge was close to a building on the other side of a slender alley. I recognized the alley though, or at least I thought I did. I was pretty sure this was the route Rome and I took. I glanced across the distance, then behind me. If I had the speed, I might make that jump, but my muscles were still trembling from the climb.

I hadn't been kidding about being out of shape.

Think...

When I spotted a drain spout, I crossed my mental fingers. It was narrow, and the chill in the air said it would be hard on my fingers, but I could live with bruises.

I'd lived with them for a long time. I scanned the area for

watchful eyes. It was a risk...then again, nothing ventured, nothing gained.

Swinging out over the edge sent my adrenaline spiking. The roughness of the roof bit into my fingers, but I made the jump on faith alone to catch the drain spout. I slid a good four feet before I had enough purchase to slow the descent.

The metal was rusted in some places and it tore at my fingers, but I ignored the sharpness as I began to monkey my way down. My quads and arms quivered with equal measure as I descended. Never look down. That advice resonated inside of me. Focus on the first step, then the next, then one after that...and then I was standing on the pavement, heart thundering and mind buzzing.

A horn blared in the distance, and I jumped. One quick sweep told me I was still alone. I rubbed my arms against the chill. The hoodie I'd grabbed wasn't enough to keep the cold all the way out, but it worked to pull up over my hair and I zipped it up for now. Damaged hands in my pockets, I hurried up the alley.

It took a bit of concentration to *not* run. Running garnered attention. People who walked like they knew where they were going were rarely noticed. I had to resist the urge to cheer when I reached the sidewalk that had been so busy the other day. The sun was still making a slow climb, and the streetlights were all still on. Most of the shops along this stretch were also closed, or at least the visible lobbies of the office buildings were darkened.

I turned north. I needed to put a few blocks of distance between me and the warehouse. Then I needed to figure out where I was. Cash or a credit card would be great right now. Hell, I didn't even have change for a payphone if there even *was* one down here. I'd have to rely on the kindness of strangers.

So, distance first.

Then a diner or place to eat.

I was half fucking frozen by the time I reached the spot where Nikki's coffee cart had been. Disappointment shuddered through me as I stared at the empty bit of pavement. I glanced across the street and then up the block like she would magically appear.

Beyond Doc, Nikki had been the only other person I'd met who wasn't a Vandal.

And she wasn't here.

I sighed.

The sun was up...well, sort of. The skies were rapidly turning a leaden gray as storm clouds moved in. The air had also grown colder and colder. Fine, no coffee cart.

Keep going. But not back to the park. I needed to switch directions. I needed to find *people* or a place I could at least make a phone call.

Then I needed to decide who to call.

I bit the inside of my lip. My list of allies had grown quite thin in the last couple of years. Even those I'd counted as my friends had moved on or focused on their careers or education. If they'd known, they would have helped me. But if I'd told them, I'd have been risking them too.

Four blocks later, my teeth were chattering and I was no closer to a destination than I'd been when I'd climbed out onto the roof. My sense of accomplishment and freedom were rapidly fading. A car swung up beside me, noticeable because while traffic had begun to increase, there wasn't as much on this route as there'd been the other day.

Was it the weekend or something?

Fuck, that would be my luck.

I kept my gaze forward as the car paced me. Curling my fingers into my palms, I steadied my breath. Was there somewhere I could run if it was one of them? I tried to map out an escape route, but then...

"Little Bit," Doc called, and I stumbled to a halt and jerked my head around to stare at him through the open window of the truck he drove. Truck, not car. There was an old camper cap on the back, but it was still a truck.

Doc.

Relief flooded me.

Concern filled his face, and he reached over and shoved the passenger door open. "I thought that was you," he said. "Get in here."

"I don't want to go back," I argued, even as I stared longingly inside what had to be the heated confines of his vehicle.

"I promised I'd help you," he said. "Remember?"

Tears burned in my eyes, and I headed toward his vehicle almost blindly. "I—"

"I know," he soothed as soon as I was in. The heat was on, but he cranked it all the way up and pulled my hands over toward the vent, then paused. "What the hell?"

"I had to get out," I admitted. "I can't really feel them right now."

My nails were broken. Two were down all the way to the quick. The skin was ragged and raw in a few places. The heat felt so good.

"Seatbelt," Doc ordered, then didn't wait for me to do it. "Keep your hands there, I got it." He snagged the seatbelt and drew it across me, then clicked it in, clucking his tongue the whole time. "Those assholes need to take better care of you."

"No," I argued. "They don't. I need to get out of here."

He let out a sigh. "Okay, have you eaten?"

I shook my head. "Well, I did. I had some protein shakes. But I'd kill for coffee."

He plucked his cup from the holder on the other side of the steering wheel and held it out to me. I wrapped my icy fingers around it. It was only half-full, but it was hot. I took a long drink and nearly had a mini coffee-gasm. It was black as my soul and twice as strong.

"So good," I murmured. The warmer it grew in the truck cab, the more I shuddered.

"I'm getting you more." He pulled out into the light traffic, and at first, I thought he was turning around, but he just took the next left and we were going north again. "Where do you want to go, Little Bit? I can get you some cash."

"Where am I?" Maybe that was a stupid question, but… "I should have paid attention, I know. I was staying at the Harbor North Hotel, that much I remember. But I don't remember the city name. We've been on tour."

"Braxton Harbor," he told me and the name meant…nothing. I had no real memory of this place. Not that I'd seen much of it. I'd been at the hotel. Used the dance studio. Then been at the theatre. And for last couple of *months*, I'd been in their warehouse place with its absolute lack of windows and too many hot, attractive guys.

I finished his coffee almost too quickly, but we were pulling through a drive-thru for a popular chain, and I swore my mouth watered.

"What do you want?"

"A big black coffee, strongest brand they have, and then one of those raspberry lattes."

He shot me a look.

"I know, I'm complicated." One was bitter and harsh. The other sickeningly sweet.

I craved them both.

"Food?"

"I don't care."

That earned me a scowl, but I really didn't want him to spend money on me. Then again, I could pay him back. He had a clinic, right? I could donate money to it. I just needed the name.

Ten minutes later, I had drained over half the latte and I was tearing into the hot croissant breakfast sandwich. The interior of the truck smelled like a coffee shop.

"I've been thinking," he said. "Did you put anything in the safe at the hotel when you were there?"

I paused mid-bite, then shook my head. I always traveled light. While Kestrel had picked up all my things, the wallet, credit cards, and ID had all been conspicuously absent from the bag. Maybe I should have hunted for it in their rooms before I left.

"Okay, but would the hotel know you?" He gave me another careful look.

"I'm all over the news, Doc," I said. "What do you think?"

He winced. "Yeah. I should have called and let them know…" The apology lingered in between the syllables.

"But the guys are your friends."

"Not…exactly, but close. Little Bit, I wouldn't have let them hurt you."

"You don't owe me anything," I reminded him. He'd been there for me when I'd woken up scared, alone, and hurting. He'd stripped down to show me his scars so I wouldn't be shy about showing mine. He'd stood up to the guys, and he'd treated me with kindness and respect.

Right now? Right now, he was helping, just like he promised.

"Take me to the hotel. I can call the authorities." It would probably open a lot of questions I didn't want to answer. "And don't worry, I'm not turning them in."

Maybe I should. But…

"You don't owe them anything either," he said after a silence that trickled on a little too long. More and more, as the coffee and food warmed me up on the inside and the heat thawed the outside, I relaxed.

"Maybe not, but they didn't hurt me." Rome had saved

me. Jasper had wanted to protect me from Eric. He'd hurt Eric for me. Vaughn had taken care of me. Kestrel, despite all his distance, he had too. And Freddie?

Another twinge of guilt hit me.

Freddie had been kind in his very Freddie way.

The only one I hadn't really cared about nor would I miss was Liam. He was a bit of an abrasive ass, but maybe that was for the best too.

"Thank you, Emersyn," Doc said quietly as he pulled over just up the block from the hotel. Not taking me all the way was a good plan. There were cameras there.

I smiled and glanced at him. "I should be thanking you."

"Nah, I didn't do much…"

That was a lie, but I didn't want to argue with him. "What's your name? Your real name?"

"Mickey—short for Michael—James." He almost looked sheepish. He'd said Mickey before, but it was this kind of half-formed memory and very vague. "Doc works, though."

"Thank you, Mickey," I said, testing it out, and then I leaned over and pressed a kiss to his cheek. He turned just as my lips brushed his skin, and then my mouth was just at the corner of his. I didn't even try to pull away. Surprise flickered through his eyes as I kissed his lips. He didn't move as I nuzzled the kiss as gently as I could, and only when I pulled back did his hand lock in my hair and pull me in for a real kiss.

My lips tingled and burned from the contact as he thrust his tongue against mine. I tasted the coffee and a hint of the blueberry muffin he'd had. All too soon, the kiss ended and he let me go. We stared at each other, and I was as far from cold as I could get.

If anything, I was too hot.

"Thank you," I whispered. "And goodbye."

Then I pushed out of the truck and onto the sidewalk

before I changed my mind. Mind and body buzzing, I shoved my hands in my pockets and started walking.

Don't look back.

Don't look back.

The mantra kept me moving, and I was almost to the doors of the hotel itself when I caught sight of *him* coming out of the main doors. He had a cell phone at his ear, and his expression was all slick and smooth. There were people around him, but they vanished.

He'd been on the news.

Of course he'd be here.

My uncle.

My father's brother.

My tormentor.

My leaden steps glued to the pavement, and I couldn't move.

No.

I needed to get out, but not back to him.

Mouth dry, I turned abruptly away from the hotel. Doc's truck was gone. Still, I hurried away from the hotel.

I didn't even make it a block before arms came around me. They yanked me off my feet, and the hand over my mouth smothered my scream.

Emersyn and the Vandals will return in *Vicious Rebel*. To keep up with Heather and all her series join her reader's group: Https://www.facebook.com/groups/HeathersPack/

VICIOUS REBEL

My name is Emersyn Sharpe. Until a few months ago, I was the lead performer for a traveling show finishing up a contract. I had been beaten, but never broken.

Then they took me.

I didn't belong in their world.

Still, they took me and I didn't know why. They promised to protect me and to keep me safe, but they had to know I'd run.

They *had* to know.

Now my world and theirs might be on a collision course and as much as I didn't belong in their world, I didn't want mine to rain down on them.

Not on Jasper, the dictatorial jerk who kissed like he wanted to own me. Not on Rome, the tortured artist who protected me. Not on Kestrel, the liar with the soulful eyes and dedicated heart. Not on Liam, the bastard who loved his brother. Not on Vaughn, the beautiful man with the beautiful voice who made me want everything I shouldn't. Not on Doc, the gifted physician who'd kept his promises to me.

I ran.

But I didn't get far and now…now I don't know what will happen next.

VICIOUS REBEL is a full length mature college/new adult romance with enemies-to-lovers/love-hate themes. This is a reverse harem novel, meaning the main character has more than one love interest. This is book two in the series.

AFTERWORD

I told you there would be a cliffhanger!

Thank you for starting this journey with me. I'm so excited to see where we go from here.

xoxo

Heather

ABOUT HEATHER LONG

USA Today bestselling author, Heather Long, likes long walks in the park, science fiction, superheroes, Marines, and men who aren't douche bags. Her books are filled with heroes and heroines tangled in romance as hot as Texas summertime. From paranormal historical westerns to contemporary military romance, Heather might switch genres, but one thing is true in all of her stories—her characters drive the books. When she's not wrangling her menagerie of animals, she devotes her time to family and friends she considers family. She believes if you like your heroes so real you could lick the grit off their chest, and your heroines so likable, you're sure you've been friends with women just like them, you'll enjoy her worlds as much as she does.

Follow Heather & Sign up for her newsletter:
www.heatherlong.net

ALSO BY HEATHER LONG

Always a Marine Series

Once Her Man, Always Her Man

Retreat Hell! She Just Got Here

Tell It to the Marine

Proud to Serve Her

Her Marine

No Regrets, No Surrender

The Marine Cowboy

The Two and the Proud

A Marine and a Gentleman

Combat Barbie

Whiskey Tango Foxtrot

What Part of Marine Don't You Understand?

A Marine Affair

Marine Ever After

Marine in the Wind

Marine with Benefits

A Marine of Plenty

A Candle for a Marine

Marine under the Mistletoe

Have Yourself a Marine Christmas

Lest Old Marines Be Forgot

Her Marine Bodyguard

Smoke & Marines

Bravo Team Wolf

When Danger Bites

Bitten Under Fire

Boomers

The Judas Contact

Deadly Genesis

Unstoppable

Chance Monroe

Earth Witches Aren't Easy

Plan Witch from Out of Town

Bad Witch Rising

Her Elite Assets

Featuring:

Pure Copper

Target: Tungsten

Asset: Arsenic

Fevered Hearts

Marshal of Hel Dorado

Brave are the Lonely

Micah & Mrs. Miller

A Fistful of Dreams

Raising Kane

Wanted: Fevered or Alive

Wild and Fevered

The Quick & The Fevered

A Man Called Wyatt

Going Royal

Some Like It Royal

Some Like It Scandalous

Some Like It Deadly

Some Like it Secret

Some Like it Easy

Her Marine Prince

Blocked

Heart of the Nebula

Queenmaker

Deal Breaker

Throne Taker

Lone Star Leathernecks

Semper Fi Cowboy

As You Were, Cowboy

Madison, The Witch Hunter

Every Witch Way But Floosey's

Magic & Mayhem

The Witch Singer

Bridget's Witch's Diary

The Witched Away Bride

Mongrels

Mongrels, Mischief & Mayhem

Shackled Souls
Succubus Chained

Succubus Unchained

Succubus Blessed

Space Cowboy
Space Cowboy Survival Guide

Untouchable
Rules and Roses

Changes and Chocolates

Keys and Kisses

Whispers and Wishes

Hangovers and Holidays

Brazen and Breathless

Wolves of Willow Bend

Wolf at Law

Wolf Bite

Caged Wolf

Wolf Claim

Wolf Next Door

Rogue Wolf

Bayou Wolf

Untamed Wolf

Wolf with Benefits

River Wolf

Single Wicked Wolf

Desert Wolf

Snow Wolf

Wolf on Board

Holly Jolly Wolf

Shadow Wolf

His Moonstruck Wolf

Thunder Wolf

Ghost Wolf

Outlaw Wolves

Wolf Unleashed

Spirit Wolf

Printed in Great Britain
by Amazon

20477396R00180